THE BROKEN VIOLIN

OWEN KORTZ

For my students

SCENE 1

Thunderstorms, those heralds of Spring, roar,
casting their dark mantle over heaven,
Then they die away to silence,
and the birds take up their charming songs once more.
— Antonio Vivaldi, *The Four Seasons,* "Spring"

*S*hel tore off her shoes, throwing them behind her, and forced her feet into the cold, wet sand. Maybe the ocean could cleanse her. Maybe she could beat the inner ache and clash it into submission by pummeling it with all her might, stroke after stroke. Maybe the pure power of the water would turn back time and make reality play out like the films she'd watched growing up, a Hollywood kiss and fade to black. She couldn't line up that picture with the way Jeremy had used her, with the shards of her friendships, with her parents' blindness to all the change she was going through, and how little they had prepared her for the barrenness that lay before her. Here she stood in the mist on Ocean Beach at the edge of San Francisco, her fists clenched, jaw tight, body rigid, wanting to scream, to yell obscenities at the universe. She might as well be on a deserted island in the thick darkness with no one in sight. Her black hair blew around her face and shoulders in the crisp January wind.

Her small body firm in the sand, she felt she could have withstood a hurricane if it plowed through, yet, at the same time, she wanted to leap out of herself. She glared into the blackness of the ocean beyond the crashing waves through tears, which she batted away, though they would refill. She ran numbing fingers over her flat cheeks and dampened nose, and her pale skin blushed red. Then she moved her hands to her chest, tensing into fists, tearing and screaming at the dark shadow that had entered her heart, but she couldn't pull it out.

The rush of adrenalin nearly lifted her feet. She had swum in the ocean before, but not at night, and not when it was so gusty and rough, but she was running before she knew what she was doing. A force stronger than her fear compelled her to free herself, somehow, from the blaring dissonance. The waves dashed her body back a few feet as she fought her way deeper into the surf, feeling the ebb of the current reloading against the backs of her heels and calves, preparing for the next blow.

Diving beneath the oncoming wave, the coldness of the water was a shock. A soft ringing began in her ears. She would show the universe what it gets for messing with her life, for not giving her what she wanted, for obviously misleading her. Her head rose above the water, and she had only a second for a breath before another wave punched down on top of her. The weight of her sweatshirt and jeans dragged her down, but she started into a powerful free stroke, ducking under the crashing water as it towered over her, threatening to swallow her body in its dark jaws.

Her heart beat fast. She tasted the saltwater that mixed with her desperate gasps. Her arms pummeled the shadowy depths beneath her. Up and down she rose with the twelve-foot swells, not knowing how far out she might be. But she knew you always feel farther out than you really are when you're swimming away from shore, so she pressed on. All she could hear was her breath, her heartbeat, the way the wind howled by her ear when she turned her head to breathe in, and how it transformed into a deep roar when her ear submerged again.

Her strokes lengthened as her core grew warm with intense effort, but she knew she couldn't stay out too long in this winter water, so she slowed and let her legs dip deep below her, turning her eyes upward to look at the billions of distant stars in the night sky.

Just as she looked up, she felt a current pull at her feet. She tried to fight it, but it grabbed with urgency to take her further out from shore. Her mind kept telling her to stay calm, but her eyes dashed to the bobbing yellow lights on the coast between leaden strokes. She kept trying to get out of this relentless funnel that held her legs fast, but her arms singed and numbed.

Shel screamed before she went under. Her body sank with the weight of her clothes, and she swallowed water in the constant rushing and cycling of air bubbles. She didn't know which way was up anymore as the ocean's current swept her along. She hadn't taken a deep breath before she went under, and her heart pounded. She struggled with might and tenacity she had never exerted before and felt the current release her. She scurried underwater, stroke after stroke toward the surface, toward what she thought was the direction of shore. But then a wave pounded the surface before she got there, and she tumbled like a rag doll in its powerful fingers. The power of nature was the weight of a mountain compared to her tiny body.

At last, she let her herself go limp, allowing the water to carry her where it wanted to. She realized these could very well be the last few moments for her on this earth. Strangely, her anxiety evaporated, and she was left with a simple calm. Her lungs made one last effort to gasp for air. They burned and wrenched.

So that's it, she thought. And then there were no more thoughts. She passed into darkness.

SCENE 2

 our months earlier

In the harsh season scorched by the sun,
man and flock languish, and the pine is on fire....
Zephyr gently blows,
but Boreas suddenly enters into a contest with its neighbor,
and the little shepherd weeps
for he hears the awesome threatening storm and his fate.
—Antonio Vivaldi, *The Four Seasons,* "Summer"

Shel and her parents sat around the dinner table in their usual spots—Shel by the window, her dad at the short arc of the oval, his back to the living room, and her mom, across from Shel, in the chair by the kitchen. Her mom was in her dark blue, hemmed pants and white blouse from work, pearls rustling in a smooth arc, her short hair combed straight but curled at the tips to frame her round face. Her dad, dressed in his usual jeans and T-shirt, leaned close over his plate of spaghetti, eating his noodles with chopsticks. The fourth side of the table was empty except for a large glass-doored cabinet that held their fine silver and a small, cracked Japanese bowl hidden to one side.

"Well, are you excited for the big day tomorrow, honey?" her mom said between bites of noodles rolled into a tight ball on her fork. She smiled.

Shel chewed and nodded, pushing up the corners of her lips and shifting in her chair.

Her mom's fork clinked on the ceramic plate. "Oh, did you remember to pack those dresses I laid out for you?"

Shel downed a sip of water. "Yeah, I have them up by my suitcase. I'll put them in."

"Good." Her mom turned her head. "Tom, did you email the dorm again today to make sure they know Shelley is arriving tomorrow?"

As if coming out of a trance, he swallowed, still holding his chopsticks at mouth-level. "Oh...yeah. Yep, yep, I did, Min." Her mom gave a curt nod as her dad slipped back into a far-off look.

Shel cleared her throat and waited to take another bite, her eyes roaming the room, the glass cabinet.

Her mom crossed her short legs under the table. "Shelley, we got the car tuned up...air in the tires, oil change, so everything should be running smoothly for you. Are you ready for the drive?"

Shel sat up straight, motionless, hoping a sound would come from her mouth. When they'd made plans earlier in the summer for her departure, she had felt so ready for this next step and said she wanted to make the drive alone. But now that the moment was imminent, she wasn't so sure. Shel felt her parents' tangible warmth around the table. How many nights had they sat there together? They were an orb she didn't want to leave. This moment had been so exciting in her mind, but now that it was here, the entire eighteen years leading up to it welled and throbbed in her heart. She was untying a rope and letting something drift from the shore, maybe never to see it again. It settled over her that nothing would be the same between them once she drove away early tomorrow morning.

"I—I'm...thinking maybe you guys could come with me tomorrow," Shel said.

Her mom and dad looked up at her and then at each other. Her dad shrugged and they traded a few words in Japanese, which they'd always done since Shel was a little girl when they didn't want her to know what they were talking about. Her dad looked back at her, his gaze a gentle flicker in the candlelight.

Her mom said, "Honey, it's a little late to change your mind on this. You told us you wanted to do this alone, and we made all the plans to support you in that."

Shel lowered her head. She wanted to throw her arms around her parents, to tell them that she didn't want to leave. Shaking herself out of those thoughts, she jutted her chest forward, focusing her eyes on her plate, and nodded.

After dinner, her dad retired to his den and her mom did the dishes. Shel went up to her room to finish packing. She stared at her shiny silver suitcase lying open on the bed and tapped her finger against its hard shell.

Her mom knocked on the bedroom door that was open a crack. "Shelley?"

"Yeah, Mom." Shel broke away and let her mom in.

"Anything I can do to help up here?"

"No, no, I've got it. I just..." Shel gathered her long black hair behind her head and sighed.

"Honey." Her mom came over and began to braid her hair. "Do you remember that time the three of us went up to that film festival in San Francisco?"

Shel relaxed her shoulders as her mom's hands moved in rhythm, and she nodded. Her mind flew back to when she was fourteen. She could see her mom and dad there next to her in the large Gothic-style theatre at the San Francisco International Film Festival. They sat in the balcony and looked down on thousands of people in the pink-lit hall, and the gigantic screen was framed between monolithic columns.

"Do you remember what you said to me that night?" Her mom paused the braiding flow, and Shel could see her lean toward her out of the corner of her eye.

Shel smiled. "That I would have a film screened there one day." She remembered her mom saying, *You'll certainly know you're successful when that day comes.*

"That's right. And now you're all grown up and have the world just waiting for you to take it by storm."

Shel glanced around her room, posters of classic films on the walls, her sophomore yearbook photo framed on a small bookcase by the window, a few medals she'd won on the swim team hanging on nails her mom had helped her hammer in.

"Yeah," she said and rolled her shoulders back. She turned around. "Thanks, Mom."

In the early hours of the next morning, Shel heard her mom down on the driveway, opening and closing the car door, probably double checking what they'd packed last night and that there was enough gas in the car. From the bottom of the stairs, she heard her dad clicking the keys on his desktop computer in the den.

Getting out of bed, she flicked on the switch in her bathroom. Her plastic *Little Mermaid* cup sat next to the sink, the graphic mostly rubbed off now. The fan rattled overhead, and she anticipated its gentle rhythm of squeaks and clicks.

She showered and put on makeup, looking in the mirror at

her pearly skin with blushed cheeks, long eyelashes painted on. Her eyes were bright, though she could see bloodshot veins if she looked close enough, and her dark black irises popped against eyeshadow. Turning her head, she followed the gentle slope of her nose rounding into rosy lips and a soft chin. She snapped shut her makeup case and went to her closet to get dressed.

She walked down the stairs past family photos on the landing: the glossy one of the three of them when Shel was twelve, the one of her mom's parents and another of her dad's, all grandparents she'd never met, though they seemed as much a part of the family looking out at them from those frames all these years. The one of her mom's parents was black and white with the couple standing unsmiling, dressed in fraying kimonos in front of a small, rectangular house, paint chipping off the wood. Their faces were grim, thin and wrinkled by the sun, and etched with the California dust. The one of her dad's parents had a faded '70s hue, her grandmother with curly short hair, wearing a sweater and black maxi skirt, and her grandfather in a business suit and tie, jacket buttoned at the top rung, his lips set, with penetrating eyes peering from round-rimmed glasses.

Reaching the bottom of the stairs, she passed her dad in the den. He made his quintessential gesture of leaning back in his desk chair, raising up his long, thin arms, and placing his hands behind his tousled hair. She wanted to hold on to his gangly frame like she did as a kid and feel on her cheek those few prickly hairs that his razor never reached through his rough complexion.

She wanted it to be a regular Friday, to come home from school later that afternoon and have her mom immersed in a Julia Child recipe, her broad, powdered cheeks hovering over a pot on the stove. *Dinner's at five-thirty sharp.* Her mom's pointed tone would find Shel across the kitchen.

After dinner, maybe they'd sit down and watch one of the classic films they all loved. As the credits rolled, her mom would sigh and say something like, "Ah, young love," pushing herself up from the sofa and going to the kitchen, and her dad would get up and go back to his computer. Shel would watch until the music ended and the screen went black, and wander upstairs to her room in a reverie. She could sleep in the next day and maybe Thelma, her bright-red-headed best friend, would come over, and they'd go to the mall and stay up late talking about the greater love they were destined for, even if they had to wait for it, and watch more classic romance films.

But today, standing at the front door on her way out of the house, Shel took one last look at the living room. It never occurred to her that a time would come when she would miss the small wooden cubby in the entryway that would no longer hold her shoes, and carefully vacuumed carpets giving way under her socks along well-trodden pathways between rooms. Her eyes landed on the dining room table, and then on the cabinet with glass-door shelves holding the fine silver and dark brown Japanese bowl that was tucked away. The bowl looked like it had been dropped but then repaired with gold along the cracks. As the morning sunlight peeked its first rays through the window, it caught those gold striations and made it look like its spirit glowed from within. They never used the bowl, but it had always fascinated Shel. It might have been the only traditional Japanese thing in the house, inherited down the generations on her mom's side. There were old pictures of Shel as a toddler with that bowl hiding in the background.

On the driveway, next to the old Honda Civic Shel had driven in high school, her mom gave her a tight, quick squeeze, and her dad came out to join them. High school had come and gone so fast, it seemed. Shel was used to driving the few miles to Azusa High, avoiding sewer dips and passing the old pool where she had her first swim lessons. The world had been small, just the three of them.

"Text us when you get in," her mom said.

"I will." Shel looked at her, large-eyed, and her mom told her to drive safe.

She turned to her dad.

"Love you, Shelley." He patted her on the back.

"Love you, Dad."

Looking at both her parents, a wave of feeling swelled up through her chest, which she struggled to push back down. Her parents would be up for Family Weekend in a couple months, but that was way longer than they'd ever been apart. She fumbled into the car and backed out of the driveway, waving through the window. Her mom stood stiff next to her dad. As Shel pulled forward, she found them both in her rearview, where they stayed, staring after her, until she turned the corner and they flew from the mirror. She looked up at it again, hoping she'd impossibly still see them there.

Once she was on the open road, her tears came and faded into a calm as she looked out over the Pacific coast. It was a longer drive to take Highway 1, but the ocean had drawn her since she was a little girl. She cast glances across the deep blue-gray expanse of water to the horizon.

The back seat and trunk of the car were loaded with her shiny silver suitcase, loose bedding, two stuffed animals, a box with some cups and plates, her laptop and book bag, and an Azusa High School mug. A rolled-up poster of Shelley Winters, the actress from the 1950s, bobbed against the pale pleather behind her.

Reaching the Bay Area, the beige finish of the car was covered in dust from her all-day trek. The Golden Gate Bridge seemed surreal in the harbor mist, arcing precisely, with mathematical perfection, across the strait to Marin County. How many films had Shel seen that featured this icon in the background of the scene? *Dark Passage*, *It Came from Beneath the Sea*, *Vertigo*,

Superman. These were classics, films Shel had watched and rewatched, placing herself in the imaginary world created on screen.

She pulled into the unloading area outside the dormitory at the University of California, Berkeley. Twilight embraced the campus with a gentle ease as birds sang their farewell to another day. Austrian-looking balconies protruded overhead with white wooden planks that had diamond shapes cut out of them. The outer walls were shingled like a roof, and two thick lodgepole pine pillars supported a vestibule that led to the main door. *Foothill* was emblazoned in metal over the dorm entrance.

Inside, a friendly young woman, evidently a student volunteer, greeted Shel.

"Hi," she said in a two-toned melody. "Are you checking in?"

"Yes!" Shel's smile rose part way.

"Great! I'm Bailey. What's your name?" She extended her hand.

"Shelley Henka." Her voice lifted at the end of the phrase as she tried to peer over the clipboard Bailey held to see if her name was there.

"Henka, Henka. Hmm, I have a Gakki Henka...." Bailey lifted the fingers of her right hand in a shrug-like gesture.

Shel knew that would happen. She always had to write her birth name on official forms, and they rarely asked for her preferred name. As a further point of annoyance, people always pronounced it "Gacki," with a nasal "a" and a hard "k" sound, like "khaki" pants.

Hiding her disappointment, she confirmed, "That's me."

Her parents, of course, pronounced her name the right way, with Japanese inflection: a low tone, then a high tone, gracing over the double "k" as more of a soft "kh" sound, "Ga-KHI." She had changed her name, unofficially, to Shel when she was thirteen. At that point, she felt she'd endured enough anglicizings of her name to last her a lifetime, which was only one of the reasons she decided to change it.

"Okay, great!" Bailey beamed. "It looks like you'll be on the third floor, room 344. Let me just grab the key, and I'll take you up!"

They ascended a few flights of stairs, passing other pods of people chattering along their way. It was now late in the evening, but everyone was buzzing and in a good mood. They traveled down a long hallway with fluorescent lights and a rough carpet that had a repeating, angular green and yellow design. The room numbers counted down their arrival: 356, 354, 352…. Shel could see that 344 was going to be about in the center of the the hallway, on the right.

"Okay, here we are!" Bailey chimed as she unlocked and opened the door, sweeping her arm in a welcoming gesture. She beamed and added, "I'm going to let you get situated. Just check in downstairs if you need anything!"

"Okay, sounds good. Thanks!" Shel said as Bailey handed her the key.

She stepped through the entryway into the symmetrical, rectangular dorm room. A window ran along the back wall with hanging vertical blinds that were slightly open, revealing Shel's reflection in the glass behind them. A twin bed was placed against each wall. The left-side bed already had a pink duvet covering it, and a large suitcase on wheels stood by the light wood desk at the foot of the bed. As she continued to look left, her eyes found the closets that covered the nearest wall on either side of the door.

"Alright," Shel spoke aloud to herself. Her voice sounded shaky, and she took a deep breath. Her knees felt weak, like they'd give if she didn't will them to hold her upright. Where was she? Was she still in her bed at home dreaming all this? She thought of her parents, and a lump formed in her throat. Her mind fought to stay focused on what she needed to do next, but her eyes blurred and pricked with tears. Where was she going to park the car? Had she locked it before coming in? What was everyone else doing? Was there a schedule she'd missed? She squeezed her fists and closed her eyes, feeling her fingernails press into her palms, then wiped her face and turned to go get her bags.

When she got back to the room with a load of bedding and her suitcase, the door was open, and her roommate was there. Shel set down her luggage in the doorway and knocked gently.

"Hello?"

"Hello?" a small voice echoed from within the room. A tall, lean girl took a few steps around the edge of the closet to greet Shel. She had brown, mid-length hair pulled back in a ponytail. Her face was clear. Each of her individual features—eyes, jaw, neck, body, arms, legs—was perfectly formed, but each seemed slightly out of proportion with the others. She stood about five feet, ten inches tall and wore a gray hoodie and Cal cotton shorts that came a quarter way down her thighs, which were very white. For such a tall girl with commanding features, she seemed rather apprehensive standing before Shel with her hands crossed in front, her shoulders rolled forward, and her head tilted downward.

"Hi, I guess I'm your roommate." Shel forced a smile and introduced herself.

"Good to meet you." The girl took an obligatory step forward, and her arm protruded from her side. "I'm Gertrude."

Shel shook her hand but noticed that Gertrude was not squeezing back, her fingers mostly limp. Gertrude smiled almost imperceptibly and made eye contact for a moment, then turned to continue unpacking.

"Hey, is it okay if I start moving some of my stuff in?" Shel wanted to get off to a kind start with this girl she'd be sharing a room with for most of the year.

Gertrude turned around, and her arm leapt from her side

again. "Oh, yes!" It seemed she was going to say more, but she re-folded her hands in front of her and turned around to unzip her suitcase.

"Thanks." Shel wanted to fill the silence but was having trouble keeping her eyes open after the long day of driving, and she decided to unpack. After hanging her Shelley Winters poster over her bed, she texted her parents to let them know she got in safe.

Gertrude sat at her desk reading what looked like the Bible, so Shel unpacked her earbuds and plugged them into her laptop, turning on the 1948 classic, *A Double Life*, one in her collection of films featuring her favorite actress, Shelley Winters, who'd been a contemporary of Marilyn Monroe. The familiar soundtrack reminded her of home, and she slipped away into the reverie of the plot's romance. The way love stories like this created tension and resolve between the fated characters moved Shel. She was entranced by the chemistry. It excited her to think of how she might fall in love for the first time someday. She closed her eyes and, after a few scenes, fell into a deep sleep.

She dreamed of two figures moving toward her from the dark distance. She could make out the silhouettes of their small bodies. It was a young couple, she could tell, as she began to make out glasses on the man's face and the curly hair of the woman. They seemed familiar to her, but she couldn't recognize them. The man's features reminded her of a young version of her father. The man was on the left, wearing a suit with the top button of the jacket fastened, and his hand sat gently underneath the arm of the woman, who wore a sweater. They slowly made their way closer to Shel. The man carried something that Shel couldn't identify in the dim light. It seemed to be cracked in two pieces, linked together in some way.

As they came near, they bowed in greeting, and Shel gasped. They were her grandparents. Their faces wore straight expressions, but there was a sense of yearning about them. Shel bowed in return. The man extended his arms and offered the object he was holding. Shel stepped forward and saw more clearly that it was a violin. The neck had snapped, and much of the body splintered, but the strings still connected the two pieces. The man bowed again and lifted his hands higher toward Shel, supplicating to her to take it, which she did. She looked back at her grandparents and found they were suddenly much older, wrinkled and hunched over. Her grandfather now stepped forward, and with a snap of surprising vigor shouted, "Gakki!"

SCENE 3

Shel splashed her face with cold water after the fitful night. She was alone in the dorm bathroom, having woken early, and all was quiet except for the background hum of the building's air conditioning and the soft click of a flickering fluorescent light above the stalls. She washed her hands, getting under her fingernails, and used the hand dryer for the full cycle, the warmth calming her.

Returning to the dorm room, Shel found a list of activities for the weekend taped to her door. She took it inside and glanced over the bold type. *Spirit rally with the Cal marching band, Pool Party at Strawberry Canyon,* and a *Movie Night* later that evening. Shel didn't particularly resonate with any of these. Actually, she preferred the term "film" to "movie," and they were going to show a slapstick comedy about a college road trip, which hardly deserved to be called a film, in Shel's opinion. It was still strange to her to be in this new place, and she decided she'd relax and re-watch a couple more of her favorite classics before braving the halls later to see if she could meet any of her dorm mates.

The late morning hours drifted into mid-afternoon as scenes of *He Ran All the Way* and *Frenchie* unfolded, starring Shelley

Winters, who was, as far as Shel was concerned, Hollywood's true "blonde bombshell." Usually, when she mentioned the actress, people didn't know who she was. If she said "Marilyn Monroe," people's eyes lit up, most likely envisioning the sex icon of the 1950s in her now-cliché pose over the sidewalk vent, white dress being blown to reveal long legs and a glimpse of underwear.

Shel couldn't understand why Monroe had been enthroned for the ages when Winters had been just as sexy and iconic in the post-war years. Besides, Shel had seen a number of Monroe's films and thought that Winters's work from the same period, her early career, outshone Monroe's. She understood, as was practically common knowledge, that Monroe had ended her life when she was still young, and that gave her a sort of immortality, but she felt Winters deserved more attention, nonetheless. She had lived a long life and acted in hundreds of films before she passed away in 2006, well into her eighties. Shel hadn't seen all of her films. In fact, she only owned a dozen, in which Winters played her quintessential gorgeous, sex-goddess roles, but there was something about the actress that spoke to her.

The ending credits of *Frenchie* flashed on the black-and-white background, and Shel took out her earbuds, her head swimming as she became aware of the room again. Gertrude had evidently decided to sequester herself for most of the day, as well, and sat propped against the wall on her bed reading *St. Teresa of Avila: The Way of Perfection.* Shel hadn't grown up religious or spiritual in any way. Her parents didn't go to church or ascribe to a particular faith. She'd grown up with morals and the importance of getting along with others, respecting them, but otherwise figured the universe or God or whatever you wanted to call it was basically an impartial abstraction that didn't intersect with anything that was important to her on a practical, day-to-day level. She didn't judge Gertrude for her interest, but it didn't strike a chord with her.

"I'm going to go wander the halls," she announced to her roommate, bouncing off the bed to her feet.

Gertrude nodded.

Shel glanced at the photo on her bulletin board of her and Thelma at graduation in caps and gowns, Thelma's curly red hair, freckles, and small nose shining from behind the cap's tassels. She remembered when they met for the first time in third grade, at Paramount Elementary, literally running into each other and knocking each other over, accidentally, on the playground. She'd dusted herself off and helped Thelma up, and that was that. They were BFFs.

As Shel shut the door behind her, her hand rested on the knob and her eyes played over the design in the carpet. The dream burned back through her mind. What did the violin have to do with anything? There weren't any musicians in her family. It was weird. She kept trying to shake the images from the dream, but the splintered wood and her grandfather's penetrating eyes seared into her mind.

She became aware of her feet drawing her down the hall, the light warming into normal tones as reality settled around her. The next door on the left was closed, but the one after that, 340, was open, and Shel heard two girls talking inside.

"Oh, my God," one of them said with a lilty, nasal voice, "did you see Danny's reaction when I told him I had a growler in my bag?" They laughed.

"Yeah," the other responded huskily, "he looked like he thought it was Christmas. As if you'd actually bring beer to, like, the first pool party of the year."

Shel peeked around the corner of the door frame as they snickered, and tapped gently on the door.

"Hey, what's up?" the girl on the left said. The roommates sat on their beds facing each other, seeming to Shel the embodiment of blonde beach girls: tan, beautifully built, wearing bikini tops and brightly-colored towels around their waists.

"Hey, I'm Shel." She lifted her hand in a fleeting wave. Her chest tightened, and she was suddenly aware of all the muscles in her face. "I was just wandering around and figured I'd say hello. I'm your neighbor, two doors down."

"Oh, right on," the other girl said. "I'm Lark and that's Cindy."

"Good to meet you." Shel tried to smile.

The two girls stared at her.

"So, where are you from?" Lark finally said.

"Oh, ah…Azusa." Shel shrugged.

"That's awesome. We're from SoCal too. Huntington Beach." Lark spoke with a rasp and bobbed her head.

"Oh, cool!" Shel said. She thought of all the conversations she and Thelma had had about the hoity-toity Huntington kids.

"Yeah, we grew up, like, right next to each other," Cindy said. "When we both got into Cal, we were, like, 'Whaaaat!' It was awesome."

Lark laughed and coughed twice, then checked her phone.

Shel stood still, her eyes roaming the room.

"Well, nice to meet you," Cindy said.

Shel felt for the door frame. "Yeah, nice to meet you, too! I'm sure I'll see you around."

"Okay, sounds good!" Lark's smile sparkled then fell to her phone again.

Shel dragged her finger along the hallway wall, looking down at her feet. Her heart was racing, and she took in a couple deep breaths. She hadn't needed to introduce herself to anyone in years, it felt like, since all the Azusa kids went to Slauson and then Azusa High. There were people she didn't know, but almost everyone in her classes was familiar, and she had Thelma. This was a part of college she hadn't thought about in her musings of what it would be like to finally be here. The images she'd had were of film classes and meeting some cute boy. A cycle of thoughts followed Shel through the hallway. Was she nice enough? Did they think she was cool? Did her smile look awkward? Did they think she was fake?

Rounding the corner to the left where the hallway teed, she saw a door open on the right and peered hesitantly into room 323.

A square character of medium build sat at his desk playing a video game on his laptop. He hadn't seen Shel standing in the doorway, and she watched him for a moment. His dark hair and a thick five o'clock shadow of a beard cut against the illuminated window behind him.

"Hey, can I help you?" He mashed the spacebar to pause the game.

Shel jumped and put her hand over her heart. "Oh, no. I'm sorry…." She shook her head and inched away, averting her gaze. Scuttering back to her room, she couldn't believe that had just happened the way it did. She wanted to go back thirty seconds and replay the whole scene. No, five minutes and replay everything that had happened since she left her room. She unlocked the door and climbed under the covers into the safe arms of her films.

The last couple nights had passed more peacefully, and the memory of the dream began to fade as the first day of classes arrived. Shel made herself up and put on a light silky dress imbued with watercolor browns, oranges, and dark greens that overlaid each other in wavy, sedimentary patterns, one of her favorites. A black belt, silver necklace her mom had given her, and black shoes tied it all together. She packed her textbooks, laptop, and a Cal water bottle into her backpack and, before leaving, looked around the room, landing on the bulletin board over her desk again and the photos she'd tacked on. There was one of her mom and dad with Shel in the middle from last winter, and the one of Shel and Thelma at graduation. She wanted to hear all their voices, but she tried to push that away so she could focus on her first day, and walked out of Foothill.

Making her way down Hearst Avenue, she followed a footpath surrounded by trees between some buildings and found herself on University Drive on campus. As she strolled along South Drive, she soaked in the forest-like environment with ponderosa pine, coast redwood, and box elder trees. The old English architecture of some of the buildings reminded her of what she thought Harvard must look like. Other buildings were very modern with sharp angles, glass balconies, and zero-scaped gardens.

Then she reached Wheeler Hall, where she'd have her first writing class. It looked like the White House. Walking up the stairs to the main doors, she saw a girl leaning against the railing who looked like her, jet black hair, smoothed features and pale skin, and compact but languid build. Time moved in slow motion. The girl seemed older, more seasoned in this ancient institution, more inducted into its traditions and culture. Her air was an etheric cloak Shel hoped might seep into her as the days and months and years went by. The girl lifted her head and smiled at Shel.

Admiringly, Shel wandered the cathedral-like hallways, light pouring in through the twenty-foot-high windows across the tiled floor. Students scurried in multiple directions.

She entered a small, woody classroom and sat down. A young black woman, no older than early thirties, dressed in a blue business suit, her hair cut short, wearing glasses, glided through the door to the front, high heels tapping. She set down her bag on the desk and opened a bright smile to the class.

"Good morning, everyone." Her inviting alto voice held a charge that drew out the good in the day.

A few hesitant, half-volume "good mornings" pinballed from the rows of desks.

"I'm Professor Ellsworth," she said as she pulled out her laptop from her bag. "I posted a short article on the class interface online. Let's all log on and read it. Then, I'll break you up into small groups to discuss."

The article was from *The New Yorker* covering a documentary called *People of the Steppe*, about Syrian refugees. Documentaries were not exactly Shel's area of interest, but she followed along. The article noted that the film carried the torch of cinematic techniques and approaches defined by earlier directors, but also outlined how the director courageously broke some of those rules—for instance, mixing expository and poetic modes and segueing between actual and reenacted footage. The article took a tone of praise for these inventive decisions but quoted other critics who were not as impressed. It reminded Shel how much she loved classical Hollywood cinema, and that is what she had come here to learn more about.

After some group discussion, Ellsworth moved on to explaining the assignment for Wednesday's class, which was to read two more articles on this documentary and write a one-page comparison. An optional part of the assignment was to watch the complete documentary.

"Any questions?" Dr. Ellsworth put her hand on her hip.

Some students started to pack up their bags.

"Alright," she said. "Thanks, everyone! Look forward to working with you this semester!"

Shel made haste to her next class, The History of Film. Two students were already there when she came in. A girl entered the room and walked toward Shel.

"You were in The Craft of Writing class this morning, right?" She sat down next to her.

"Yeah! I'm Shel."

"Good to meet you. Ellana."

"Alana?" Shel repeated her name with the usual 'a' sound at the beginning of the name.

"No, *E*llana," the girl repeated, this time emphasizing the "e."

She had long, dirty-blonde dreadlocks that were tied back by a black scrunchie and came down over a forest-green, v-neck T-shirt. She was thin, but fit, no makeup. Otherwise, she wore a faded ochre cotton skirt and Chacos.

"Oh, *E*llana, sorry," Shel corrected herself. She realized she was doing the same thing to Ellana's name that others did to her with *Gakki*.

"No prob, it happens all the time." Ellana made an elvish grin.

Her green eyes seemed old—not in the tired sense, but they looked wise. She had some wrinkles under them, even though she was surely no older than Shel. Her teeth were crooked here and there, but they were clean, as was her skin, which shone. She was pretty in a different way than Shel had seen before. It was a natural, inside-out beauty, instead of the airbrushed look which she had learned from her mom and her friends in middle school. Shel could also smell her body odor, which, again, was natural and pungent, but not unpleasant.

The professor set up his computer at the podium by the door. Probably in his late fifties, he had short hair, balding in front, and a goatee.

"Alright everybody, we'll go ahead and get started. I'm Professor Raskell." He sounded like a Victor Talking Machine, and this was the thousandth time he'd replayed the same message.

Outlining the course, he explained there would be sections on classical and post-classical Hollywood cinema, experimental documentary, avant-garde cinema, Italian neorealism, French poetic realism, Third Cinema, and film in the era of global multimedia. Shel could feel a growing buoyancy as these areas were introduced. Of course, the classical Hollywood era was her all-time favorite, but "French Poetic Realism" sounded like it could have promise.

It sent her drifting off into a world of her imagination where she walked the streets of Paris in a lost time of fine dresses and men in suits, tipping their fedoras at her as she passed. She stopped at a fruit stand and chatted with the madame about the beautiful springtime weather, and she smelled the fresh-picked flowers. Then a young man in slacks and a white button-up work shirt came up beside her. She could tell he was only pretending to look at the fruit while trying to steal a glance at her. His skin was smooth but hardened by work, maybe as a dockhand along the Seine, his hair dark and forearms strong beneath his partway rolled-up sleeves.

The bustling of students packing up their bags brought her back, and she tried to collect herself, drifting out of the classroom.

When she got back to the dorm that night, she lumbered up the stairs toward her room. Her mind swam as she reached into her purse to grab her phone. Seeing her mom's face on the icon, Shel felt her heart swell, and she fought back tears. She was about to dial, but one of the Resident Advisors burst through the stairwell door and reminded her there was an ice cream social in the courtyard. She put her phone away and, after going through the dessert line, sat on one of the metal benches. The boy she'd awkwardly been watching play the video game in his room arrived and she watched him go through the line. Shel was surprised when he came over to where she was.

"Hey," he said, motioning with his bowl. "Weren't you outside my room the other day?"

Shel blushed. "Oh, yeah. I'm sorry I interrupted you. I was going to introduce myself...." She looked down at the sidewalk, but then lifted her head and extended her hand. "I'm Shel."

"Royson," he said, and gave her hand a quick shake.

Shel had never heard that name before.

"I take it you weren't in the mood for the pool party that day, either." She turned her head and looked at him out of the corner of her eye.

Royson smiled, but Shel could see he was using it to cover his gaze, which still searched her.

"No," he explained, "I was just taking a break from starting to get a handle on my O-Chem text." He took an incredibly thick book from under his arm and opened to a page with an illustrated pentagonal compound.

"Oh, wow," she said. "That sounds like a tough class. What's your major?"

"Pre-med."

Shel knew that pre-med usually led to a lot of schooling after undergrad, and Royson certainly had the gravity of one bracing himself for that long haul. She respected that, but his seriousness was also humorous to her.

She said, "So, you're gonna be, like, the next mad scientist brain surgeon of the Bay Area, then?"

But this time he didn't smile. "No, I'm not going to stay here... maybe work for Doctors Without Borders."

"Oh, that's cool." Shel sobered to match his intensity.

"How about you?" he asked. "What's your major?"

"Film," she said, grinning. She took a bite of ice cream. "Are your mom or dad in medicine?"

"No. My mom lives in Sacramento. I'm not sure what she's doing for work now. I haven't seen her in a few years. My dad's in San Jose. He works for American Airlines as a plane technician."

Shel nodded.

"How about you?" he asked, coming out of a momentary distance. "What made you want to be a film major?"

"Oh, I fell in love with the classic black-and-white films when I was just a kid. My parents and I used to watch them together." Warm memories flashed by of being with her mom and dad for movie nights. It was the only occasion they'd bring out the

Tokyo Banana cakes, a treat they ordered from Japan once a year that her parents loved from when they each visited as kids. Shel loved biting into the soft, bready exterior and feeling the gooey banana cream against her tongue as the title scenes began to roll. "I guess it got in my head early on that I wanted to be involved with these kinds of films, so I took a couple classes in high school and started making some short videos, and…that led me here."

Royson nodded. "Where are you from?"

"Azusa."

"Right on," he said, seeming to log that info into a file in his brain.

They finished their ice cream and sat in silence, looking at the streamlets of vanilla.

"So," said Royson, "I guess I'd better get to the library to go over some notes from today."

"Sounds good."

Shel smoothed her dress and searched the courtyard with her eyes. Royson waved as he departed.

"Have a good night!" Shel called, and watched after him a moment as he walked away.

Just then, her phone buzzed. Shel beamed as she saw Thelma's name pop up on her screen. She swiped opened the text.

Shel! I miss you already!! How was your first day of COLLEGE?? Ahhh! :) We don't start till next week, but I'm getting so excited! How are classes? How's the dorm? Any cute boys? :)

Shel smiled to herself. How many nights had she and Thelma stayed up until the early hours of the morning in middle school talking about boys? She felt homesick thinking about her base-ment where they had their sleepovers. They used to take turns describing their perfect "prince charming" and imagining the glorious futures they'd have. At that time, high school was just around the corner, and the possibilities seemed endless.

Shel wrote back, *Thelma!! OMG…I feel like I'm on an alien planet. So many new things…I miss home already! Yes, a few cute boys so far, but just barely getting to know people, so fingers crossed! When are you heading to UCLA?*

Oh nice, haha :), Thelma wrote. *I'm there with you in spirit, Shel! I leave on Friday. I'm getting nervous, but also can't wait!!*

Shel smiled at her phone. *Love you, Thelma! Can't wait to hear about your first days! Don't hack a lung! Haha :)*

Shel glowed with the memory of their sophomore year when they had one of their many sleepovers and ate spaghetti for dinner. Shel choked for a second on one of her bites and made this ridiculous hacking noise that made them both laugh so hard their faces turned red. Since then, they'd dropped *hack a lung* into infinite conversations. Thelma texted back two laughing-so-hard-I'm-crying emojis.

Back at the dorm, Shel washed the first day from her face. Saying goodnight to Gertrude, she thought of the last seventy-two hours, which felt like a blur. How had she gotten here? Watching her parents disappear and the drive up the coast were echoes from what seemed a long time ago. It was only getting started, but college was not turning out like she thought it would. Maybe she could stick out this semester, but then she'd move back in with her parents, go somewhere closer to home. She looked at her Shelley Winters poster, streaked with shadow bars from the blinds, and wrapped her arms around her pillow.

Classroom C-25 opened through double doors to an amphitheater with rows of padded seats. There were at least two hundred of them, tapering off at the front of the room into a carpeted, open area with a single podium on the right. The focus of it all was the gigantic screen, which justified the rest of the room's features.

In spite of all the seats, there were only about thirty students scattered around the room as the seconds ticked down to begin the Tuesday 11 a.m. period. A young man entered and began setting up items on and around the podium. Shel wondered if he was an upperclassman, or maybe a graduate student teaching assistant. He looked twenty-five at the oldest with his fair skin, medium height, and lean body. He had short black hair that contrasted with his light complexion. His ears were small and stuck out noticeably, his eyes calm, and his countenance relaxed and confident. As the time for class to begin arrived, no professor-type entered to greet the youngster and thank him for setting up.

Instead, the young man came out from behind the podium, smiled at the small group of students in the overbearing room, and with a clear, resonant voice and a welcoming gesture, said, "Good morning, everybody! Do you all mind coming down to the first couple rows here?"

He raised a hand over his eyes as if peering across the distance of an open sea. Shel and the other students gradually started to repack their bags and mosey down to the front rows. Once everyone was seated again, the feel of the room was different, suddenly more intimate and personal. The young man thanked everyone. His smile spread only on the lower part of his face, while his eyes sat tranquil and unchanged.

"I'm Dr. Hadaway," he started. "I'd like to get to know each one of you. Do you mind introducing yourselves? And tell me your favorite film soundtrack, too." His lower-face smile appeared as he pointed at a student at the end of the row, far to the right of Shel.

The roll call of voices panned across the room toward her. She didn't hear many of the names or soundtracks as she began to plumb her own mind's archives for an answer that would fall somewhere between her true favorite and what might impress her teacher and peers. The approach happened faster than she thought, and a voice next to her brought her out of her inner searching.

"Charlie Bassett. My favorite soundtrack is from the original version of *The Diary of Anne Frank.*"

Shel immediately recognized the name of the film. Shelley Winters had acted in it further into her career, around 1960, and it was one that Shel hadn't seen. She loved the romantic films, and *Anne Frank* seemed too heavy for her. She knew that Winters had won an Oscar for her portrayal of Mrs. Van Daan. Somewhere in the back of her mind, Shel was also thinking, "Who is this guy who loves classic films?" Charlie was short, black-haired, clean-shaven. He looked older than he probably was, had a small build but a large presence. Shel hadn't noticed him when surveying the students in the room earlier. Suddenly, it was her turn to share.

"I'm Shelley Henka. I would have to say *Jaws.*" Did she really just say that? *Jaws*? She hadn't fully decided on an answer, but *Jaws* slipped from behind her fumbling thoughts. Shel wasn't sure if she did have a favorite. She always focused on the plot more than the music, but she knew the music added a lot to the emotion of a scene. If she could do it over, she'd probably say her favorite was a score to one of Shelley Winters's films, like *Frenchie.*

Her focus eventually returned to Hadaway as he transitioned into presenting the syllabus, which covered camera angles, various digital media to capture shots, lighting techniques, formats and styles including trailers, short feature, essay, and web material. They watched a few clips that demonstrated these approaches, and Hadaway asked questions that were left open for anyone in the class to answer.

Charlie responded to a couple. He seemed poised and sure in his answers but nonchalant, as if this was everyday conversation for him. Shel admired his demeanor. His eyes, she noticed, pinched in the outside corners which became very pronounced when he smiled, and his nose was a little flattened.

Hadaway showed a few clips from films over the decades, and

the last was from the 2007 *Transformers*, demonstrating CGI, but Shel was locked on the heightened chemistry between Shia LaBeouf and Megan Fox. As soon as he closed and thanked the class, a guy in a matte-black starter cap from across the room said in a deep voice that carried, "Megan Fox is hot." Some people laughed as they began to pack up.

Shel noticed Charlie shake his head, and he turned and rolled his eyes at her.

The guy must have seen him because he said, "You gotta a problem with that, little man?"

Charlie kept packing his backpack. "I don't know." His voice was narrow and higher pitched compared to the guy's in the starter cap. "I just don't think we should objectify women."

Everyone paused.

"Hot is hot, man. I don't think there's any debating it." The guy smirked, shouldering his bag.

Charlie zipped his bag.

A few people chuckled and the guy shook his head, pulling his cap down over his brow and walking out. Others meandered toward the door, amused. Shel and Hadaway's eyes met, and he shrugged.

Shel walked behind Charlie on the way out of the room and watched him for a moment as he disappeared down the hall.

Shel went to the Golden Bear for lunch, and, by the time her food was paid for, she realized she was going to be late for her next class, so she stuffed the packaged sandwich in her bag and ran. There was something fresh about the air here. She made her way through a wooded pathway to the large entryway of Tolman Hall, a water-stained building with Parisian façade. To her relief, the professor was just starting with what sounded like a brief history of psychology.

"...which contrasts with Jung's philosophy of the importance of each individual's personal journey toward harmony. Maslow called it 'self-actualization.' Czichzemihaly calls it 'flow.' All of them were trying to understand the mind, our thoughts, in relation to the big questions of life: Why are we here? What is our purpose on earth? So, we'll be diving into more of that as the semester unfolds."

The professor's light hair followed the shape of her jaw, revealing triangular earrings and a golden necklace. Though she didn't have the accent, this lady reminded her of British upper class. Her face, with her high eyebrows and poised chin, was like that of royalty, but her eyes also looked tired, somewhat aloof to life in her older age.

"Dr. Bath" was typed on the syllabus beneath the course title as the professor brought it up on the screen at the front of the room. There were a lot of names of psychology pioneers on the syllabus, some of whom Shel recognized: Sigmund Freud, Abraham Maslow, Ivan Pavlov, and some of whom she didn't: Mary Whiton Calkins, Alfred Adler, Albert Ellis, Eleanor Maccoby. She found the topics intriguing: development of the mind, learning theory, cognitive behavioral therapy, emotion, motivation.

Dr. Bath had the class do an interesting experiment of closing their eyes and watching the thoughts, not trying to control or change them, but just being aware of what they were. Shel found this fascinating and scary at the same time. Her thoughts seemed to jump around at a hundred miles an hour. First, they jumped back to Hadaway's Digital Film Production class, Charlie, the guy in the starter cap, then to one of the films they had watched. A pair of boots she remembered seeing in that film reminded her of home, the cubby in the front entranceway of her house in Azusa. Then it flashed to images of her mom and dad's faces, their waves on that day less than a week ago that she drove away to college. Then to Gertrude reading her Bible each night, then to the uneaten sandwich in her bag.

Shel became conscious of something else she had never perceived before, which was that there was a kind of running commentary from her inner voice along with all of these images. It was her voice, but it repeated what someone else had said, or what she had said, or commented on the scenes being played in her memory.

Dr. Bath invited them to open their eyes.

"What did anyone notice?" she invited. No one raised their hands right away, and Shel felt she could simply share what she observed, so she spoke.

"I noticed my thoughts jump around a lot, either replaying memories or projecting forward."

"Very good!" Dr. Bath encouraged. "Anyone else?"

A young woman with dark skin and glasses near the front of the room said it felt peaceful. A stocky guy in sweatpants said, in a comical tone, that it was scary to actually just have to sit with himself. Most of the class laughed in camaraderie with that statement.

"The point of this exercise," Dr. Bath said, "is that all of what we'll be studying this semester has to do with what you just observed. Does anyone know what the Latin root 'psyche' means?"

A guy in slacks and a light blue button-up shirt said, "Phyche means 'mind.' Hence 'psych-ology': the study of the mind."

"Yes, exactly." Dr. Bath let his words gather momentum as she turned toward the board. "Interestingly, it originally meant more than just the mind, though."

On the board, she wrote:

Psyche = mind, soul, spirit, breath, self, ego, persona

"The ancient Greeks were wrestling with the same questions we are: who are we, really? What are these thoughts that can make us feel high or low, happy or sad, tense or resolved, that we like or dislike something so much?"

The class let that sink in.

"The question I'll leave you with for today is," she continued, "what happens when the thoughts stop?"

Shel's phone buzzed, and she reached for it in her back pocket. It was a text from her mom.

Shelley, please call me right away, it said.

Shel threw her laptop in her bag and ran down the stairs and out the front entrance of Tolman Hall. Rounding the corner of the building, she found a bench between some bushes and called her mom.

"Hi, Shelley," her mom answered.

"Hi, Mom. Everything okay?"

Shel heard clicks.

Her mom's voice became clearer. "Sorry, I'm on the road. Just hooking in my headset. How are you, honey?"

"I'm fine." Shel stood up. "What's going on?"

"Well, I hadn't heard from you since you texted Friday, and wanted to hear how your classes are going."

Shel's shoulders relaxed. "Oh! Well…I don't know, Mom. I mean, they're not exactly what I expected." She kicked a pinecone from the sidewalk on to the grass.

The phone crackled on the other end. "You still there?"

"Yes, I'm here." Shel checked her service.

"Listen, Shelley, it's only been a few days. Give it a little time, honey. I'm sure everything will work out okay."

She knew her mom would say something like that. "Yeah. I just miss you guys." She remembered them waving in her rearview mirror as she drove away.

"Shelley, you know we miss you too, but stay strong, sweetie. You have so much opportunity there."

"I know." Shel looked across the courtyard, and her heart lunged as she saw a guy in shorts and backwards cap kiss his girlfriend and walk with his arm around her toward the Golden Bear.

Her mom's voice sounded far away through the narrow bandwidth. "Alright, well, you give us a call this weekend, okay?"

"I will."

"Okay, bye, sweetie."

"Bye, Mom."

Shel clicked the screen off and looked past it at the sidewalk. She eased the phone into her back pocket and wended through the waves of faces toward the dorms.

SCENE 4

"So, do you have a boyfriend, or...." Shel looked across the table at Ellana.

It seemed that Shel would blink and another day and then week had already gone by. Most Mondays and Wednesdays she and Ellana got lunch together at the Golden Bear between Ellsworth's writing class and Raskell's History of Film. Ellana was from Ohio, which surprised her because she figured she was from California or Oregon with her hippie style.

"Ugh, boys." Ellana rolled her eyes. "I'm not sure I've met a member of the male sex who's not thinking with his groin."

Shel laughed. "That's probably true." She went along but didn't necessarily think of it like that. "Well, they're not *all* bad, are they?"

"I don't know. I'm sure there are some good guys out there. I guess I just have more important things to focus on right now."

"That's fair. I have to be honest...I really want a relationship. I didn't date anyone in high school. I've never even been kissed, much less...anything *beyond* that." She looked to gauge Ellana's reaction and found her eyes still open and unmoving, so she went on. "I guess I'm just curious. I mean, I want to find the right guy, you know. I just hope he's out there soon!" Shel lifted her hands, her fingers stretched.

Ellana smiled at how passionate she got about it. "Well, you have to start getting out and meeting guys if you want a relationship. They're not just going to come knocking on your door!"

"You're right. I've been so focused on school for the last month, I haven't even gone out on the weekends or anything."

Ellana shrugged and nodded, a lock of knotty hair dropping over her forehead.

"When did you start wearing dreadlocks?"

Ellana always looked Shel straight in the eye when she spoke. "When I was fourteen. That's when I started my rebel days." She smiled and took a bite of her cucumber, tomato, and sprout sandwich.

"Tell me!" Shel said.

Ellana swallowed. "My older sister took me to a rally for women's rights. I wasn't old enough to know why we were going, but it totally changed my perspective. They showed a short feature that night which was going to be a big release to bring more awareness around gender roles. My sister went nuts for it. I think that was the first time I thought about being a filmmaker. I don't think I knew about gender roles before that, or expectations people put on women to start a family, but I just made up my mind right then and there that I wasn't going to play the game, so to speak, when it came to my role as a woman."

"How much older is your sister?"

"A few years."

"Are you still close?"

"Yeah." Ellana pulled her elbows in front of her on the table.

"So that's when the dreads started?"

"Mm-hm." Ellana nodded and grinned with her lips closed to hide a last mouthful of sandwich.

Ellana put her Tupperware into her reusable grocery bag, and Shel cleared her tray and put on both straps of her backpack.

They weaved through the crowd and headed on to Raskell's lecture.

The next day, after classes were over, Shel took a deep breath and walked down the hall from her dorm room to Cindy and Lark's, whose door always seemed to be open.

She tapped to announce her presence. The two blonde girls sat on their beds, as usual, across the room from one another, each in black tights and sweatshirt tops, typing on their phones.

"What's up?" Lark smiled as her husky voice came through.

"How's it going?" Shel said, feeling for the door frame.

"Livin' the dream, you know," said Cindy, wryly.

Shel forced a laugh. "I was just thinking...I've been working away since school started, and I need to get out and *do* something, you know? I wasn't sure if you knew of anything going on this weekend, or...."

The girls paused and looked at her.

"Um...yeah, some of the guys we know are throwing a party at Sigma Chi on Saturday night. You should come out!"

Lark's invitation was exciting to Shel, but it felt somehow impersonal, too easy.

"Oh, okay." Shel roused her enthusiasm. "What time?"

"Things usually get bumping around eleven p.m." Lark put a hand up and pumped the air twice, looking over at Cindy, who glanced up from her phone and rolled her eyes.

"Cool!" Shel nodded. A few seconds passed. "Well, I guess I'll just see you there, then!"

"Right on! See you there!" Lark said, and looked back at her phone, typing.

Shel had taken a few steps back down the hall when she heard one of the girls whisper, "What was her name again?" She slowed and turned her ear back in the direction of the girls' room.

"I don't remember!" They both giggled.

Shel let her head sag. She remembered her freshman year of high school when she tried, for a while, to sit with Veronica and her friends at lunch. She could see herself back in the cafeteria squeezed in on the end of the bench, her hands in her lap, looking over Veronica's shoulder. She had turned in toward the others to show them her necklace. Shel peered around the side but couldn't see the necklace. What she did see was a circle of faces that she didn't seem to belong to. *But what the hell?* she thought to herself. *I'm in college. I gotta live it up.*

"Woah, where are you headed?" Royson said as Shel walked down the dorm hallway in a shimmery blue dress. His plaid pajama bottoms and worn-out Aerosmith T-shirt were both wrinkled.

"I'm going to a party!" Shel half-curtsied. "What are you up to?"

"Oh, I've got a big chemistry assignment due Monday and have to get a lot done in the lab this weekend, so I'm gonna get up early tomorrow…." His tone fell, but he looked steadily at Shel.

"You sure? You can go with me if you want," she said, turning her hips left and right, the dress sparkling in the overhead light.

Royson smiled. They'd had a few short conversations passing in the hallway over the last few weeks, and this was, she realized, the first time she'd seen him fully smile.

"Alright," Shel said, pouting. "Well, don't work too hard."

Royson stiffened, and his eyebrows met. Her words were, of course, meant lightheartedly, but he just said, "See ya," before pushing open the bathroom door. Shel didn't move for a few moments but then shrugged and skipped down the stairs.

.   .   .

She could hear the subwoofer down the block from the Sigma Chi house as her heels clicked along the sidewalk. As she approached, there was a group of people playing cornhole in the front lawn and a few more on the small concrete porch outside the front door. Everyone had red plastic cups in their hands, and it smelled like beer as Shel passed them on the walkway to the entrance.

When she opened the door, the number of people was astounding. There didn't seem to be any place to walk once she was inside. She kept having to belt, "Excuse me!" and squeeze between people to get through the hallway. People were inches from each others' faces but had to yell to communicate anything because the music was so loud. Shel pressed on through the crowd. She wasn't sure where she was going, but figured she'd keep moving until she found a drink. Fortunately, the kitchen was at the end of the hall, and a pocket opened up around a metal keg. She grabbed one of the red plastic cups that were stacked on the counter and filled it with beer.

Drink now in hand, she took a few sips and rose on her toes to see if she could find Cindy and Lark, or if she recognized anyone. No familiar faces caught her eye, so she continued on her self-guided tour of the house, snaking her way through the crowd. The next room off the kitchen to her left was the living room. This room was, evidently, the source of the music because, as Shel passed through the archway into the area, the music reached a new level of clarity and volume. Shel almost covered her ears but then shook out her hands. She was here to have fun. Taking a few more sips of her beer, she joined the mass of grooving bodies, feeling the subwoofer hit her chest. Memories of dancing with Thelma at high school homecomings and proms came pouring back to her.

A while later, refilling her drink, she noticed the door to the basement had been behind her as she entered the kitchen, so she'd missed it. She pushed through toward it and walked down the staircase. It was a more chill vibe below the main floor, less crowded and much quieter. In fact, all that could be heard of the music upstairs was the gentle thud of the bass. The overhead lights were off, but white string lights were hung along the tops of the walls, and a couple lava lamps churned in the corners of the room. Not a large space, it was perfectly rectangular with a built-in bench covered in pads and pillows that ran the circumference.

Shel spotted Cindy stretched out on the bench in the back, surrounded by a few others, and shuffled her way there. Cindy was in the middle of reenacting something that sounded like it happened last weekend. She was animated and loose. A girl with brown hair and two guys stood by laughing, passing around a joint. Shel wasn't sure if the story was through or not, but she had worked her way close enough to the group that Cindy's attention latched on her.

"This is the girl from my dorm!" she screamed, standing up and giving Shel a hug. Shel waved with both hands out to her sides, introducing herself. The people around the circle said their names.

"Clive."

"Jenny."

And the guy closest to Shel, "Jeremy." He had deep black eyes that struck her. His handsomeness, altogether, struck her. He looked like a film noir actor. It only took a couple seconds for her to take in his slick black hair and clean, short beard, the perfect ratios of his facial features, his elegant smile, his lean but shapely body. She felt a debilitating excitement streak through her chest and into her bowels.

Cindy held the small audience with a reprise of her story for another few minutes before she unceremoniously left them mid-sentence for Lark and another girl who had just come downstairs.

"Laaaaaark!" she squealed as she waddled across the room in

her heels and tight dress. The faces of her recent audience followed her and then turned to each other, and they threw back sips of their beer. Shel's eyes met Jeremy's, and they smiled. Jeremy shrugged and seemed like he was going to walk away.

"Some party, huh?" Shel felt her face flush.

"Yeah!" Jeremy turned toward her, bobbing his head and looking around the room. Shel sped through the options of what she could say next.

"Do you come here often?" Wasn't that from a song? She wondered if Jeremy could see her heart moving her chest, beating twice its normal rate.

"Ah, every once in a while," he said. His voice was smooth, and he looked at her as if sizing her up. "You want to go upstairs and dance?"

A lightning bolt of fear and excitement flashed through her body again.

"Sure!" She was impressed with the calmness she was able to muster.

Upstairs, "Shut Up and Dance" came through the speakers. The room undulated and jumped, and Shel and Jeremy joined in. They were welcomed into the mouth of the beast, and soon found themselves surrounded. Jeremy reached for Shel's hands and pulled her closer, their knees slightly bumping now and again, but neither seemed to mind. Shel couldn't stop smiling. She was truly happy. Another song came on, and Jeremy pulled her against him. She could feel his body and smell his cologne. She surrendered into the ecstacy of it and wrapped her arms around his neck.

The song ended and transitioned into a ballad, so Shel and Jeremy took a break. She was still holding his hand as they walked out of the room. He motioned toward the keg, so they got another beer.

"Oh my God, that is so fun!" Shel yelled between sips.

Jeremy nodded and swung his hips, playfully bumping Shel's side each time. She laughed and nudged him with her elbow.

The slow song was ending, and another upbeat, electronic groove started pulsing. Jeremy walked backward away from Shel, inviting her back to the dance floor with a rotary hand motion, and he mouthed, "Come with me!" Shel set down her empty red cup and followed him.

"Baby Got Back" revealed itself from the electronic remix. The buzz flowed through Shel's veins. She glanced down at her shimmering blue dress and couldn't believe how sexy she looked. She smiled and looked at the ceiling as Jeremy nuzzled into her neck. She ran her hands over his hair and opened her mouth.

Jeremy had his hands on her hips, sometimes moving down lower. She felt a little nervous when he did that but just kept letting go. The more she let go, the more she enjoyed herself, and liked how free she felt. At one point, he took her hand and twirled her, then came up against her backside. She could feel him rub against her, his hands moving over her hips, her arms, her stomach, the beat pulsing through them. She was in a trance, her whole body alive with a tingling fire.

Two more songs played. They took another break, had another drink, and went out on the back patio. The cool late-September air tickled Shel's skin after working up a bit of a sweat on the dance floor. She was relaxed and at ease with Jeremy now.

"Oh, what a beautiful night!" she said.

Jeremy took a sip of his beer and looked up at the stars that were dim above the city lights.

"Have you always lived in the Bay Area?" Shel ran her finger along the rim of her cup.

"Yeah, for the most part," he said with a small amount of breath, then released the rest. "How about you?"

"No, I'm from Azusa." Shel thought of mentioning she was a freshman, but held back, not sure of Jeremy's age, and if her being eighteen would make a difference to him.

"You live close to here?" He scratched his beard.

Shel froze, searching for a way to not have to tell him she was staying in the dorms. "Yeah, a few blocks toward campus."

"Roommate?"

"Well, yes." She eyed him, hoping she was catching on correctly to his line of questioning, holding a line of decency while not turning him down. "How about you?"

"I have an apartment a short drive from here," he said, pointing his chin in the general direction. Shel wanted him to invite her there. She didn't think she'd go, not tonight, but at least she'd know how he felt. "Well," he motioned with his head back toward the house, "you want to dance a little more?"

A few more songs played, and Shel checked her phone to see that it was 2:16 a.m. She didn't want to leave Jeremy.

Maybe sensing that she was struggling with what to do next, he said, "I'll walk you out."

Shel was starting to come down from the buzz of the alcohol as she and Jeremy walked hand-in-hand out of the party.

He turned toward her, and they stood in each other's arms, their faces close. "My car's right down the block. Do you want a ride home?"

"Maybe," she said, rising on her toes and moving her nose against his. She could feel his soft breath against her lips. She pushed forward and kissed him. His mouth was soft, and her hand ran along the roughness of his fine beard. Lowering again onto her heels, she batted her lashes and looked into those crystal black eyes.

"Now what?" She clasped her hands in front of her and swung them a few times.

He hesitated. "You want to come back to my place?"

She wanted to say yes, but with the alcohol wearing off a bit, she didn't feel inclined to "let go" that much. Besides, she felt like this was just the beginning of something beautiful.

"I would...." She breathed in, then out, not finishing the

sentence. She looked down, then back at him, smiling. "I will give you my number, though."

Jeremy punched the number into his phone. He kissed her again, then turned with his hands out to his sides, as if saying, *You sure you know what you're giving up tonight?*

But he said, "I'll see you soon," with that smooth tone. Shel was floating.

She stood there for a few moments watching Jeremy, then turned and sauntered back to her dorm. She texted Thelma, not able to wait to share the exciting news.

Gertrude was sleeping on top of the covers in a fetal position when she returned. That poor girl, Shel thought as she undressed and crawled into bed.

SCENE 5

The peasant celebrates the pleasure of the happy harvest
with dances and songs;
and inflamed by the liquor of Bacchus,
many end their rejoicing with sleep.
Antonio Vivaldi, *The Four Seasons*, "Autumn"

Shel talked with her mom and dad over the weekend, and her mom mentioned how bouyant she sounded, but Shel told her it must be all the new film techniques she was learning. She kept her hand on her phone all through classes on Monday, and now, as she climbed the stairs to her dorm after her second day of classes that week, her thoughts split in two.

I was an idiot. I should have asked for his number. No, if he's really the right guy, he'll call. You have to trust that. What a jerk! He totally led me on. Well, maybe he's just trying to not seem overeager. Overeager? How about he's over me?

Closing her dorm room door behind her, Shel squeezed her head. She tried to practice what Dr. Bath taught about being the observer of her thoughts. *What happens when the thoughts stop?* Shel remembered Dr. Bath asking. Just then, she got a text and swiped open her phone.

Hey Shel, it's Jeremy. How have you been since Saturday night? :)

Her heart skipped. She typed back, then waited a couple minutes to send her message so she wouldn't seem overeager.

Hey Jeremy! I've been great! I had such a good time with you. How have you been?

Can't complain. I had a great time too! You wanna get together again soon?

Shel jumped up and down a few times when she read his text. "Happy day, happy day!" she sang softly.

Sure! What do you have in mind? she wrote.

She waited a couple minutes, but he didn't write back right away, so she hopped onto her bed and re-watched *South Sea Sinner,* another early Shelley Winters film. This was one of Winters's blonde bombshell roles where she was made up with bleached hair, skin-tight top and feathery cabaret skirt and gloves, finished off with high heels. Winters was singing a classic number in the nightclub scene when Shel started to worry again.

It was hard for her to concentrate on what she was watching, and as more time passed, her worry took on an edge. She wanted to give Jeremy the benefit of the doubt that something came up and he couldn't text right back. She adjusted the brightness of her screen, tapping the buttons harder when she couldn't get it just right.

At the end of the film, just as the detectives were putting all the pieces together, Jeremy's text came through.

How about the Raven on Friday night?

Her worries flitted, and she sighed.

Gertrude came in and dropped her backpack heavily on the floor next to her desk and fell into bed, rolling over on her side toward the wall. Shel glanced a few times between Gertrude and her phone.

The Raven? She looked it up and found it was a dance club in downtown San Francisco. Her mind fell into an image of being close to Jeremy, her arms around him at the club. She typed her response but then hesitated to send it.

Her frustration made one last flare. *Maybe I should wait three hours to text him back!* But the other part of her reasoned that maybe he was getting info on the venue and that's why it took him so long, and if she delayed getting back to him, he might think she wasn't that interested. So she sent it.

That sounds fun! Count me in! :)

Cool, I'll pick you up at 8. What's your address?

I'm in the Foothill dorms on Hearst St. near campus. I'll meet you out front! Can't wait!!

See you then!

Shel read those last few texts a few times, beaming. Then she turned and looked at Gertrude, who was still curled up facing the wall.

"Gertrude, you okay?"

In a small voice, she heard her say, "I'm fine."

"Just one of those days?"

"Sometimes I think God is punishing me." Her words were muffled against the pillow.

Shel thought that was a little melodramatic and didn't know what God would be punishing her for, or if she even believed it worked like that. She fought her mind from drifting back into Jeremy's arms.

"Look, you'll be alright, it's probably not that bad…." Shel knew these weren't the right words, and the rest of her breath released from the back of her throat. She crossed her legs on the bed. "Maybe you just need to get out more. You know, go to a party, laugh it off a bit!" Shel giggled to try to lighten the mood.

Gertrude condensed into a smaller ball, tucking her legs up against her body, and she turned her face down into her pillow.

Shel burned a hole in her with her eyes and then shook her

head and sighed and jumped down from the bed. "I'm just going to go brush my teeth and get ready for bed, okay?"

Gertrude didn't respond, so she grabbed her toiletry bag and walked down the hallway toward the bathroom. A part of her felt guilty for not trying to connect more with her roommate, but another part of her tightened up and argued that she wasn't Gertrude's shrink, and it was an inconvenience on *her* that she had to share a room with a depressed girl.

She brushed her teeth, washed her face, and watched her thoughts flit between Jeremy, Gertrude, the paper she needed to write for Ellsworth's class, the dream she'd had about her grandparents and the broken violin. *Gakki!* Her grandfather's voice echoed. Shel shook her head to beat it away.

When she came back in, Gertrude was asleep in her clothes again.

All Shel could think about was getting together with Jeremy on Friday. In Ellsworth's writing class, they were doing peer editing on their first essay assignment: a comparison of French Impressionist Cinema and American silent films from the 1920s. She and Ellana paired up to trade papers, which they read through fairly quickly and shared a few critiques with each other.

"Ellana, your writing is really good. It totally reads like a real review," Shel said.

"Oh, well… I'm not sure it's *that* good!" Ellana reached across to Shel's desk to grab her paper back.

"No, seriously." Shel leaned forward in her desk. "I feel like your voice really comes across through your writing and it's, like, powerful. Have you ever thought about…*being* a writer?"

Ellana shifted in her chair and shook her head. "I don't know. I mean, thank you, but…." She looked at Shel through a masking smile, shaking her head.

Shel smiled back and shrugged.

When they got to History of Film, Raskell's voice was a drone to Shel. They were covering silent films and, as they watched some clips, Raskell pointed out that, even though there wasn't dialogue, there was a score.

"Music has always been an integral part of film from its earliest conception," he said, "light and sound inseparable."

Though she tried to concentrate, her mind slipped back to memories of the weekend and envisioning what Friday would hold. Thelma texted her in the middle of class, and she couldn't help opening her phone.

Shel! That's so exciting about Jeremy!! Have you seen him again?

I know!! I feel like I'm dreaming. We're getting together this Friday to go DANCING!!

Oh my God, so romantic :) What's he like? You have to send me pictures!

Haha. He's honestly like what I've always envisioned. I don't know, there could really be something there. It was like mega sparks flying :)

Yes!! You HAVE to tell me how it goes Friday, K?

K :) How about you, how are the digs at UCLA?

Well, not as exciting as you in that department, but classes are going well. There are some cool people. Joined the Latin club. Miss you though!

Nice! I know, miss you too, Thelma. Thanks for the text. We gotta chat again soon!

Yeah, like Sat morning first thing haha!

Haha, sounds good.

On Thursday in Digital Film Production, the young professor Hadaway had them compare classic black-and-white films with *The Artist*, the 2011 feature film that won an Oscar for Best Picture. As he usually did in class, Hadaway facilitated more discussion, this time by breaking them up into small groups. They numbered off, and Shel found herself in a group of four with two students whose names she didn't remember, and Charlie. Hadaway had posted a few questions on the front screen to guide their reflection on the films.

One of the students in Shel's group read aloud, looking at the screen, "What elements did director Michel Hazanavicius pull from these older films that give *The Artist* an authentic 'classic film' feel?"

This was Shel's strong point in terms of genres, so she jumped in. "One thing I noticed was that Hazanavicius stays true to the 'hundred-and-eighty-degree rule,' filming *The Artist* as if it were a play happening on a stage. Also, there is linearity to the scenes and plot development, as opposed to jumping around in time."

Another student added, "Yeah, there are some axial cuts where the camera suddenly jumps to a close-up of the actor speaking, but definitely no cross cutting between various characters and storylines."

Charlie said, "I know we're supposed to be commenting more on film production techniques, but as a music major, I can't help but notice the scores behind these different examples. It's interesting to me to hear a contemporary film score composed specifically to sound like music from the 1920s. It's kind of like going back in time, because the sound quality is impeccable in the score for *The Artist,* whereas there's a lot of lo-fi hiss in the old recordings for the classic films."

"I didn't know you were a music major," Shel said.

"Yeah! I'm actually interested in film scoring. That's why I'm in this class," Charlie replied. The other students in their group nodded.

"That's cool." Shel looked at him as if noticing him for the first time again. Something about him felt familiar to her. It was in the subtleties of his movements, mannerisms, tone of voice. She couldn't place it, but it was like she'd met him before this semester even though she knew she hadn't. It was déjà vu. She could almost predict what he was going to say next. Or at least when he did say it, it was exactly as it should be.

Later that day, in Psychology, Dr. Bath explained a video showing what looked like an alien world with a network of cartilaginous webs and occasional lightning bolts erupting across their latticework.

"What you're seeing here is a 3D rendering on a microscopic scale of neurons firing in the brain. The neurons are electrical signals that are associated with particular sensations, thoughts, and emotions related to our experiences of the world around us."

She paused the screen. "This process begins from the moment we're born and continues till the moment we die. Studies have shown that experiences we have, particularly family-of-origin patterns set in our early life, form so-called 'grooves' in our brains, or habits of electrical firings that register as pleasant or unpleasant to our various body systems. So, most of us love chocolate cake, but if, on your sixth birthday, your parents got in an argument after you took your first bite, which led to them getting a divorce, that particular firing of neurons associated with tasting the cake becomes deeply 'grooved' through that emotional experience to be associated with dislike."

Dr. Bath's mention of family brought to mind Shel's parents, and a warmth radiated throughout her body. A gentle cascade of images fell on the screen of her consciousness. Light imbued the memory of her dad talking to her the night she was getting ready to go to prom her junior year. Some guy she wasn't very attracted to, Steven, had asked her, but she was glad to get to go. When she'd told her parents, weeks earlier, that she'd been asked, they were excited, and her dad told her to buy any dress she wanted. When Steven came over to pick her up the night of the prom, she wore her new shimmery blue dress, and her dad and mom took photos of them. Then her mom went to the kitchen, and Steven had to go to the bathroom, so Shel and her dad had a moment together. He got a little teary, which hardly ever happened.

"You're growing up so fast," he said, his eyes warm.

He wiped his tears as Mom came back from the kitchen. Shel didn't know how to respond, but her eyes glistened, looking back at her dad.

A soft radiance suffused a memory with her mom. Shel had just finished eighth grade and was doing a two-week junior life-guard training at the beach. Her mom rewarded her with a shopping day. She canceled the one client she had, and they went to the mall. After checking out clothing and jewelry, they went into a poster store, and her mom bought her the poster of Shelley Winters.

As the joy in these memories washed over her, a darker lens stabbed through. It conjured a gloomy cloud around her at eight years old when she was sick, staying home from school. Her dad worked from home, so it was just the two of them in the house that day. He was in the den on his computer and, as Shel was feeling better in the early afternoon, she came downstairs, crawled into her dad's lap, and rested her head against his chest. She could hear his heart beating rhythmically, and it was nice to feel his warmth. She realized he was listening to classical music, the violins leaping vigorously in flourishes of melody.

"What are you listening to, Daddy?" She could feel his chest drop. Then he stiffened, clicked off the music on the computer screen, and lifted her by the arms to set her back on the floor.

"I'm trying to work, Gakki," he said, not looking at her. "Go rest." She turned and walked upstairs, tears brimming though she tried to hold them back.

Her dad apologized later, but ever since then, she'd always hated being sick, beyond just the physical discomfort of it.

The shadow played on and formed into a scene at the beach on a Saturday. Shel saw herself at seven years old, swimming in the waves, when suddenly she couldn't feel the sand beneath her feet anymore and began to flail. Between gasps, she screamed for her mom to come help her but couldn't see her among the blur of colors and figures on shore. She felt the firm grasp of her mother's arm wrap around her chest and pull her to safety. Once on solid ground, she let her small body collapse in the sand, and she cried while all the people around them stared.

In the car on the way home, her mom said, "Gakki, you were barely beyond the sand bar. Was it really necessary to scream and cry like that?"

Gakki crossed her arms and looked out the window.

Her mom shook her head. "One of these days you're going to have to learn how to toughen up instead of breaking down like that."

Shel tried to shake these memories from her mind. Where had they come from? She hadn't thought of them since they happened. They were spots of darkness in the floodlight of her childhood, and she tried to forget them again.

Friday night could not have come soon enough, and Shel bounced on her tiptoes as Jeremy pulled up in a small red Mazda convertible outside Foothill dorm. The autumn weather was still warm, and Shel stood in her tight black dress and heels, showing off her legs and figure. Her straight, dark hair blew gently in the night air. The Mazda came to a quick halt in front of her, and Jeremy reached across to pop open the passenger door.

"Jump in!" He smiled as The Weeknd's music played through the car speakers.

Shel sat down and closed the door, her fingers and right leg trembling beyond her control. Jeremy pulled away from the curb and sped off down the road. Taking a few deep breaths, she told herself to be cool and flipped her hair in the breeze as they rocketed down Clermont Avenue.

At a stoplight, Jeremy drummed on the steering wheel to "Can't Feel My Face." He turned and smiled at her, and she did her best to smile back. She was searching for something to say and was about to tell him how excited she was when the light turned green and Jeremy revved the Mazda into motion. Shel let go and moved her hand in a flying motion through the wind in rhythm with the music.

They took highways around the outskirts of Oakland and found Bay Bridge, the portal to the mystique of the big city. Shel thought back to just a month earlier when she crossed that bridge, arriving at college. So much had changed in a short time. Only in her best dreams would she have seen herself on a date with a gorgeous guy who was driving her to a San Francisco nightclub in a convertible.

They slowed down outside a row of renovated warehouses. Shel read the signs as they passed: SF Bicycles, Flannery's instrument repair with a violin silhouette making up the two Ns. Then she saw the blue neon *Raven* sign above a black awning. There were no spots to park on the street, so they continued down the block. A car was pulling out, and Jeremy swung in.

"Here we are!" Jeremy hopped over the side of the convertible without opening the door.

Shel's heels tapped as they walked the couple blocks back toward the Raven, her hand holding Jeremy's arm.

"You look really hot tonight," he said.

"Thanks!" She dipped her head, looking up into his eyes. "You look"—she nodded her head a few times as if words weren't adequate to describe—"*great*, too."

He had on a light gray sports jacket over a white, V-neck T-shirt and khakis that tapered at the bottom. His black and white Converses were spotless. It was the clothes, but it was the *way* he wore them, mostly. They looked like an extension of his body, which was candescent.

When they got to the door, Jeremy whispered back and forth with the bouncer for a moment, and he patted Jeremy on the back and waved them both through. The atmosphere was electric. Pink and blue lights cast soft glows on rows of alcohol bottled behind the bar and on black curtains and walls that absorbed and bounced the color palette around the room. It was packed. Shel held Jeremy's hand as he led her to the far end of the bar.

"Pretty cool place, huh?" He ran his hand along Shel's lower back.

"This is awesome," she said, looking around.

"What'll you have?" He nodded toward the beverages.

Shel had never been to a fancy bar like this and had no idea what to order.

"I'll have what you're having!" she said loudly, close in to his ear, for him to hear over the music. Shel recognized a remix of J-Kwon's "Tipsy," repeating "E'r'body in the club gettin' tipsy" over and over with sirens and stutter effects. She felt the primal vibes of the music, the driving pulse and heavy breathing between lines. It was hypnotic.

Jeremy ordered two vodka Red Bulls, and they stood off to the side of the room sipping and moving gently to the bass thuds that vibrated through their bodies. They watched others on the dance floor in the middle of the club. Shel loved seeing all kinds of people, dressed up and grinding to the infectious beats, as if at a ritual.

Shel could feel the buzz of the drink, and when they both finished, Jeremy set the glasses on the bar and pulled her onto the floor. He wrapped his arms around her and moved with Rihanna's "Love on the Brain." She could feel his breath against her neck, and she closed her eyes as they rolled back in a blissful blush of feeling.

The rest of the night was a blur of drinks, dancing, and laughing. Jeremy kissed her neck and back, and his hands explored her. She merged with the people around her as the room spun, and they all became entranced deep down in their bodies. It was a strange dream where she suddenly became aware of where she was and what she was doing, but not knowing why or how she had gotten there.

She came to and found herself dancing with Jeremy and another girl. She came to again and found herself in the bathroom. She came to again and she was pressed against the wall, Jeremy making out with her, and she found herself kissing him back hard. The last time, she was aware of the brisk outdoor air and her heavy weight against Jeremy's arm as her heels click-clacked back toward the car. She was laughing and kissing Jeremy when she could.

This was all she could remember when she woke up late the next morning in her dorm room, still in her black dress. Her head reeled and throbbed. She changed into her robe, grabbed her water bottle, and went to the bathroom. Drinking the water down, she turned on a hot shower and let it massage her brain, her skull, her shoulders. Everything was still spinning when she got out.

She checked her phone when back in the room. No text from Jeremy, so she got dressed and went down to the cafeteria. There was a strange sensation of hunger and nausea at the same time, but she figured it would be best to get some food in her, so she loaded up with pancakes, fruit, and yogurt and sat at a table by herself. Her head felt better as the food hit her belly.

Still no text from Jeremy when she got back to her room. It was almost noon. She reached out to him.

Hi :) I just rolled out of bed!

She waited a couple minutes, but he didn't respond, so she got dressed in yoga pants and her Cal sweatshirt. Maybe she'd go see what Royson was up to. She walked down the hall to find his door open. He was sitting at his desk in front of his laptop.

"Knock, knock!" she said, tapping on the door.

"What's up, Shel?" he said, his eyes glued to the screen.

"Not much, what are you up to?"

"Playing…uh…World of Warcraft." His monotone voice trailed off. "I should really be studying for my Bio midterm. How about you?" He closed his computer.

"Not much. Just recovering from a late night. Figured I'd come by and say hey."

"Late night, huh? Seems like you're becoming a regular partier." He winked.

"I guess." She smiled. "No, it was fun. I met this guy, Jeremy, last weekend, and he took me out to a club in San Fran."

"That's cool," Royson blurted. "Well, I was going to head to the library to study."

Shel thought for a moment. "You know, could I actually go with you? I could get some work done, too."

"Sure. Meet you downstairs in five?"

"Sounds good."

Shel grabbed her backpack from her room, and Jeremy texted back.

Hey there. I'm glad you survived. I didn't know you were such a lightweight!

She jerked her head. She couldn't tell if he was joking or being mean. She didn't have much time to respond with Royson waiting for her downstairs, so she quickly typed back.

Haha. I know. That's the most wasted I've ever been. I had so much fun, though. That was such a great club!

He didn't respond right away again, so she put her phone in her sweatshirt pocket and jogged down the stairs.

Shel and Royson walked in silence for a while. The wind

brushed through leaves and swept down streets and alleys. As they passed onto the campus grounds, there was a calm, protected by the large buildings that surrounded them.

"So, you said you're from Azusa?" Royson tucked his hands under his backpack straps.

"Yep. Born and raised," Shel said.

"Have you ever been out of the country?"

She hesitated. "No. I know it sounds crazy, but I've actually never been out of the state!" Shel looked at him but he just nodded.

"How about your parents...are they originally from California?" His lips, somehow, barely ever moved.

"Yep. They both grew up in SoCal and met at USC."

"Ah, the University of Spoiled Children." He smiled.

"Yeah, yeah." She played along. "Actually, they were about as far from spoiled as you can get. They both went on scholarships...my dad's was academic, but my mom's was for swimming. I was too young to remember my grandparents before they passed, but evidently my dad's folks were pretty hard core. I can't remember if they both did, but at least my grandfather actually migrated from Japan. He was only nineteen when Pearl Harbor happened and was put in one of those internment camps for a couple *years*. He was evidently a pretty no-nonsense guy after that and ran a tight ship. They didn't have much money, and my dad was the only child, so there was a lot of pressure on him to... keep the family honor. So my grandfather pushed him pretty hard to be successful."

"Wow, that's intense. What did he end up studying at USC?"

"Computer science."

"Nice." He paused. "What about your mom?"

"She studied design. I think that's why my dad was so attracted to her. I think some part of him wished he was artistic, so he admired my mom's creativity."

"What does your mom do now?"

"She's a freelance interior designer."

"That's cool." Royson seemed to be digesting all this information as he usually did.

Their footsteps clapped along. The campus was mostly empty on Saturdays.

"What about you?" Shel tugged on the bottom of her shirt. "You said your dad works for American?"

He shrugged and said, "Yep."

"Are you close with him?"

"I mean, he's all I got." Royson seemed to be searching for what to say next. "My mom left when I was pretty young, and my dad had to work the overnight shift a lot, so we didn't really spend a lot of time together. I mean, I know he cared about me, but I just saw what a stupid woman and a stupid job were doing to him. He didn't have much left for me."

"Mm." Shel let their conversation rest for a time as they walked.

When they arrived at Moffit Library, they found a table in the main hall. A few other students hovered over their books, ruffled pages and muffled coughs echoing in the large, cathedral-like space. Royson pulled out his biology textbook and his laptop.

Jeremy still hadn't texted back. Shel wanted to squeeze her phone. She tried to put it out of her mind for the moment. In any case, she needed to complete an assignment for Raskell's class on the portrayal of women in two different films from the 1960s.

As she watched the scenes from *My Fair Lady* and *Guess Who's Coming to Dinner,* both of which she had seen multiple times, it occurred to her that she'd never watched them for any kind of assignment. She always turned her mind off and enjoyed the quaint dialogue.

She opened the course interface online and clicked through to the worksheet Raskell posted. She read, "How might the roles of women illustrated in these films have influenced social expectations at the time?"

Shel thought about it and typed,

These female roles played a powerful part in setting an impossible image that women be simultaneously loyal to their husbands and loving mothers to their children, while also sexy and free-spirited; humble and soft-spoken, while also intelligent. This paradoxical existence must have put a lot of pressure on women at that time, setting an expectation of perfectionism.

She read back over it and shrugged, moving on to the next question: "Why are films particularly influential in defining and reinforcing social standards and expectations?"

She wrote:

It's always difficult to determine whether art reflects culture or vice versa, but Hollywood is, and was in the 1960s, deeply interwoven with the fabric of American culture. So, it's likely that audiences looked to films almost as social instructional manuals.

It felt strange to Shel to see these words appear on the page from her thoughts in a more analytical mindset, like there was a part of her turning against herself. Wasn't it okay to just enjoy these films for the entertainment value they offered? She had so many fond memories of watching them, sometimes with her parents, sometimes with Thelma, and other times alone, able to drift off in the fantasy world they created. Real life was complicated with a million shades of color.

Shel looked down at her hand and saw it shaking. Her knees

felt weak, and she was glad she was sitting. A dark feeling pulled at her heart, her stomach was empty, and a pang shot in her side. She'd never felt this before, like she was inhabiting some strange new body or mind. Some schism was cracking down her middle, and she breathed shallow, trying to hold them together. Her vision became dizzy, and it was difficult for her to focus on her screen. She needed to get out of whatever this space was that she had stumbled into. She threw her laptop into her bag.

Royson looked up from his book.

"I gotta go," she said. She pushed her chair out, and it roared in the empty space.

His eyes were wide, searching her. "Okay, see ya, Shel."

She rubbed the back of her neck and scurried across the checkered floor.

SCENE 6

*J*eremy was over to Shel's dorm room at least a few nights a week. They'd been to dinner, a couple bars, and another nightclub since the Raven, but as the weeks went on, Jeremy seemed less inclined to go out and more interested in just hanging around in her room. It was a challenge, at first, to figure this out with Gertrude, since she liked to be in the room in the evenings, but Shel explained to her one night when Jeremy wasn't there how important this was to her that she be able to spend time with him, and that they could only go out on the town so many times a week.

"Well, is it possible to go to *his* place some nights?" Gertrude said, interweaving her arms across her midsection.

"I asked him," Shel said, "but it's just easier this way because then he doesn't have to drive me home and then drive back to his place."

"Why can't *you* drive to his place?" Gertrude threw one of her palms up and jabbed her head forward.

"I don't know. I've asked." Shel noticed the bite in her own voice. "He just prefers to come here, okay?!" She sat down. "Look, if you'd just be willing to be out from seven to nine-thirty on

Tuesday, Thursday, and Friday, that's all I'm asking. I'll go to the library or go out with Jeremy on the other nights, deal?"

Gertrude's eyes fell to the floor. Without looking at Shel, she said, "Fine."

Since then, Shel and Jeremy had been spending those nights in the dorm room. She told him about some of the classes she was taking and asked if he'd seen any of the classic films that were her favorites. He said he hadn't but that they sounded cool. She asked what he did—if he was a student or was working—and he told her that he had moved to the Bay Area right after high school and worked a bunch of jobs that never lasted long, and was currently between jobs.

"What do you do during the day?" She lay by his side on the bed, running her finger over the faded wording on his Corona T-shirt.

"I've been trying to get a band together," he said. "It's with my cousin, who I live with. Sometimes we hang out and try to write. I mean, not a lot. It's pretty chill right now. Hopefully I'll find a job soon, but it's kinda nice to not have any obligations."

That did sound great to Shel. Especially in the midst of midterms, that seemed like an ideal life. She wished she could come with him instead of having to be in class all day. Over the weeks, she had learned that he grew up in Indianapolis, living with his mom, and loved to skateboard in high school. His stories about himself were always brief and involved some crazy thing he or his friends had done back home, like getting fake IDs or pushing each other around in a shopping cart they'd hijacked.

Their talk would always lead them into making out for the rest of the evening. Jeremy tasted like Old Spice, and his kisses poured through her body as a soft rain. Hardly a thought passed in her mind in these moments with him. She was immersed in the sensation of his touch, of the way he moved her body, of his weight against her.

Tonight, as they talked like they usually did on her bed,

Jeremy nuzzled into her neck, and Shel leaned in and gave a soft "meow." Jeremy told her about how he'd rescued a stray cat when he was fifteen. He begged his mom to let him keep it, and she didn't care, as long as he kept it in the garage.

"I used an old towel to make a bed and poured some milk in a bowl for him." His body relaxed, and his eyes were soft and open, connecting with hers. Shel felt a tremor move through her heart and thought, *So this is the real Jeremy.* Then he started to laugh in the same way he usually did when he told about his past and said, "Then he just ran off one day." But he stopped short, as if catching something in himself.

As they made out, Jeremy gently pushed a little further, kissing down her neck, moving his hands up the back of her shirt. He had wanted, a few times, to take off her shirt, and she had always hesitated at this. But tonight she felt like it was right to lean into these next steps with him. Shel kept her eyes on Jeremy's face, trying to read behind his sharp features as he ran his fingers over her bare chest. She knew there were lots of girls who had sex in high school, but that was always a fantasy to her, and it was a rush to be bringing it into reality, even partially.

Nine-thirty came too soon as Gertrude knocked politely on the door. Shel had to pull herself from an almost inescapable magnetism in Jeremy's arms to let her in, straightening her hair and buttoning her shirt over the interval to the door.

When Gertrude walked in, Jeremy leapt down from the bed and walked right past her, rapping on the top of the doorframe on his way out. He pulled Shel into the hallway. She stumbled and felt his weight press her against the wall. She tried to laugh, but his lips mashed into hers, pinching against her teeth, and she felt his hips gyrating against hers. Her eyes wide, she glanced down the hall to see if anyone was watching. A part of her wanted to pull him closer, to tear off his shirt right there in the hall, and another part wanted to use the door as a shield against his closeness. Then, as fast as he had pinned her, he backed away and laughed, turning his eyes away from Shel's.

"I'll see you soon, Shel." He howled and ambled down the hallway toward the stairs.

"Okay, goodnight, Jeremy! I'll text you tomorrow!" Shel hoped her words could put a balm on what had just passed between them. She wondered if it was just her, though.

Cindy walked out of the bathroom as Jeremy reached the door to the stairs, and she saw him exit. Her eyes shot down the hallway to meet Shel's.

"She-e-e-ll," she said. "Is there a man in your life?"

Shel didn't feel like talking about it at this moment but nodded and said, "Yes."

Cindy was in silk red pajamas and flip-flops, which clicked as she came toward Shel.

"Wasn't that guy at the party you came to?"

Shel cocked her head slightly to the side. "Yeah, Jeremy. I thought you knew him."

"Oh, no, that was the first time I'd seen him at the party. Seems like a catch, though!" Cindy put her hand on her hip and raised her eyebrows at Shel.

"Yeah, he is. He's amazing." A pang went through Shel's chest. She hoped she hadn't messed anything up tonight and wondered if she should text Jeremy to make sure everything was alright. But she thought twice about it, because that might seem too overbearing.

Cindy smiled and did a mock cheerleader arm-in-the-air move and bobbed her head while she sang, "Shel's gonna get some. Shel's gonna get some…." She giggled and flipped around, twirling her towel as she skipped to her room.

Shel grinned and shook her head. It was nice to get attention from Cindy. That kind of girl would never talk with her in high school, and it made her feel like she had taken a step up the social ladder now that she was in college.

After Ellsworth's writing class the next day, Shel told Ellana about what had happened with Jeremy. They followed their usual routine at the Golden Bear but had started sitting inside with the cold, late-October fog hovering in the trees.

"I don't know how objective I can be here," Ellana said. "I get that you're smitten with this guy, but there's just, like, red flags around some of this. Well, maybe yellow flags, but you know when something doesn't feel right."

"He's such a sweet guy when we're alone together, though. I feel like I see who he really is, and I bring that out in him, but he's just got another side to him that's… I don't know, but I feel like he's opening up to me."

"Well, just be careful, Shel. You're my friend, and I don't want to see you get hurt."

"Thanks, Ellana." Shel focused on her soup. "Hey, are your parents and sister still coming out for Family Weekend?"

"Oh, yeah! Well, it turns out it'll just be my parents. My sister and her husband I guess are not gonna be able to make the trip, but…." Her voice lowered and she mumbled the last words.

"Oh no! Why not?"

"Ah, that's just the way my sister is. She always has some important thing to do with a rally or strike, or soliciting people to call their senator. I guess something like that is happening that weekend."

"That seems like a lame excuse to not come out and see you in your first semester in college."

"Yeah. But that stuff is important. I admire that she takes it so seriously." Now Ellana was looking into her soup.

After lunch, they headed on to Raskell's class. They were covering the Hollywood depression years of the late '60s and early '70s and relaxing restrictions on censorship around sexuality and violence. Raskell showed clips from *The Graduate* and

The Godfather, and Shel found it compelling that these film-makers were new to their craft but were following their vision and redefining the industry.

That night in her room, Shel sat in front of her open laptop at her desk, but her eyes played over her photos and the poster of Shelley Winters on the wall. Jeremy said he had band practice and wouldn't be able to hang out. She was trying to work on her paper for Ellsworth's writing class, but her mind was in a tug-of-war between a part of her that thought it was great that Jeremy was following his passion and that it was probably good for them to spend a little time apart now and then, and another part of her that couldn't help but wonder if he really did have band practice, or if it was a cover for him spending time with another girl or something. Then she'd catch herself thinking all this, shake her head to break out of that hypnosis, and try to focus on writing, only to be sucked back into the *what if* vortex again. She was hardly making any progress on the paper and shoved her computer to the back of the desk.

Maybe the familiar cadence of her mom's voice would calm her down. She dialed and waited while the phone rang, but it went to voicemail. The automaton woman answered, "You've reached six-two-six...." Shel hung up and pressed her palms to her temples.

She decided to practice what Dr. Bath showed them at the beginning of the semester. Sitting up straight in her chair, she put her hands in her lap and rolled her shoulders back. Then she inhaled and exhaled deeply a few times, focusing on her breath moving in and out. Just as she had experienced in class the first time she tried it, she was amazed that her thoughts settled down and a cool breeze resolved over her chest and shoulders.

Realizing she could do nothing about how Jeremy was spending his time apart from her, she would need to learn to trust him, as they couldn't be together all the time. She let it go.

Her eyes returned to the computer screen, and she pulled the laptop forward and wrote.

By the time she got to Digital Film Production the next day, Shel was ready to jump in. She pictured seeing Jeremy that night and getting to be close with him, and her eyes glowed. Hadaway introduced a guest lecturer who happened to be the director of the San Francisco International Film Festival. Her name was Nora Bellinsky. Shel thought back to when she and her parents attended the San Francisco International Film Festival, the giant columns framing either side of the silver screen, and her mom saying, *You'll know you're successful when you have a film screened here.* The class was rapt with the clips she showed from last year's festival. Shel spun her pen around her fingers with the thought of making her mark in the industry.

After she and many of the other students chatted with Nora at the end of class, everyone filed out of the theatre. Shel turned her head and saw Charlie just behind her.

"That was awesome," she said, slowing to let him catch up with her.

"Yeah." He stared at her and tilted his head. "That'd be amazing to get to go to that festival sometime."

"Oh, it sounds incredible!" Shel said. "It makes me want to start making a film right now. I don't know where to start, but it's that rush where I feel like I could do anything."

"I know!" Charlie's eyes widened.

"I feel so overwhelmed, but super excited at the same time. Sometimes it's like I'm drinking from a fire hose with all the info from my classes, and I don't have time to just…process it all and do something with it!"

They were now standing outside Dwinelle Hall, and Shel was

facing him, talking with her hands, fingers stretched. Charlie smiled at her, and she blushed, dropping her hands.

"Sorry, I guess I get a little passionate about wanting to dive in and *do* more. I came here to make films! I've been watching Shelley Winters films all my life. She's what made me want to come here and major in this, and this lecture feels like it woke up a part of me that gets buried beneath all my assignments." Shel liked that her voice sounded deeper, more thoughtful and connected.

"No, no need to apologize. It's awesome."

He's so calm, she thought, *and awkward.* They stood there for a few seconds, no one saying anything. Charlie didn't seem uncomfortable, just not in a hurry to speak. Shel found herself comparing him to Jeremy. Physically, he wasn't anything like Jeremy. He was shorter and smaller, almost impish. In a subtle way, he was attractive, but it was more because of his sincerity and an intangible quality Shel couldn't put her finger on that was magnetic about him. Part of her wished she felt that with Jeremy, but the other part of her was glad for the incredible physical chemistry with him.

"Well, I've got an advising meeting across campus," he said. "See you next Tuesday?"

Shel nodded. "Yeah, yeah, absolutely, Charlie. See you then!"

She skipped a few times into a fast-paced walk to lunch. The birds chirped in the bushes as she passed, and the sun's warm rays turned her head to the sky. She closed her eyes and wanted to jump and holler, her heart a balloon trying to lift out of her chest, but she let her arms open at her sides and smiled. She couldn't wait to see Jeremy that night.

Jeremy was late. Shel had texted him a little after 7 p.m., when they had agreed to meet, but it was getting close to 7:20, and she still hadn't heard from him.

I hope he's okay, she thought.

She'd made herself up for this night, wearing a new blouse, wood-brown with black cursive f-shaped patterns and string-like tassels that hung from the neck. She put on her best pair of skinny jeans, ivory-strapped sandals, and wore her hair pinned and taut.

She was sitting on the edge of her bed, letting her legs dangle, clicking her phone screen on every half-minute to check the time. She was starting to wonder whether, after their strange interaction last time, he decided he was done with the relationship. Then there was a knock at her door. Gertrude was supposed to be away visiting a girl she knew in high school for the weekend, and Jeremy usually texted before coming up, so she wasn't sure who this would be. But it was Jeremy.

"Sorry I'm late," he said, moving past her into the room. She closed the door and turned toward him.

"It's okay," she said. "Everything alright?"

"Yeah, everything's fine." He was playing with a Hollywood snow globe on Shel's desk, watching the glitter fall from the iconic sign.

"Come here." Shel reached out to him. They stepped toward each other and began kissing. Shel felt Jeremy's attention shift to her, and he became passionate, grasping at her body. Her heart beat fast, silencing her mind. She was happy he was all hers again in this moment. If the physical connection was what he needed right now, she wanted to give that to him.

The chemistry was afire. Words weren't necessary, Shel thought, when you have this kind of magic. As Jeremy began to undress her and kiss the skin revealed, her eyes drifted over her poster of Shelley Winters and the photos of her parents and Thelma. The film of her life had all led here, and what a glorious scene to be playing…living. It was real. She was ready to give herself for the first time into the arms of a man, this man.

He whispered to her, "Everything's going to be alright." She wasn't sure if he was saying it to her or to himself.

Shel woke to the warm sun feathering in through the dorm blinds. Her whole body tingled, and she stretched in the warm sheets, feeling them like silk all over her. Then she caught herself and cocked her head to see her brown blouse wrinkled on the floor and Jeremy putting on his clothes.

"Oh, where are you going? Gertrude's visiting a friend in Oregon." She lifted the corner of her lips. "She won't be back until Sunday."

Jeremy didn't say anything right away but buckled his belt and put on his shoes.

"Jeremy?" She sat up in bed, pulling the sheets to her chest.

"I'll call you later, okay?" He ran his hand through his hair, avoiding eye contact with her, then grabbed his jacket and left.

As the door clicked behind him, the sheets suddenly felt like not enough to cover her naked body. She pulled them up beneath her chin and coiled her legs into herself, sitting there a long time, her eyes wandering the stark, white-walled room, wondering what had happened and what would come next.

Shel's thoughts turned to home as she waited for Jeremy's call. Family Weekend was two weeks away, and she was looking forward to seeing her mom and dad. It had been almost two months since she left early that mid-August morning. It was Saturday afternoon, so she wasn't sure what her parents would be up to, but she needed to hear their voices, so she called.

"Hi, honey!" her mom answered.

"Hey, mom!" Shel tried to sound like her usual upbeat self.

"Sorry to have missed your call yesterday," her mom said.

A muffled voice came over a loudspeaker in the background, and Shel figured they were at the store.

"How's everything going?" Her mom spoke in a louder-than-usual volume.

Shel wasn't sure if she was glad or disappointed that it didn't seem like a good time to talk about what she was dealing with. In any case, she could predict her mom's response once she started hinting at the topic of romance. *Oh, Shelley, it's a fun and crazy time of life. I'm sure you'll figure it out*, she could hear her mom say. And with her dad, there was a realm of topics and activities where they met, and this type of issue simply fell outside those boundaries.

Shel forced a smile. "Everything's good! Yeah, fine. How about for you?"

Her mom paused. "Good. Kind of an unusual week for your dad. He had to go downtown for an annual conference, which he said was mostly unessential. But it got him out of the house, so I think it's good for him. And I had a new client this week wanting some help with a home in the Hollywood Hills. He wanted to put in shoji sliding doors and a chabudai table to make it feel like a Zen dining room, but I talked him into more modern materials."

"Oh, cool." Shel tried to follow along, but her thoughts pushed her mom's voice into the background.

"Tell me about your week, honey."

"Classes are going well." The tone of her own voice also sounded far away.

"That's good. Are you getting enough to eat?"

"Yes, Mom." She let her eyes go out of focus.

"Well, do you want to talk with dad?"

Shel felt her eyelids burn, so she took a breath. "No, I should probably go do some homework."

"Okay, Shelley. Well, you let us know if you need anything. We love you."

"Thanks, Mom. I love you too. I'll talk to you soon."

She had tears around the rims of her eyes, and her heart hurt. There was a part of her that longed to be a little girl again, to get picked up in her mom's arms, but another part that bore its teeth at that notion.

Staring up at the ceiling from her bed, Shel watched her thoughts. They were thunderclouds in her head. She tried to stay positive, snapping herself out of the shadow settling over. *Jeremy will probably call soon, and all of this will vanish like rain when the sun comes out.*

She wanted to call Thelma and tell her what had happened. They had dreamed so often about what it would be like to have sex for the first time. Shel always visualized it happening with someone like Jeremy, but the conditions had been much more idyllic in her mind. In her fantasy, the guy was much more straightforward and romantic with her, and they stayed in bed all morning talking afterwards. In her situation now, she wasn't sure what to tell Thelma, because she didn't know what was going to happen next with Jeremy.

For the time being, she cheered herself up by watching another film from her Shelley Winters library. As much as she wanted to be pulled into the plot, her mind kept drifting to the look on Jeremy's face when he was leaving, and it worried her. It was a look she hadn't seen from him before. The energy was drained from his features, and his eyes were dull and dark.

Her thoughts darted between the film and her attempts to reason that maybe Jeremy was just tired, and she was reading too much into his body language. She wondered if she had done something wrong. Finally, it was too much for her heart to handle, and she drifted off to sleep.

Her grandparents glared at her in her dream again. The first part went by more quickly, and suddenly the couple was before her, and she was holding the broken violin.

"Gakki!" her grandfather snapped.

This time the dream continued. Lifting the violin toward her grandfather, she tried to give it to him. He held out his hands in front of him, and they ghosted away, his feverish eyes turning up to hers and his brow pulling into a wavering crest. She opened her mouth to scream, but nothing came out.

Shel was jolted awake as Gertrude came into the room midday on Sunday, closing the door behind her and dropping her backpack on the floor by the closet. She started to unpack, sniffling. Shel rustled in the sheets and knit her eyebrows. She could hear Gertrude's breath shudder as drawers opened and closed.

"Do you mind not doing that right now?" Shel's sharp tone was muffled through the pillow.

Gertrude stopped, covered her eyes with her hands, and then bolted from the room, pulling the door closed with a solid smack behind her.

Shel lifted her head and threw her pillow at the door. She dropped her face and buried it in the mattress. Everything in her wrenched. Her head hurt from sleeping so long, her heart was raw from having exposed it. Her body was lead. She didn't like who she was today and wanted to sleep it away, but she had assignments due tomorrow, and there was a sliver of will left fueling her hope that Jeremy would call, so she lumbered out of bed.

The image of her grandfather's eyes replayed in her mind. The Winters film she'd been watching before falling asleep had ended and was looping the DVD main menu screen. She closed her computer, checked her phone. Nothing from Jeremy. It was early afternoon. Hunger punched, and she realized she couldn't remember the last time she'd eaten, so she showered and went to the cafeteria for a late lunch.

Royson was at one of the tables alone, his *Organic Chemistry* book open beside his tray.

"Hey, Royson," she said.

"Hey, Shel."

"You mind if I join you?"

He motioned for her to take a chair and leaned back in his own. "How's your weekend going?"

Shel had just taken the first bite of a tuna fish sandwich, and she chewed for a while. "Um, it's okay." Her tone was dull, and she swallowed then looked up at him. "I've been having this recurring dream about my grandparents."

"What about?"

Shel gave him the gist of it, and he nodded.

"That's interesting." Royson ran his hand over his cheeks and closed his textbook. "I mean, there are some theories that dreams come from the subconscious mind, which is a part of the brain that picks up and processes information in a different way than the conscious mind. I don't know if it's, like, scientifically proven, but it evidently works in symbols and synthesizes things that happen in our lives that we may not even be conscious we're experiencing."

Shel thought about it. "What does a violin symbolize?"

"I don't know. It's supposedly all contextual. What does a violin mean to you? Did you used to play?"

"No. I don't know anyone who does, and I never knew my grandparents. That's why it seems so strange."

"Did you tell your folks about it? Did it mean anything to them?"

"No, I haven't told them about it."

Royson had finished his lunch, but he picked at chip crumbs.

Shel looked at her food as she ate. "Is your dad coming out for Family Weekend?"

Royson thumbed the corner of the book. "No. I try to keep my life here at school separate from him."

Shel nodded. "I'm sure he'd love to see what you're doing

here. You must be the top student in all your classes with all that studying you do."

Royson shook his head. "I don't think he'd really fit in here. He never went to college, you know. Barely finished high school, for that matter."

Before today, Shel wanted to have her parents here. She had hoped to introduce them to Jeremy, but that was starting to look unlikely.

The rest of the day was long. Shel meandered between reading posts on her phone, finishing some reading assignments for classes, and letting her mind wander as she looked out the dorm window. She couldn't stand not hearing from Jeremy and ached to call him, to hear his voice, to go back to the way it was when they'd lie on the bed together for hours, to at least understand what was going on. But she would seem desperate and maybe would annoy him if she called, so she didn't. But eventually she left a voicemail, and then another.

She didn't understand. How could someone do this? She called once more, and her message was soft.

"Jeremy, I want to be with you. If I've done something wrong, please let me know. Let's work this out. I'm confused...please call me." Her tone limped, and she hung up.

How could someone ignore a person he's been intimate with? She squeezed her phone, wanting to turn it off but not wanting to miss its illuminating comfort. She typed Jeremy's name into a search window, but nothing came up. She scowered for his profile until she screamed at her phone and pounded it into her mattress. In her mind, he wore a mocking smile and magazine clothes, his hair slicked back. Later that day, she went to the window and looked out at the bike rack where he used to wait for her to come down and get him. Then she lay on her bed and cried a long time. The next evening she did the same, and the next. Her heart felt like it had been snapped inside her chest.

When her phone finally buzzed, she grasped for it, but it was Thelma calling. What was she going to tell her? That Jeremy hadn't texted or called back in over two weeks? That she had tried to track him down so she could smack him and scream in his face if she could find him?

She couldn't answer Thelma's call. She would ask about Jeremy, and Shel would start crying as soon as she started to talk about him. Her finger pressed into the phone to decline the call. Something happened as she did that. A dark encasement closed around her, saving her from having to feel either the warmth of joy she had with Jeremy, or the cold pain after he'd ripped himself from her. Her parents were coming into town that weekend, so she just needed to hold herself together through these next few days.

Shel thought about how weak she'd been to let her emotions get the best of her. It put her behind on classwork. At least she had tonight to get caught up before her mom and dad arrived on Friday. Maybe Royson would be up for one of their library work sessions. She jutted out her chest and hurried down the hall from her room.

Lark was coming out of her door as Shel approached.

"Hey, Shel!" Her raspy tone grated against Shel's ears.

She was in a boyfriend-fit Cal sweatshirt and leggings and smelled like Bath & Body Works. Memories of asking Lark and Cindy about the party and dancing with Jeremy leapt out from a place Shel was trying to keep shut in her mind. She looked down to keep her pace and ducked into the bathroom.

A few moments later, Lark nudged open the bathroom door and found Shel bent over the sink, red-eyed.

"Shel, what's going on?"

Shel shook her head.

"Does this have to do with Jeremy?"

Shel shot a look at Lark. "How do you know about Jeremy?"

"Cindy said you met him at that party, and that he was with you here at the dorm."

Shel looked at her own puffy face in the mirror. "Yeah, things were going so well, and then...I haven't heard from him in over two weeks."

"I'm so sorry, Shel." Lark's eyes darted in the reflection. "I didn't want to interfere, but I'd heard about Jeremy from one of the sorority girls. She told me she met him at a party. He really came on to her over a few weeks. You know, she let him in, and then...radio silence."

Shel took deep breaths, hyperventilating, as she leaned over the sink, Lark's words reeling through her mind.

Lark started toward her, but Shel waved her away, and she stormed out of the bathroom and down the hall.

Royson was predictably at his desk, leaning back in his chair when Shel got to his room. She wiped her eyes and beat on the open door.

"You want to go to the library?"

"Uh...." He brought the front legs of his chair to the floor and pulled a couple pages of notes into his hands, looking at them front and back. "Yeah, let me just get this stuff organized."

Once outside, he had to walk faster than usual to keep up with Shel. She was quiet.

"Hey, everything okay?"

"Yeah, fine. I just feel behind on work." Shel tightened the straps of her backpack.

They were silent the rest of the walk.

When they were seated in the library, Royson kept looking over his laptop at Shel as his fingers clicked away at the keys. Shel knew he might be worried about her, but she didn't feel like talking.

She needed to finish an assignment for Dr. Bath's class on left- and right-brain hemispheric communication, which she wanted to punch out as fast as possible. The textbook said that synapses in the brain formed patterns of firing based on repeated action or thought. Many of these patterns develop early in childhood from family environment and are reinforced through events throughout adolescence and young adulthood. But the point here was that something called "neural plasticity" could occur through left- and right-brain hemispheric communication.

A quote from an article in *Your Maximum Mind* by Dr. Herbert Benson was included in the text:

> When you are in this state of enhanced left-right hemispheric communication… "plasticity of cognition" occurs, in which you actually change the way you view the world…. If you focus or concentrate on some sort of written passage which represents the direction in which you wish your life to be heading, this more directed thought process will help you to rewire the circuits in your brain in more positive directions…. When we change our patterns of thinking and acting, the brain cells begin to establish additional connections, or new "wirings." These pathways or wirings that kept the phobia or other habit alive are replaced or altered…. Changed action and a changed life will follow. The implications are exciting and even staggering.

Shel wasn't in the mood for a positive message, and the words mocked her. She felt overheated and leaned on her hand to keep her head up. How quickly could she get this over with?

"What is 'neural plasticity'?" was one of the questions on the worksheet Dr. Bath posted. Shel pulled together some of the ideas presented in the chapter and wrote:

Neural plasticity is the brain's ability to become more flexible—less locked-in to the synapse patterns developed in childhood and early adulthood. The brain can begin to harden like clay, and certain activities, like playing an instrument or being mindful of the breath, add water to it so it becomes more malleable again.

She sensed Royson looking over as her eyes pierced her computer screen.

The textbook went on, explaining that synapses were linked with thoughts, which were linked with memories. In class, Dr. Bath had described it with the phrase, "What fires together, wires together." So, every time a particular synapse was triggered through a face, a place, a word, it would bring up all those associated experiences. And thoughts were linked with emotions. Shel remembered the chocolate cake example from class. In her current state, all her memories of her near and distant past were filtered through a dark lens.

Shel closed her laptop and looked at the cover of her textbook then around at the endless library shelves. Royson peered at her.

"What's the purpose of all these books?" Shel whispered, staring across at him.

"What do you mean?" He tried to get his voice loud enough without drawing attention to them.

"Every one of these books...Someone had to spend so long writing, but what good do they do us?"

Royson held her gaze, trying to decipher where she was going with this. Finally he whispered, "They pass on info so we don't have to reinvent the wheel."

A girl sitting a few chairs down the length of the long table cast them a rebuking glance, but Shel continued, in a loud voice now.

"Everything's still so fucked up, though. All this knowledge, and the world's still broken."

Heads turned, and Royson tried to become smaller in his chair.

Shel lowered her eyes and put her psych book and laptop in her bag. "Let's go," she said.

They walked back through campus. The rhythmic trace of their soles on the concrete blended with breath and distant sounds of cars passing. When they reached the dorms and then their hallway, Shel waved goodbye but noticed Royson wasn't turning to go toward his room.

Looking first at her and then just beyond at the wall, he said, "Shel, you and I get along well. We're different in some ways, but our personalities seem to line up. I'm wondering if you want to… define this."

"Define what?" She threw her words like a blade before she had time to think.

"This!" He motioned back and forth between them.

Her tension leapt from inside her. "Royson, we've had a couple short conversations and have studied together a few times." She jutted her chin out at him. "That doesn't mean I want to go to bed with you."

He stared back at her. "I didn't say I wanted…" He stopped himself. "You know what, fine. Don't come to me the next time you need someone to hold your hand to get your assignments done."

He turned his back and walked away.

Shel wanted to spit at him but stormed to her room. Gertrude was there, reading on her bed when Shel came in. Her roommate didn't look up to greet her, and neither said anything to the other. Shel glared at her and felt her eyes flare with the burning in her chest, so she shut it all away again in the dark case of numbness. As she looked at herself in the mirror, taking off her makeup, she met her own blank stare in the glass, and wasn't sure who she was looking at anymore.

 *e just landed!*

The text from her mom buzzed Shel's phone as she lay in bed. A few weeks ago, she couldn't wait for Family Weekend, but now her lack of any feeling made the coming days into a chore, a façade she hoped she'd be able to uphold.

Her mom had already let her know they were renting a car, so Shel texted back, *Sounds good, see you soon*, choosing to leave off the exclamation.

When they arrived at Foothill forty-five minutes later, Shel met them at the car, and they drove to the hotel where her parents would be staying for two nights. Her mom asked the basic questions about her classes as they drove, and Shel ticked off the answers, looking out the window more than speaking directly to her mom. Her dad fidgeted with his phone, trying to navigate the narrow streets.

The hotel was an upscale Marriott a few blocks from campus, and Shel admitted to herself that it was refreshing to get away from the dorm. Her dad checked them in, and the three of them took the elevator to the eleventh floor. The room was simple and crisp and smelled of recirculated air. Shel flopped on the king-size bed and wished she could sleep the day away.

"I was looking online and found the schedule of events for the weekend," her mom said, flicking her thumb along the screen of her phone. "It looks like we can check in tonight or tomorrow morning in Moffit Library. Then there's all kinds of fun stuff tomorrow starting at nine a.m.—a welcome breakfast, some tour options, and, of course, the football game."

Shel fidgeted at the thought of going to the football game, rubbing her forearms. Her mom's voice scraped at her brain: the way she was speaking, how she assumed that Shel wanted to participate in the activities. She lay there, not moving, as if gravity were stronger on the mattress, her muscles lead-like.

"What else do you want to do tonight, honey?" Her mom unzipped her suitcase.

Shel was a rag doll, her arms drooping in front of her. "I don't know. Should we get some food soon?"

Her dad perked up. "That sounds good. Do you want me to look up some options?"

"Well, how about you show us where you usually have dinner on campus, Shelley?" Her mom shrugged, holding her electric toothbrush.

Shel didn't really want to go back to campus and thought it would be strange to have her parents there with her.

"I don't know." She tugged at her collar. "Let's go out somewhere."

Her parents acquiesced, and they went to dinner at California Pizza Kitchen. Shel plodded through more updates about her classes and that she was liking Dr. Bath's psychology course. Her mom asked about Gertrude, and Shel rolled her eyes, saying she wasn't sure it was the best roommate match. She asked if there was anyone else they should meet. Shel didn't know if she was hinting at whether or not Shel was romantically involved, but then her mind drifted to Royson and Thelma, seeing those relationships also splinter across her consciousness.

"No." She took a bite of fig and arugula pizza.

Shel sensed her mom squinting at her, searching for the right thing to say. Then she shrugged.

"Well, what sounds good for tomorrow?" Her mom sighed as her dad handed the check back to the waiter with a card.

They agreed on meeting at the hotel then going to the welcome breakfast by 9 a.m.

Shel yawned. "Well, I should probably get back to the dorm."

They scooted back their chairs, and her parents dropped her off at Foothill.

The next morning, they walked into the dining hall on campus for the freshmen welcome event. Round tables were set with white tablecloths and linens and glasses holding ice water, dripping with condensation. People mingled with cups of coffee in hand. A podium was set up on a small stage at the far end of the hall.

Shel spotted Ellana, who was with her parents a few tables away. When Shel's parents returned with coffee, she pointed out her friend, and they went to join Ellana.

"Good morning!" Ellana smiled as they approached. "Mom and Dad, this is my good friend Shelley Henka and her parents."

Min and Tom introduced themselves.

"It's a pleasure to meet you. I'm Robert," Ellana's father said, standing to shake all of their hands. He was tall and lean and wore a blue suit. The blazer sleeves were too short for his long arms and slid up almost to his elbows when he extended his hand. He looked like he didn't naturally belong in a suit but wanted to. His gray-brown hair was brushed, covering over a bald spot on the crown of his head.

"This is my wife, Gina." He motioned, and she extended her hand. Gina reminded Shel of Ellana, her facial features sharp, cheek muscles defined when she smiled, and a genuine quality to her brown eyes. She didn't wear much makeup, and the wrinkles under her eyes showed but held a beauty of their own. Her forehead peaked high, with dark blond, almost brown hair, pulled back and extending over her shoulders.

"Great to meet you!" Min said, and they sat down at the table together. "So, is Ellana your only child?"

Robert hesitated. "Ah, yes. Well, I have an older daughter…"

"Oh, wonderful!" Min smiled. "You must be proud parents of your girls," she said, looking at both Robert and Gina.

"Yes." Robert adjusted his jacket, looking at his wife. "Well, Theresa, Ellana's half sister, is my daughter from my first marriage, so it's a little complicated, but…"

Shel tapped her thumb on the table, replaying what Robert just said, and she shot a glance at Ellana.

Gina picked up her glass, and the ice rattled as she took a sip, some drops of condensation falling onto her white dress.

"Oh, yes, well, that does sound wonderful." Min smoothed her dress. "So, you all are in from—"

"Ohio," Robert said.

"And what do you both do?"

"I'm in…sales, and Gina's a journalist with the *Dayton Daily*."

They continued with some small talk, the conversation driven by Min and Robert, though they coaxed in Tom and Gina with occasional questions. Soon they all got up and brought back food from the breakfast buffet. The welcome event officially started as a woman in a light green business dress with a gold name badge too far away to read spoke at the podium.

Shel's thoughts picked at what she'd heard, and she wondered why Ellana had never told her that she was the daughter of her dad's second wife. Was that why her sister didn't come to things like this? Shel heard a voice, like a shadow, telling her she should never be lied to, and a part of her felt quenched, thinking about giving in to it. Why should she suffer alone?

A student in a tux came on stage as the crowd applauded. He lifted his arms to reveal a violin, which he brought to his shoulder, and he poised the bow over the strings. Shel remembered her dream about her grandparents but pushed it away.

As the young man played, Shel heard her dad humming the melody under his breath behind her. No one would have heard it, except that she was so close to him. Shel had never heard the piece before and didn't recognize the name of the composer in the program as anyone particularly renowned. It was strange that her computer-programmer dad somehow knew this song. What lies was *he* telling her? Her head swam.

The program ended with announcements about the various other activities on the day's schedule. They were thanked and dismissed, and everyone meandered into the courtyard. Min and Robert continued their conversation, standing with their spouses in tow when they got outside. The two girls followed, and Shel pulled Ellana by the arm a short distance from their parents.

"You didn't tell me the truth about your sister." Shel trembled.

Ellana's eyes welled, and Shel felt some satisfaction in that. What was she doing? But it felt too good, letting her waves of pain come crashing out.

Ellana opened her mouth, but no words formed right away. After a moment she said, "I don't really share that with…anyone."

"Is that why your sister isn't here?" Shel raised her eyebrows.

Ellana drew her shoulders back. "Are you trying to make me feel bad?"

Shel rolled her eyes.

Their parents came over on trickling laughter and asked if everyone wanted to go to lunch together. Ellana and Shel avoided eye contact, and Shel cleared her throat.

Min flapped her hands. "Maybe we all need a little rest, and we can meet up later in the day."

As they walked back to the hotel, Shel looked at the ground and stayed silent.

"Shelley," her mom said, "we made this trip up here for you. If you're just going to sulk all weekend, I'm not sure why we came at all."

Shel's back stiffened. "Yeah, well, maybe I don't need you here. I can take care of myself."

Her mom snorted. "Well, I think that's the last straw. Tom, we're flying back this evening." She snapped her chin in the opposite direction, her short black hair whipping around, and her heels pounded the sidewalk.

"Shelley." Her dad's large eyes met Shel's. He took in a breath and brought up his hands, but then exhaled and dropped them, turning away from her.

Heat climbed through Shel's throat and eyes, but she pushed it down and willed her legs to carry her back to the dorms. When she closed the door behind her and saw that Gertrude wasn't there, she couldn't hold the wave of feeling anymore and collapsed onto her bed and wept.

The weeks that followed were a hollow doldrum. Shel had set her alarm for 8 a.m. one Wednesday but kept snoozing until she finally turned it off, deciding to skip her morning class, and couldn't force herself to get out of bed until noon. She figured she may as well try to get to one class for the day, but her head throbbed, and she didn't get up until 4 p.m., shuffling downstairs to the cafeteria.

She didn't sleep well that night and couldn't remember the last time she had slept well. The dream of the violin haunted her, waking her over and over until she covered her head and her ears with her pillow, wanting to squirm out of the pang it left echoing in her heart. In the morning, she walked with her eyes closed, feeling along the walls in the hallway until she reached the bathroom door. She hadn't showered in days, and her hair was frizzed and oily, her eyelids pink and heavy. She splashed water on her face but didn't bother with makeup. She picked up off the floor by the foot of her bed the same wrinkled and pungent jeans and sweatshirt she'd worn the day before and drifted down the streets of campus, people staring at her as they walked by. The air was cold and damp, and an empty breeze swept dead leaves around Shel's feet.

Dr. Bath had asked them to work in groups for a project on learning differences. When she reminded them they'd be working with their partners that day, Shel realized she hadn't done her write-up on elementary school curriculum accessibility. She said she'd forgotten to email it but would send it to the group that night. When she got back to the dorm, her bed looked so enticing, she dropped her backpack and fell into it. She thought of sending the write-up the next morning, but just couldn't force herself to sit down at her computer and type. Later that afternoon, the incessant voice in the back of her head hammered her about how the group was waiting on her, but she lay there on her bed, looking at the ceiling, unable to move. What was the point? Everyone had told her to do well on all her homework and tests in elementary school so she could do well in middle school, then high school, so she could get into a good college, but what did any of this have to do with what she really wanted to be doing for a career? What was the point of even doing film anymore? All the films were lies. They promised romance, that everyone gets a love story and there's some perfect match out there for everyone, if you just wait long enough for it. But look what happened with Jeremy.

And her parents telling her to stay strong so she can be successful. Why? Just because they had to work so hard for it?

But look at them, were they happy? They had fallen in love when they were young, but now they just got along and coped. She'd vowed to do it differently, but now she was pretty sure it was unavoidable, a trap that everyone had to fall into eventually. Why had she ever thought she could one-up it, escape it somehow? And "stay strong so you can be successful"? Was it because her grandparents had to work so hard to overcome the racial shit of their generation? What did any of this have to do with her? She wanted to leave it all behind, to start over somehow. She'd done everything everyone had told her to, followed all the steps, checked all the boxes. And for what? Years of holding on to all that dropped from her hands and cracked on the floor in a single breath. That's all it took. The pieces could stay there, for all she cared.

The next week, as Shel was on her way out of writing class, Ellsworth stopped her.

"Hey Shel, I just wanted to check in with you. I noticed you haven't turned in a couple of the most recent assignments. Is everything okay?" Her brow wrinkled as her brown eyes scanned Shel's clothes.

A part of Shel wanted to tell her what was going on. She hesitated a moment but then jutted her chest forward and leveled her gaze. "Yeah, everything's fine. It's just been a hectic couple of weeks. I'll get those to you later today."

Ellsworth frowned, and then a soft smile washed over her face. "Okay, well, you come by my office hours if you need anything, alright? Or call me."

Shel wanted to roll her eyes but caught herself and nodded, not looking at Ellsworth.

Ellana glanced at her on the way out, but they hadn't spoken to each other in over a month. Ellana blinked in rapid fire as she continued on her way out of the room. Shel froze for a moment, furrowing her brow, then shook her head and walked out.

Her mom called that evening, but Shel watched the phone flash, sitting still at her desk until it stopped vibrating and the "missed call" message popped on the screen. Then she lost track of time, unmoving. The sun set so soon, now, and Shel walked over to the mirror by her closet and stared at her fading reflection, wishing she were someone else.

The semester-end tests came and went. In Raskell's class, Shel read over the first page of questions and didn't remember talking about them in class. She let out a quick snort and flipped the page, expecting to find some familiar material there. She'd glanced over her notes last night, thinking that'd be enough to ace Raskell's test. She knew the answer to the first question on the second page, and then another on the third, but that was it. Her palms began to sweat. She faked her way through a few other short essays, the weight of her hand leaving sticky indents in the paper, smudging the ink, her handwriting scribbly and faint.

She finally answered a text from her mom, and they booked a ticket for her to come home for the winter break. When she walked in the front door, she saw the wooden cubby for her shoes, the vacuum lines in the living room carpet, the dining room table, and the glass-door cabinet where the Japanese bowl hid, its gold striations dull in the evening's pale light. In her room, the eyes in her sophomore-year photo looked past Shel, waiting to greet the girl who'd left four months earlier.

There was nothing to do over break. Shel listenend to the clock ticking by the dining room table as she sat on the gray couch in the living room. She took out her phone and tried to look up Jeremy on social media again, this time through Lark's and Cindy's profiles, but couldn't find him anywhere. She stroked along the screen through her high school friends' posts with photos of end-of-semester parties and keg stands, or at their hometown José's eating the grande burritos they'd missed for months. She looked up Evan Miller, a guy she'd tried to ask out once, and stared at one of his photos. He had his shirt off on a hike in Minnesota, where he evidently ended up going to college. She was being left behind. All her friends were moving forward, and she was stagnating, festering, drowning alone in this silent living room. Why did this have to happen to her? How did she end up being the one utterly unprepared for this change of going to college? All had seemed fine on the surface before she left, but there were these currents underneath pulling her down.

Shel groggily answered the door a few days later when Thelma came over. Her friend was sad to hear things hadn't worked out with Jeremy but wanted to know all the details. Shel rattled off the skeleton of events, and Thelma kept adjusting her position on the side of the bed, pushing her long curls of bright red hair into a position that would hold.

"You know what I kept remembering during finals?" Thelma smiled. "Oh, if *God* was just!"

Their math teacher in high school had asked Thelma about one of the questions she'd missed on the final. "If all was fair and God was just, what would have been the correct answer to number five?"

Thelma answered with a different number but still got it wrong. "Oh, if *God* was just," she'd said, covering up her making a mistake again. Shel had laughed, and they couldn't stop after that, so Shel had to excuse herself to go to the bathroom. But today, she shrugged off Thelma's words, trying to be polite. She really just wanted to be alone. They walked downstairs, and Shel gave a strained smile, waved, and shut her parents' front door, leaving her hand on it for a few moments before allowing herself to collapse onto the couch.

On Christmas, Shel argued with her mom when she said she needed to eat more because she looked too skinny. She watched the Times Square Ball drop on New Year's. She let her vision go fuzzy, and the screen turned into a mass of light and shadow as she sat on the couch next to her parents, just the three of them in front of the TV. Each day bled into the next, and on another blurred morning she was back at the airport and flying to San Francisco.

That Friday night, the weekend before school started again, Shel couldn't sleep. She clicked her phone and watched the minute change to 2:05 as her mind stormed over the stale hollow in her chest. Her legs churned the sheets in tightening knots until she slammed her fists into the mattress, wanting to scream. She needed to beat this darkness out, to shock herself back to life. She threw off the covers and struggled into her sweatshirt and jeans, scrambled to the Civic, and floored it to Ocean Beach. As she stood in the mist at the edge of the water, she couldn't hold back the tension that threatened to explode at any moment, and ran out into the crashing waves.

SCENE 8

Trembling with cold amidst the freezing snow,
while a frightful wind harshly blows,
running and stamping one's feet every minute,
and feeling one's teeth chatter from the extreme cold.
Antonio Vivaldi, *The Four Seasons,* "Winter"

She woke up under neon lights. A tube filled her nostrils, and she felt the tape on her arm where the IV was inserted. Her breathing was slow and rhythmic as she took in the sharp white corners of the room and paneled ceilings. She drifted in and out of sleep a few times. Soon, a nurse came in. She saw him as her eyelids yawned open.

"Hello there," he said in a kind tone. He placed his hand on her forehead and took some readings from the computer next to her. She tried to speak, but the back of her throat was dry and swollen. She swallowed and managed a few muffled words.

"Where am I?"

"You're at the UCSF Medical Center, just down the street

from Ocean Beach. You've been unconscious for about eighteen hours since we reached you there. Do you remember what happened?" The nurse lowered his glasses and peered at her, one oily eyebrow lifted.

She was quiet a long time and then whispered, "Yes, I remember." She reached for details and then shook her head. "I don't know."

"That's okay." The nurse adjusted her pillow. "Can you tell me your name?"

"Gakki," she said, with the Japanese inflection. "Henka." He asked her to spell it for him, and she did.

"Okay, Gakki. You're alright. Just rest for now. I'll bring you some food." The nurse padded away down the hall, and she fell back asleep.

When she woke again, she heard the gentle beeping of the heart monitor to her right and moved her arm, feeling the medical tape pull against the fine hairs on her skin. She heard a tremulous whisper just beyond her vision at the foot of her bed.

"Tom, she's waking up."

Her mom's face came into view at the side of the bed, and she felt a warm touch on her hand. Shel could see the wrinkles strongly etched on her mom's forehead and the puffiness around her eyes. Her dad's face moved in next to her mom, the prickly hairs on his chin a little longer than usual. She could feel through the covers that he placed his hand gently on her leg.

"Oh, Shel! Can you hear us, honey?" her mom said.

Shel nodded and squeezed her mom's hand.

"You're going to be alright, sweetie," her dad said, giving her calf a squeeze.

Shel felt more in her body than the last time she woke, and a pleasant but throbbing sensation of emptiness came forward from her stomach and muscles.

"I'm hungry," she whispered.

A few minutes later, the nurse came in with a tray of food. He pushed the button on the bed, and the back of it propped her up. She shoveled applesauce as her parents pulled up chairs next to the bed.

"I'm so happy to see you awake and well, Shelley," her mom said. "You really gave us a scare there!"

"I know...." She leaned her head back and took a deep breath. "It all happened so fast."

"What were you doing on the beach, honey? Why did you go out in the water at night?" Her mom squished her eyebrows together.

"Well, it's kind of a long story, really. I...I just felt like I needed to get away from something."

"Away from something?" Her dad tilted his head.

"Well, not like danger, but... Look, there was some stuff that happened before winter break...." Shel sank, and she could see the lines etched in her parents' faces. Her eyelids felt heavy, and she closed them. "Maybe I can tell you some other time."

The nurse came back in to bus the tray, and Shel slept. A while later, he returned to read her vital signs.

"Well, you're healthy as ever," he said. "It's a real miracle you survived such long exposure to the water and that someone found you so late at night. But you're in good shape." He took out the IV.

"Someone found me? How did I end up back on the beach?" Shel replayed those last moments in the water, the current pulling her farther out, swimming as hard as she could, darkness.

The nurse pulled her chart. "I only know what the EMTs told me, but it sounds like you were lying on the beach, unconscious, and someone had been out walking and came across you, performed CPR, made the call." He shrugged. "The waves must have brought you in."

Shel looked down at her hands and the plastic bracelet around her wrist. "Is there any way I can track down who found me? They saved my life."

He smiled at her. "The police might have taken his name. You could check with them." He recommended she get some more rest and, when she felt up to it, to walk around and see how she was feeling. If she felt good over the next twenty-four hours with some activity, he said, she would be fine to go home.

When she woke again, her parents helped her out of the bed. She felt stable on her legs, so they walked with her through the halls.

"What was it that happened before break that you were going to tell us, honey?" Her mom held tight to her left arm.

Shel opened her mouth but then breathed out through her nose.

Her dad walked along behind them. "We're concerned about you, Shelley. We just want to make sure you're alright."

"Well…" Shel's legs were heavy, and she had to concentrate to move them. "There was this guy I was hanging out with a lot…." What was she going to tell them? That she'd slept with him and then he'd left her? She'd never talked with her parents about anything romantic. This seemed a dramatic way to start.

"Shelley," her mom cut in, "now, listen. Don't let a relationship get you down. We all go through that at your age. It's just a part of life, sweetie."

Shel heard her dad let out a quick breath, but he didn't say anything.

Her mom turned and looked at her with soft eyes, hugging her arm closer. After they rounded a hallway corner, her mom asked about the classes she would be starting next week for the spring semester. Shel said she hadn't registered yet and saw her parents look at each other out of the corner of her eye, but she assured them she would.

When they'd completed the loop back to the room, Shel felt tired, but her body was in check. The nurse brought some paper-work for her to sign and then discharged her. Her parents expressed their thanks, shaking the nurse's hand. Shel changed into clothes her mom brought for her from home, and they left the hospital in her parents' rental car.

They stopped by Ocean Beach to pick up the Civic. It had a ticket on it for being parked in a No Overnight Parking zone. Looking out at the ocean, Shel wondered how and why her life had been spared. Maybe in that last struggle she'd been able to break free from the riptide. Maybe the waves had brought her in, like the nurse said. She made a point in her mind to call the police and try to figure out who found her on the beach and revived her. Shel rode with her mom in the rental while her dad drove the Civic.

Shel looked at her mom in the driver's seat, and a soft warmth started over her heart, like a far-off voice. How many times had they done this after she'd won her heats at swim meets? They'd laugh together, and she felt so close to her. But they sat in silence now, and a chill flowed in as Shel thought of Jeremy, everything that had happened over Family Weekend. She looked through the windshield at the headlights of a passing car and felt dizzy, seeing dark spots in the flood of light. A flat metallic taste panged her mouth, and she blinked herself back, but her heart had gone numb and heavy.

Her parents walked her to the door of Foothill, and Shel thanked them for making the trip under the circumstances. Her mom asked if she'd like her and her dad to come up. It was getting late now, and Shel knew Gertrude would probably be in the room, so she said it wasn't the best time.

Her dad gave her a hug then her mom held her tight, and Shel could sense she was holding back tears but then she straightened and jutted out her chest. "You're going to be okay, Shelley."

"Yeah, I'm sure I'll be fine," she said, looking away. She wanted to feel something, to cry, to yell, but she couldn't. "You know, when I went under and lost consciousness…" Her eyes searched inside herself then she shook her head. "I'll be fine."

Shel's phone alarm went off at 7:38 a.m., and she tapped Snooze for the fourth time, a pattern she'd fallen into over the past few weeks since her near-drowning. Her floral comforter lay ruffled at a diagonal across the mattress, mocking her for still being in bed.

She'd had the dream about the broken violin again, her grandparents' harrowing stares boring into her and the splintered instrument she still held, not knowing what they wanted or what to do to put the pieces back together. This time, the dream ended with her screaming and shaking the violin.

She was a zombie walking down the hallway to the shower with her hair jutting in random directions. Showering and putting on makeup, she felt like she was watching herself from beyond her body. Two girls were a few sinks down from her in the bathroom, one dressed for the day in Capri pants and a low-cut T-shirt, the other in black tights and a white sweater that hung off her shoulder. They were brushing their hair, applying mascara, and talking about some other girl they both despised. Their indifference to Shel's presence confirmed her fear that she was a void. Why hadn't her war with the ocean been able to make things right again? She was living someone else's story, not the one she imagined for herself.

Back in her room, she put on jeans and flipped through her pile of T-shirts. She found one that she'd begged her parents to buy her in seventh grade, of Einstein with an old video camera superimposed against his eye and an equation beneath reading "$E=M(Scene)^2$". She hadn't worn it in years and wondered, now, why she'd brought it to college. She picked out a black top and pulled it over her head.

Scanning through her phone, the "recent calls" screen was open, and she saw the 415 area code number she'd called last week for the San Francisco police department. They'd said they didn't have a name on file for the caller who found her on the beach. He'd slipped away shortly after the paramedics arrived, before they had time to question him. She clicked her phone off and looked at the blank screen before putting it in her pocket.

The crisp early-February wind refreshed Shel on the walk to the music building, Morrison Hall. The milieu passed by in her periphery like the gentle fog of the morning, which the pine trees held on to, not wanting to release it in exchange for the daytime sun. Morrison was a beige brick building, unimpressive in comparison with the pillared giant, Wheeler. But it was welcoming and without pretense.

Music Appreciation class, the only elective left that would fit her schedule after she registered for her other classes, was not her favorite. The professor, Mr. Tarlaigh, had plodded through two weeks of Gregorian chant and modern performances of ancient songs for lute. Shel didn't see how any of this would relate to her making films, if she even wanted to make films anymore. All she really felt like doing was sleeping.

The classroom was nothing fancy. It felt like a high school room with squeaky plastic chairs connected to flip desks, an outdated tile floor of orange and off-white, and a sliding chalkboard. It had been updated with a newer sound system and speakers, however, which may have replaced the tape deck, Shel thought. She was two minutes late to class but shuffled in and found her usual seat. It wasn't assigned, but most of the students locked in on a spot in the classroom and didn't waver. Charlie was already there, and Shel sat next to him.

"Good morning," he whispered.

"Yeah, it's alright." She meant it with gravity, but with Charlie's stare, she couldn't hide a slight smile and then shook her head.

Mr. Tarlaigh, an older man Shel thought in his mid-60s, had unruly white-gray hair and bushy eyebrows, which often rose above his thick glasses. He almost always wore denim shirts and a fleece jacket, which rounded over his slight potbelly where it met his loose-hanging trousers. He had just queued up the first listening of the day, and everyone was awaiting the highfalutin voice of an Italian castrato at the syllabus's cue. Instead, a piano playing open-sounding chords along with a low thudding came through the speakers. Shel lifted her head. The low instrument plucked a short melody which was then followed by a long and short note from the piano and what sounded like horns, maybe a trumpet. The tones were warm but had a dry edge that felt to Shel like guileless words.

The trumpet took over the melody and played as if the phrases were already in the air and it was simply pointing out what already existed. The song, the sounds, pressed their palms to her heart. They spoke to her of what she was experiencing and understood and lightened the burden. As the trumpet solo ended, Mr. Tarlaigh slowly turned the volume knob, fading out the track. Shel looked blankly at him, awaiting an explanation for this departure from the expected.

"Miles Davis," he said, more to himself than the class. "You know, I've been teaching this class for almost twenty years, and something hit me last night while I was listening to this song that had never occurred to me before."

Shel looked around and saw the other students starting at him.

"I've always taught this class as an appreciation for the musicians who created the music, and for the importance of the concepts or techniques that certain composers or performers introduced into the annals of music history."

Wasn't that what a music appreciation class was supposed to be about? Shel thought.

"But I've never taught an appreciation for what music *is*." He paused for a long time, his white eyebrows peeking over his glasses and his hands extending toward the class, as if everyone was in on this revelation. A guy in the front shifted in his chair. Shel and Charlie exchanged a brief glance.

Shel sensed a difference in Mr. Tarlaigh today, though: his voice more sonorous and his eyes embers. Before, he droned on, but today his vigor belied his age.

"Look...." He stumbled for words. "How did this music make you *feel*?"

Silence.

"I mean, not even *feel,* as in emotions, but...what did it feel like in your body? Moving through you?"

"Kinda jazzy?" A guy on the far left of the classroom flung this response, maybe hoping to bring Mr. Tarlaigh back to the measured world of Antiquity-to-1750. Mr. Tarlaigh smiled and reset, seeming to become aware of his intensity but not letting go his point.

"Okay, it's a start." He motioned toward the student. "Thank you, Ross. Anyone else?"

A girl with dark braids in the front row raised her hand. "It felt kind of like it cut through. Not in a harsh way, but just direct."

"Good, Imani!"

"It swung, made me feel more relaxed," another student said from just behind Shel.

Mr. Tarlaigh gathered air with his hands. "It cut through, was direct, made you feel more relaxed." He paused. "Why do you think it affects you that way?"

Silence again.

He turned back to his computer and clicked on another song. Immediately Shel recognized the iconic electric guitar motif, but wasn't sure what the song was called. The drums thundered and distorted guitars layered to set up an ominous cloud for the singer's grit to stab through. After the lyric, "I'm off to Never-never land," the guitar became a demon with flourishing, screeching wails.

Mr. Tarlaigh eased the volume knob down again. "How do you feel now?"

"Agitated."

"Angry."

"Pumped up."

Answers flew from around the room.

Mr. Tarlaigh held out one hand to his left. "Relaxed, direct." Then he held out his right hand. "Agitated, angry, pumped up." He dropped both hands. "Why?"

"It's the vibe," said a student from the back.

Mr. Tarlaigh pointed where the voice had come from behind Shel, jumped toward the blackboard, and wrote:

Music is vibration.

"But what causes different kinds of vibrations? Why do we feel relaxed listening to one song and angry listening to another?"

Shel noticed her grip had tightened on her desk, and she relaxed, trying to follow the stream of ideas. She couldn't get over the drastic charge of enthusiasm and energy Mr. Tarlaigh suddenly had and wondered what caused it. It certainly made class more interesting, but she couldn't help but think it was a little over the top. Was she weird for not wanting to jump into this new direction? She looked around again and saw that a few students were on their laptops checking email or scanning posts, but Imani and Charlie, Ross in the front row, and a couple others were homed in on Mr. Tarlaigh.

"Listen to this." He clicked another clip on his monitor. A Native American flute flowed gently into their ears. Shel sensed a tingle along her spine. He went to the board again and drew a wavy line:

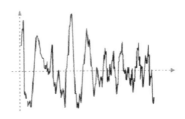

"This is what the waveform looks like for a flute. You can imagine those vibrations undulating our eardrums. What do you notice about it?"

"It has a pattern," Charlie said, dipping his head.

"Good. And how about this one?" Mr. Tarleigh continued. This time a loud cymbal crash surprised everyone, and repeated a few times, biting into the classroom walls. A few students covered their ears. He made another illustration on the board:

"Here's what the cymbal waveform looks like." His eyebrows rose again and he peered at the class over the rims of his glasses. "So, why do these songs affect us differently?"

Imani said, "Because one has nicer waveforms and the other more...erratic ones?"

"Yes," Mr. Tarlaigh said. "And why are we affected by those waveforms?"

"Because...they hit our ears?" Imani tried again.

"True," he said, "but there's more. Think quantum physics!

Einstein!" He rapped the desk with his knuckles. "What do those high-powered microscopes show that this table is made of?"

The guy behind Shel said, "Electrons, protons."

"That's right, and what are those electrons and protons doing all the time?" He tapped all his fingers on the tabletop.

Shel noticed a few of the students look up from their laptops.

"Vibrating," Charlie said.

"Exactly." Mr. Tarlaigh pointed at him. "So, why are we affected by these waveforms?"

Shel spoke up. "Because *we* are waveforms."

"Bravo," he said, pausing a moment as if recognizing Shel anew. Then he went to the board again and began to make concentric circles. "But remember, waveforms aren't linear like I've drawn them over there. They expand in all directions."

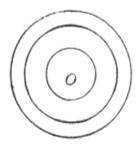

Shel snapped into a flashback. In her mind's eye, she was running out into the ocean again, struggling against its current, gasping for breath. She went under, and her lungs seethed for air. "So that's it," she remembered thinking, and her thoughts stopped, and all went dark. But then her awareness returned. She saw her own body drifting there in the water, as if she was above it. There were no words, just silent knowing. A gentle wave of vibration deeper and more peaceful than anything she'd ever felt echoed on the horizon of her awareness. She found its center at the core of her heart, which melted in awe as rings of luminous golden waves undulated outward. She followed them as her sense of self expanded into the water, the vast sky, and out into the universe. All planets and stars, light and shadow, tension and resolution, melted in that golden light, resounding with the most intimate and overwhelming harmony she'd ever felt. Time extended into infinity, and she didn't ever want to leave. Something like words, but not spoken, unfolded in her, communicating on a deeper level than words could express. The meaning began to reveal itself again.

Shel gasped and then exhaled, steadying herself in her desk back in the classroom. Charlie turned to her.

"You okay?" he whispered.

She nodded, looking straight ahead.

Mr. Tarlaigh continued on about vibrations and the power of music to affect the way people feel. For a few moments, Shel felt like she was in an echo chamber, distanced from what she was hearing, and from her body sitting there in the classroom. But she settled in, and Mr. Tarlaigh's next words caught her attention.

"So, if music has this power to affect us, what about our and others' actions, words, even thoughts?"

A tableau of events and feelings from the last few months dominoed through Shel's mind. It was true. Her choices, Jeremy's choices, their words, her thoughts, were so powerful that at times they were a knife cutting into her heart.

Mr. Tarlaigh went on. "Because what are actions, words, and thoughts?"

Finally Charlie said, "Well, they're all different kinds of vibration, too: action is movement, words are wavelengths of sound forming words, thoughts are synapses firing in the brain."

"Exactly." Mr. Tarlaigh sobered, looking at Charlie. "Action, words, and thoughts are all a kind of music." He paused and dipped his head.

"Look," he picked up again, "what I'm trying to say is that I think we have a tendency—I certainly do—to relegate music to old, dead composers...to Spotify playlists and Muzak in the grocery store. It's something we study, we listen to for entertainment, and put back on the shelf when we're done. But music is a living, breathing thing that not only affects the way we feel, but it *is* us. We *are* the music. We are creating our own compositions around us all the time."

"Alright," he said. "I want to end today by paraphrasing one of my favorite quotes by philosopher Alan Watts: 'Life is a musical thing...Sing and dance while the music is being played.'"

Sing and dance. Shel thought about what college had become. She wanted to sing and dance, but all she could hear was static.

"I want to give you all the opportunity to create a documentary of your own." Professor Sobol, who taught Documentary Film, addressed the class. He was short and stocky, bald except for a band of fine hair that ran around the back of his head, and wore a dark brown beard and fine-rimmed glasses. He always wore some variation of a collared, button-up shirt.

"I think it's one thing to learn *about* something, but it's another level of learning to do it yourself," he said. "This being a one-thousand-level course, I'm not expecting professional film quality here, but I am asking you to conceptualize and execute, with whatever video recording devices you have at your disposal, a five-to-seven-minute documentary that reports on a topic of your interest."

Shel sat toward the back of the room with her laptop closed. As Dr. Sobol continued into the details of the assignment and the components the film needed to include, she felt a weight on her chest. Sobol probably couldn't see her face from the front of the room, but she tried to keep her head forward as she eyed the exit sign over the door.

She remembered the documentary analysis assignment Ellsworth had given in writing class early last semester. Shel slouched in the hard desk chair and rewound to a brighter, happier version of herself those few months earlier, playing through alternate endings. Her leg fell asleep and throbbed, bringing her back to Sobol's voice.

"I also have some exciting news," he said. "The head of the film department, Dr. Marlin, told us in the faculty meeting last Friday that we're going to be able to sponsor an undergraduate short-film contest again this semester during finals week with multiple categories, including animation, film noir, and documentary, among others. I wanted to let you know about it in case you want to submit the documentary you'll be working on for this class, or anything else you've been creating. I'll even give ten percentage points extra credit if your film places in the top three, just to give some additional incentive to submit. Here's the info, which I'll also email to you."

The screen in front of the whiteboard lit up with a document outlining the details of the contest, when and how to submit, and what the prizes would be. The first-place prize was a chance to shadow Nora Bellinsky, the director of the San Francisco International Film Festival, the woman who had visited Hadaway's class last semester, and to have your short film screened there. Second place was an internship at Pixar that next fall, and third place was a professional-quality JVC camera that the department evidently didn't need anymore.

Shel thought about how amazing it would be to get to shadow Nora and showcase one of her films at the festival. That was what she and her parents had always talked about as the "you'll know you're successful when…" type of achievement. She felt lighter, like she was floating, but caught herself. She'd had such little experience and had only made novice films. From what she could tell, this contest was open to juniors, seniors, everyone. There were sure to be many filmmakers with a lot more talent and skill than she.

Dr. Sobol got into the day's lecture. He used PowerPoint with bullets outlining his topics, so Shel found it easy enough to follow along. She opened her laptop and typed in spurts to flesh in the outline about using archival footage.

Her other class of the day was Japanese I. It wasn't required for her major, but it did pique her curiosity and filled an elective credit. Her parents never taught her Japanese, but she had always thought it would be interesting to learn. Her mom and dad rarely spoke it between themselves, and Shel sometimes wondered if they were fluent or just knew enough to communicate when they didn't want her to know what they were talking about.

The professor, Mr. Fujimoto, had a humble demeanor and straight black hair and mustache. He made it clear on the first day of class that he was not a "doctor" but had earned his master's degree in education from UC Berkeley "many, many years ago." He chuckled as he said this in a mock-Japanese accent. He did have a faint Japanese accent when he spoke normally, but it was evident that he had spoken English for a long time and was perfectly fluent.

They had begun the semester learning some of the basic Japanese characters and the sounds that went along with them. Now, Fujimoto was leading them into simple combined characters that gave deeper meaning. Shel found it fascinating that a series of stacked lines and swoops on her page could contain a whole sentence's worth of information.

At some point in each class, Mr. Fujimoto wrote more advanced characters on the board and explained their meaning, having the students copy the figures. He introduced interesting proverbs, like:

苦あれば楽あり

Ku areba raku ari / There are hardships and there are delights

He would explain them in the context of Japanese culture and history, sometimes telling ancient stories. This one, he said, could also be translated as, "After the rain there is sun," which ties in with Japanese lore that when rain and sun occur at the same time, the foxes get married.

As she traced the lines of the characters in her workbook over and over, she thought about Mr. Tarlaigh's music class and what he had talked about in terms of vibrations and how they affect people. As she drew the Japanese characters, she wondered if they held vibrations like English words did for her. "I love you." A warmth came over her, remembering her parents saying that. "You look hot tonight." A rush of adrenalin replaying Jeremy's words. "It's all gonna be okay." Thickness in her throat. Her pen traced on.

As the weeks passed, Shel hit snooze fewer and fewer times on Music Appreciation mornings. Last week, Mr. Tarlaigh had covered the concept of "resonance." Resonance, he said, was an instrument's ability to amplify sound to a maximal degree, which could best be accomplished in the *tessitura,* the range of pitches most naturally produced by the instrument. He did a demonstration with a tennis ball tied to a string where he held the end of the string at chest-height, the tennis ball tethered down by his knees. He moved his hand back and forth at different speeds to see how it affected the ball.

First, he moved his hand very slowly and the tennis ball simply followed from left to right, not moving much.

"Enthralling, right?" he said.

Then, he moved his hand quickly back and forth. The tennis ball barely moved at all because it never had time to catch up with the direction Mr. Tarlaigh was leading it.

"Still pretty uneventful." He scratched his beard.

Finding a steady rhythm left-to-right, the tennis ball caught on and arced into a swing that grew wider and wider until, with still only slight movements of the hand, the ball was completing a near 180-degree arc. His movements were effortless and simple, but causing a lot of response from the tennis ball.

Shel leaned forward, but wasn't sure how this connected with music.

Mr. Tarlaigh brought out a violin and pretended to blow some dust off it. He began to play in the low register, which sounded like a nasal growl. Then he played in the uppermost register, stretching his fingers up the small neck over the body. Shel thought of her dream as the sound screeched and whistled.

He stopped, looked at the class, and then bowed in a note in the middle register. It started softly, and as he pulled across, it drew out the richness of the tone. He added vibrato, wavering his left hand against the pressed string. The body of the instrument came to life as the vibrations leapt off the walls around them. It didn't look like Mr. Tarlaigh was playing any harder or louder than his approach in the lowest and highest registers, but everything was working together to produce a vibrant, more resonant, sound. Shel's skin tingled.

She had continued to think about that concept of resonance a lot last week and what did or didn't resonate in her life now. She remembered how enthusiastic she was last semester to be starting college, which had made getting up and going through each day almost effortless. Since Jeremy left, everything took effort. Other thoughts did the opposite of resonate: how she hadn't talked with her parents much since they came up from Azusa when she was in the hospital. She replayed that image of screaming at her grandfather to take back the violin. But then she thought of Mr. Tarlaigh playing his violin, and Charlie sitting next to her in class each day, his simple smile and jutting ears, and resonance came again as a clean breath.

Today, Mr. Tarlaigh was talking about musical form and variation. He turned on a song that featured a woman's fluttering voice. Shel recognized it as belonging to an artist her parents listened to from time to time. Mr. Tarlaigh leaned back in his chair while the verses unfolded, his gaze far off.

The innocent soprano sang about clouds and how you could look at them as something wonderful, like "ice cream castles in the air," as she put it, and also as something not so great, like when they rain on you. The next verse was about love and that it could also have two sides to it. It can make you feel happy and light when you're in the honeymoon phase, and completely torn apart when it doesn't work out. The last verse was about life and its double-sidedness. Even through all these experiences, her final words were, "I really don't know life at all."

They all were still after the song played and Shel watched Mr. Tarlaigh's eyes soften and come back to settle over them.

"Does anyone know that song?"

No one did.

He smiled. "That's called 'Both Sides Now.' It was written by Joni Mitchell in 1969. She was only twenty-seven years old when she wrote it. A lot of wisdom for a twenty-seven-year-old."

He wrote the form of the song on the chalkboard, showing how the verses were about clouds, love, and then life. Then he turned back toward the class. "Why do you think Joni Mitchell chose to put the verses in that particular order?"

Maya, two seats to the left of Shel, raised her hand. "Because they get bigger, as concepts. Clouds are very specific. Love is more intangible, but still relatively contained in the sense of romantic love. But life is huge. It's...everything." Her palms turned upward.

"Well said." Mr. Tarlaigh nodded. Then he drew a circle on the board and put 'A' at the top and 'B' at the bottom. "If there was no variation from section to section in a song, we could represent it like this."

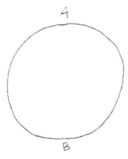

"But with a song like Joni Mitchell's, we can introduce this concept of variation."

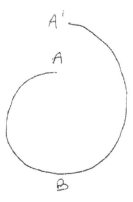

"Here we see that we come back around to a similar 'A' section, but this time, with the lyrics being different and expanding on the core concept—like Maya said, the concepts getting 'bigger'— we can represent it with an expanding spiral. The same theme comes back around, but it's evolved."

He drew another spiral next to the one he'd just drawn, but instead of writing 'As' and 'Bs', he wrote:

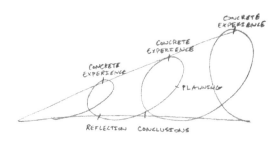

"Just like with vibration and resonance, form and variation aren't just concepts relegated to the musical world. They reflect and inform our everyday experience. How many of you have ever tried something new, succeeded in some ways but maybe failed in others, but learned something from the experience and tried again, most likely with more wisdom for better results?"

Everyone nodded.

He pointed around the new spiral he'd drawn and commented, "This is called the Krebs Cycle. Concrete experience, reflecting on it, creating a new concept around it, actively experimenting with this new knowledge, and then having a new, more evolved, concrete experience. Clouds, love, life. Ups, downs, both sides. Expansion."

Shel pressed the desk with her palms. The lyrics from "Both Sides Now" cycled in her head: "The dizzy dancing way you feel / As every fairy tale comes real / I've looked at love that way / But now it's just another show.../ And if you care, don't let them know / Don't give yourself away." She slumped and fixated on the closed circle Mr. Tarlaigh had drawn on the board. Her eyes followed it around and around. Then she found his illustration that spiraled upward and felt as if it drew a peaceful breeze up through her and over her mind.

"That's good for today." Mr. Tarlaigh put his hands in his pockets. "Remember, 'Life is a musical thing...Sing and dance while the music is being played."

Shel peered at Mr. Tarlaigh as he put his things away. He caught her eye, and his expression warmed. His eyes sparked, almost winking at her, and they both bowed their heads. A trace of a smile came over Shel. As she turned to leave the classroom, she looked back over her shoulder. Mr. Tarlaigh was humming to himself, packing his bag. She let her shoulders relax then walked out.

. . .

That night, in the dorm, Shel lay face up on her bed, trying to form familiar shapes from the pocked patterns on the ceiling panels. She was glad Gertrude wasn't around. They seemed to have landed on an unspoken agreement as to who got the room on what night and rarely saw each other. The marks on the ceiling formed under Shel's eye into a busty silhouette, and her thoughts fell back through time.

She was eight years old with her Barbie dolls in her room, alone in the evening after school. She could hear her mom come home from work and the sounds of pots and running water as she started dinner. Coming down the stairs, through the dining room and past the hiding Japanese bowl and into the kitchen, she could hear her mom's crisp voice, "Hi, Gakki." Shel remembered staying and watching for a few minutes, smelling the bread, but there was not much she could do, so she went back upstairs and kept playing with the dolls. There was a whole world in her mind where the dolls came to life and had glorious clothes and convertibles, and Barbie and Ken's kisses lit up the night. When her mom called her down to dinner, she didn't want to leave that world.

A new reel began in her mind. In this one, she was fourteen, and she and Thelma were in Shel's basement sitting in bean-bag chairs in front of a big TV screen that doubled as a computer monitor. Thelma said they should get online and chat. Shel, as she had recently begun calling herself by this time, wasn't sure what chatting online was all about but sat next to Thelma as she pulled up an instant-messenger site. Thelma said she knew this boy from another high school that was really hot, and sometimes they chatted online. She sent "SteelMan4343" a message, and within a couple seconds he responded with, *What up girl?* They started sending messages back and forth, sneaking in more and more obvious sexual innuendos, like Thelma typing, *I wish you were here right now*, and SteelMan4343 typing back, *Oh yeah? What are you wearing, or not wearing? :)* Shel found herself in a struggle between feelings of enthrallment with the topic and jealousy that Thelma had this online lover. She wanted to dive deeper into this conversation alone and felt strange that Thelma was there.

Later, on her laptop at home, Shel found a chat room where she could connect anonymously with people. She was curious and started messaging with a boy who seemed interested in her. She told him her age, fourteen, and described how she looked. As the stranger described himself, Shel formed an image in her mind. He was a tall, skinny, but fit sixteen-year-old with dark hair. Eventually, their language became more suggestive. She tingled as he wrote back to her. It was a thrilling combination of romance and eroticism, and she wished she could meet this boy in person. He actually asked, but she was in Los Angeles and he in New York. Logging off, she pinned her arms against her stomach, swearing she wouldn't do it again, but every once in awhile the urge drew her back throughout high school.

Lying on the bed, the reel in her mind jumped again and showed her sitting behind Evan Miller in physics class her junior year. Evan was one of the "hot guys" at Azusa High. He had a tattoo on his left arm and always smelled of cigarette smoke, which clung to his black T-shirt and jacket. Her time in high school was getting on, and she hadn't had a single romantic relationship, so she'd decided it was time to muster the courage to ask someone out. She'd never talked with Evan before but figured she never would if she didn't ask him out. So, that day after physics class, she was going to ask.

Her palms were sweating, and her heart began to pound in her chest when the teacher explained the homework and everyone put their books in their bags. Shel was dizzy standing up but followed after Evan as he turned down the hall toward his locker. When he opened the latch, she came up to him and smiled.

"Hi," she said.

He pinched his eyebrows.

She felt the urge to look down but kept her eyes on him. "We're in physics together," she said, pointing back toward the classroom. "I've been noticing you...well...for some time now. We had geometry together last semester...I don't know if you remember me from that...."

He stared.

"No, I—I didn't think you would," she said, "but...well, I just... think you're...cool, and would like to go out with you sometime —I mean, if you want to."

Evan turned to grab a book from his locker. "Look, I really appreciate it, but I'm already seeing someone."

He closed his locker and spun with a snap, pointing at Shel, and walked down the hall to his next class, the chain connected to his wallet clinking with each step.

Shel felt a tremor, and her arms seemed out of place at her sides. She'd had it all lined up, finally found the courage to reach out and start a real relationship. How could she be so stupid to not think he already had a girlfriend? That snap, point, and clinking chain played over and over in her mind. It was like he could see into her and was making fun of her for thinking he'd be interested. She also kept replaying the lame look on her face at that moment, and her just standing there in rejected silence as he walked away. She didn't ask anyone else out after that. No one asked her out, either, except the guys she went to dances with, whom she wasn't attracted to.

Shel sat up on her bed in the dorm and took her head in her hands. Where was her guy? The man of her dreams? She had thought Jeremy was it. But maybe something was wrong with her or the way she was programmed through these experiences of life. She always thought it would go like the films, that she was a very attractive girl who would find her ideal guy. She was healthy, her parents loved her, she had friends, had gotten into one of the best schools in the nation. But when she looked closer at these films, holes began to melt through, the fantasy world in her mind curling up around burning edges. She'd had so much time to build that scene, holding out for the perfect guy. All it took was one singe of reality to wisp that away.

She jerked her legs under her, stood up on the bed, and tore her Shelley Winters poster off the wall, stuffing it in the back of her closet. Then she walked over to her desk, where she kept her collection of Winters DVDs. Her eyes blurred over remembering her younger self, those times with her parents or with Thelma watching the actress as the blonde bombshell who stole men's hearts. She saw it all, now, as a lie. She picked up the films off the shelf, her jaw tense in the darkness, and dropped them into the wastebasket.

SCENE 9

Shel made out her mom's cursive handwriting on the package. That weekend, she'd found a slip in her dorm mailbox and checked in at the front desk to pick up the medium-sized box. She took it back to her room and split the layers of tape with her key, finding a note on top of some plastic bags and Tupperware containers inside.

Shelley,
   Here are some treats to keep you going strong.
   We love you,
   Mom and Dad

She dug into the box and pulled out a ziplock bag full of home-made peanut butter cookies and another of trail mix with dried fruits, which she set aside on the thin carpet. The two Tupperware containers held Tokyo Banana cakes. Those nights as a kid came back to her when she and her parents would watch Shelley Winters films together. She tossed the containers on top of the plastic bags on the floor.

Shel was about to close the box, but one more item caught her eye. It was a book with a bright red cover that read: *Shelley, Also Known as Shirley*, with a photo of a middle-aged Shelley Winters on the front and the actress's name at the bottom as the author. Shel turned the book over. "Imagine being Shelley Winters!" it said. There was a photo on the back of Winters in one of her blonde bombshell roles. Shel wanted to throw it onto the pile on the floor, too, but something moved her to open it.

On the first page was scribbled:

Shel,

I was at the store recently and picked this up for you. Just thought it might shed a new light on SW, in a good way.

— Dad

Shel blinked over and over at the words. Keeping her eyes on the book, she maneuvered onto her bed and fanned the pages, landing on chapter one and reading the first sentences.

"Who is Shirley Schrift? What happened to her, and what metamorphosis took place that changed her into Shelley Winters, movie star?"

Shirley Schrift. Shel realized she'd never looked up much on Shelley Winters, but only knew her roles in the films she watched growing up.

The next paragraph read,

Adolescence is the time when most children struggle with their identity. I have come to feel that when adolescents are forced by circumstances to change their name, for whatever reason, they somehow bury part of that identity, and for much of their adult life are compelled to try to reclaim and rejoin it into a unified feeling of a complete self.

Shel ran her fingers along her throat. It was as if her own thoughts were speaking through these words on the page. The cords on either side of her neck stiffened, and she closed the book and tossed it on her desk, looking at it. It was a sweet gift from her dad, in any case.

Later that evening, her mom video-called her. She'd been doing that every couple of weeks since they'd come up after her incident.

"Hi, Mom." Shel saw herself in the small screen in the upper left corner and straightened her hair.

"Hi, honey! How was your day?" Her mom was seated at her usual spot at the dining room table. They'd probably just finished dinner.

Shel shrugged. "Fine. I got your care package. Thank you." Shel gave a soft grin in the yellow light of her desk lamp shining over her bed.

"Oh, good! I was hoping that arrived today. Did you eat the banana cakes?" She smiled.

"No, I just opened the box, so…." She smoothed the comforter by her leg.

Her mom nodded. "How's your room? Is your bed warm enough…you sleeping alright?"

"Mm-hmm." Shel bobbed her head.

Her mom straightened something on the table and then looked back at the screen. "Classes go okay this week?"

"Ah, I fell behind on some reading for Documentary Film and didn't do so great on the first test, but otherwise everything's coming along."

"Okay." Her mom's brow came to a point. "You know when I was in college, I remember" she looked up toward the ceiling

—"…I had to take a crash course in speed reading to keep up." She gazed off into the distance and grinned, shaking her head.

Her dad came into the screen and waved, smiling at Shel. She waved back.

"Hi, Dad."

"Did you get the book I sent?" He extended his long, thin arm to adjust the camera angle.

"Yes, I just started reading it. It seems like it'll be…great." Her eyes widened as she nodded. "Thanks, Dad."

Shel looked at her parents in the screen and then over at the photo on her bulletin board of the three of them huddled together. She had so much going for her then, and her parents looked so proud of her. She refocused on her mom and dad in the call, then the box around the dimly lit image of herself in the upper-left corner, and didn't know how to connect with them anymore. Maybe if she could pull herself back together, find some way to make them proud of her again, things could be like they used to.

They talked for a short time and said goodnight. Shel eyed the book on her desk. The words were as simple and beautiful as the Miles Davis song they'd listened to in Mr. Tarlaigh's class. Then she thought about the poster she'd torn down and the DVDs she'd thrown away. She turned off the light and tried to forget them.

The following night, Shel rearranged the snow globe, books, and photos on her desk, stealing glances at the Shelley Winters cover. She grunted and paced to her closet, beating a steady rhythm of sliding coats on hangers until she reached the end of the rack. She shoved them all back and closed the door, slouching before her swinging wardrobe. Then she turned, hesitated, and ambled across the room, picking up the book again.

The next pages were about Shirley Schrift's childhood, growing up during the Depression in Brooklyn. Her father was wrongly imprisoned for allegedly burning down his own store, since the insurance on the property was worth so much. Without her father around, her mother scrounged for money.

"We were taken to the Ambassador Theater every Saturday because Uncle Joe got us in free," Shel read. Shirley and her sister would stay there for the whole day, evidently. "We would see *Buck Rogers, Flash Gordon, Movietone News,* a vaudeville show, and sometimes two pictures. My sister swears I never moved; my eyes would stay riveted to the stage and screen."

Another paragraph said,

I developed a whole fantasy world during my childhood; reality was too unbearable. The ability to fantasize has been a powerful tool in my acting. But it used to play hell with my real life. Even later in my life I often refused to see things as they really were and would fantasize them into something nicer.

Shel's eyes consumed the pages. She remembered all those sleepovers when she and Thelma watched films and then fantasized about which famous actor they'd marry. *How much did we live in fantasy?* They always slept over at Shel's house, instead of at Thelma's, she realized, and she wondered why. And Shel was always the one choosing the films they'd watch. She was surprised she'd never registered these details before, or realized they were happening in the moment when she was younger. She always thought of her and Thelma like sisters, choosing and doing things together, but now she saw Thelma in a new way in those same memories, her blue eyes stark against curls of red hair, looking to her for guidance and following along with whatever Shel wanted to do.

She thought of all the time she'd spent as a child watching films, getting ideas about how the world should be and what love should look and feel like. She'd always considered her parents' relationship so plain and figured she was bound for some greater love. But her parents had stayed together all these years. Their love wasn't some Cary Grant and Audrey Hepburn fiery romance, but she remembered coming upstairs from the basement late at night to get more pizza after one of the sleepover films ended and seeing a large bouquet of flowers on the kitchen counter. Only then did she remember that the next day was her parents' anniversary. Her dad must have left them there after her mom went to bed so she'd find them first thing in the morning. She knew they loved each other, and maybe there was something deeper there than she gave them credit for. Shel rollicked between these worlds that felt like they were falling apart. She reached out and grabbed her bedpost, which was solid and cool, but shards of rubble tumbled from her mind, and she gripped the post tighter.

Mr. Tarlaigh started class by bringing in an old, beat-up guitar. It was out of tune as he started to strum "Free Fallin'" by Tom Petty, and students squinted as he sang along off-key. After how well he'd played the violin earlier in the semester, Shel figured this was an act, but some in the class started to laugh because he wailed on, "'Cause I'm freeeeeeee!"

After everyone settled down, he pointed to the top of the instrument where the strings connected. "What are these different parts of the guitar called?"

"That's the headstock," Ross said.

"Right! How about this?" He ran his finger along the section where he had been holding down the strings.

Shel said, "The neck?"

"Good! And how about this?" He knocked on the largest, hollow part of the instrument.

"The body," a guy in the front row said.

"Exactly, Greg. So, what does this remind you of?" He held the guitar next to himself, lining up the headstock with the top of his unkempt hair.

Shel sat back. One of the students said that it was like the human body. Mr. Tarlaigh nodded then put the guitar away and pulled out his violin.

As he tweaked the strings, Shel fidgeted in her seat, stretching the muscles along her spine, the clash of notes and sudden ache in her back waking that scene of Jeremy leaving. Her cheeks grew heavy, and the heat rose through her shoulders. She cranked her neck and found Charlie, replaying the memory of Nora Bellinsky's visit last semester. She yawned and pressed her arms forward and remembered Charlie smiling at her as she talked with her hands about the film festival. Her heart lightened, and she grinned.

Mr. Tarlaigh read them part of a poem called "The Touch of the Master's Hand" by Myra Brooks Welch. The story of the poem was about a broken violin being auctioned off.

'Twas battered and scarred,
 And the auctioneer thought it
 Scarcely worth his while
 To waste time on the old violin,
 But he held it up with a smile.

"What am I bid, good people," he cried,
 "Who'll start the bidding for me?
 One dollar, one dollar. Do I hear two?
 Two dollars, who'll make it three?
 Three dollars once, three dollars twice, going for three..."

    . . .

But, No,
> From the room, far back, a gray-bearded man
> Came forward and picked up the bow,
> Then, wiping the dust from the old violin,
> And tightening up the strings,
> He played a melody, pure and sweet
> As the angel sings.

Mr. Tarlaigh played a gorgeous melody that brought his violin to life, his eyes closed and his chin resting on the body of the instrument. Then he went on:

The music ceased, and the auctioneer,
> With a voice that was quiet and low,
> Said, "What now am I bid for this old violin?"
> And he held it up with the bow.

"One thousand, one thousand. Do I hear two?
> Two thousand! And who'll make it three?
> Three thousand once, three thousand twice,
> Going and gone," said he.

The audience cheered,
> But some of them cried,
> "We just don't understand.
> What changed its worth?"
> Swift came the reply.
> "The touch of the Master's hand."

. . .

Mr. Tarlaigh held the violin straight up and down, and bowed, and then set it back in its case, easing the bow into the black felt seam. Shel thought he made a good "master" in his telling of the poem. That image of him holding the violin next to his body, and the guitar, as he had done earlier, flashed in her mind. If her body was an instrument, then what was the master supposed to represent?

Shel walked the path through the tunnel of trees on her way back to Foothill that afternoon, glad to have the quiet alley all to herself. Before she reached the street, Royson turned in, probably heading to the library. His thumbs were laced under his backpack straps, and he squinted in the fading sunlight that snuck between branches. Shel's heart beat faster. He looked up at her and snapped his gaze to the ground. They both kept walking. Shel wondered if she should have said something to him. Blood rushed to her face, and she tried to avoid her reflection in the glass door of Foothill as she grabbed the cold metal handle to pull it open.

When she got upstairs, Gertrude was changing and jumped behind her closet door with a gasp when Shel came in the room.

"Sorry." Shel rolled her eyes and threw her bag down at the foot of her bed. She thought she'd figured out Gertrude's schedule and knew when she wasn't in the room. It didn't matter. She just needed to get some of that reading done for Documentary Film.

Gertrude rustled and banged drawers, finally stretching into a cardigan. She walked over to her desk and stood over her computer, clicking. Shel looked across at her rounded shoulders. She couldn't wait to try to get a room to herself next year. Gertrude threw her laptop and a couple of books in her backpack and left the room. Shel sighed and scrolled through the article on her screen, which seemed to go on and on.

A week later, Mr. Tarlaigh wrote "Interpretation" on the board. He played "Here Comes the Sun" by The Beatles, singing along with the guitar, in tune this time. Then he said he was going to play the song again, but the class should listen for what was different. The second time, the melody was the same, but the chords were darker.

When he asked what had changed, Charlie raised his hand.

"It sounded like you harmonized the song using chords from the relative minor this time, instead of the usual major chords."

"Good ear, Charlie," he said. "What effect does this have on the mood of the song?"

Imani said, "It made it sound sadder, like a happy memory that could never be again, or something."

"Very good." Mr. Tarlaigh smiled. "This is one way we can interpret music. How we harmonize a melody plays a strong role in the message communicated to the listener."

Then he put the guitar away and took out his violin and began to play a classical melody that Shel recognized. It was long and connected, fluttering at the peaks of phrases, and Mr. Tarlaigh swayed with the instrument, his eyes closed. After a short segment of the piece, he stopped.

"'Prelude in D' by Bach," he said. "This is probably how you're used to hearing it. But what if I played it like this?"

The notes came faster with fire as he dug the bow into the strings and they growled under the attack. Mr. Tarlaigh's hair flipped while he wrestled the violin.

"Or like this?"

Now the same melody bounced toward them as if puffs of smoke rising off the strings. The bow hopped, reminding Shel of the "Sugar Plum Fairy" song from *The Nutcracker*.

"So you see," Mr. Tarlaigh said, "it's all in how you frame the music. It's just inanimate notes on the page until the musician interprets them and gives them meaning."

The class nodded.

Mr. Tarlaigh wrote "Here Comes the Sun" and "Prelude in D" on the board.

"In life, you see, events happen. Those are the inanimate notes on the page. But it's how we respond to, or interpret, those events that gives them meaning. We're often pretty quick to call something a 'good' or 'bad' experience and let it affect us in that way. But circumstances are always neutral. The interpretation is up to us."

The following day, in her Japanese class, Mr. Fujimoto told them a story associated with some characters he had written on the board that translated to the phrase, "Is that so?"

"There was a man named Hakuin who was praised by his neighbors for being a good role model," he began. "A young woman whose parents owned a small store in town lived near him. Her parents were surprised one day to discover she was pregnant. This made them very angry. She would not confess who the father was, but after much harassment, she at last named Hakuin. In great anger the parents went to Hakuin. In response to their accusations, all he said was, 'Is that so?'

"When the child was born, the parents brought it to Hakuin, who was now held in low regard by the whole village. They demanded that he take care of the child since it was his responsibility. 'Is that so?' Hakuin said calmly as he accepted the child.

"A year later the young woman could stand it no longer. She told her parents the truth that the real father of the child was a young man who worked in the fish market. The mother and father of the girl at once went to Hakuin to ask his forgiveness and to get the child back again. Hakuin was willing. In yielding the child, all he said was, 'Is that so?'"

Shel felt something ancient in her heart awakening as Mr. Fujimoto finished the story. She had never heard it before, but it felt like a memory from some distant past. She was connected with herself, more noble and interwoven with a heritage that extended beyond her eighteen years, beyond her parents and grandparents, beyond all the culture of L.A. and Hollywood and San Fran.

Shel didn't feel like going right back to her room, so she strolled past Foothill and continued down Euclid Avenue. It was blustery, and the clouds moved fast, high in the sky. Along with the rhythm of her footsteps, *Is that so?* repeated in her mind. Across the street, she saw the dark wooden beams of a peragola and jogged between waves of cars to investigate. The sun peeked through the clouds and made shadows through the beams, which reminded Shel of pictures she'd seen of the entrance to the Forbidden City. On the other side of the peragola, cascades of rose bushes descended into an amphitheatre of green. The roses weren't in bloom, but the sun was warm on her face, and she had the place to herself. She meandered down the stairs to an inter-section of pathways at the bottom. She closed her eyes and spread her arms wide, leaning her head back to take in the light. Then the clouds moved, casting shadows again. The wind stirred, and the leaves on the bushes shook and lost their color. Shel rubbed her arms and looked around at the same scene, which grew dark and barren. She narrowed her eyelids and frowned at the overcast sky, but then she remembered when she'd looked up into the stars before she'd gone under in the ocean. She thought, now, about how the sun was just one of them in the vastness. The sun was still there above her, burning brightly, giving off all its warmth. The clouds weren't covering it. She just happened to be in a spot where she couldn't see it.

Sitting down on the bottom stair and pulling her legs to her body, Shel's mind drifted over her memories of last semester. She thought of Ellana and felt bad that she hadn't made any effort to reach out to her since their argument in October. And then there was the awkward interaction with Thelma over break. Thelma had called a few times since then, but that black numbness had closed around Shel each time, and she let it go to voicemail. It all clashed in her mind.

"Tension!" Mr. Tarlaigh began Wednesday's class with a jolt. "Anybody know Frank Zappa?"

A few hands went up, including Charlie's. Shel fought her sluggishness as she was learning to flow with Mr. Tarlaigh's spontaneous teaching style.

"Oh good, I'm glad a few people know who Frank Zappa is," he went on. "Zappa, a master contemporary composer, once said that 'music without an ebb and flow of tension would be like watching a film with only good guys in it.'"

Shel didn't agree with the overgeneralization of plots into the hero-versus-villain archetype, but she appreciated Mr. Zappa's use of the world "film."

Mr. Tarlaigh drew a music staff on the board, squiggled a treble clef on the far-left side, and wrote out a C major scale.

He plunked out the notes on the upright piano in the corner of the classroom. It was the "do, re, mi," sound Shel had heard many times before. He then played two notes together: C and E, then G and B. This, too, sounded familiar and pleasant to Shel's ears.

"If the whole song only had those few notes in it, repeating over and over again, it might start to get boring, right?" he said. "But if I add some tension…." He played a series of notes that started the same as his last example but evolved with sounds that pulled at Shel's ear, suspending it, holding out a chord that hung in desperation to be released, and finally resolving it to the original C and E notes again. Shel leaned forward with her arm under her chin.

"Could you imagine if we had no tension like this in the music we listen to? What if composers thought that having tension in their music was something to be embarassed about, or to be avoided? We would be missing out on a lot of beauty."

Mr. Tarlaigh played more music examples, showing how composers managed the balance between tension and resolution.

Setting the chalk on the desk, he ended, "Okay everyone, remember, 'Life is a musical thing….'"

This time, some of the class joined in, "'Sing and dance while the music is being played!'"

He smiled.

Shel kept repeating in her mind what Mr. Tarlaigh had said. *What if tension was something to be avoided? We would be missing out on a lot of beauty.*

Shel still couldn't quite imagine beauty in the midst of all that had happened but was trying to understand what Mr. Tarlaigh meant—what music was trying to tell her. She felt as if the vibration she'd experienced in her vision was intimating to her, speaking to her through light and shadow. *That*, at least, she was beginning to see clearly through the mist.

Shel and Charlie walked out together.

"How's your project going for Documentary Film?" he asked. Shel shook her head, remembering that she'd mentioned the assignment to him weeks ago, feeling overwhelmed about it.

"To be honest, I haven't started it yet. I just… I don't know what direction to take."

Charlie's piercing eyes seemed to pick up more than what Shel said, but they held her. He stood there, silent, and Shel blushed.

Weighing each word, he said, "If you need help with the music for it, let me know," and he smiled.

The thought relieved her. "Really?!" She lit up. "That would be amazing, actually. I'll let you know what I decide to focus on. Um…." She kept her hands on her backpack, adjusting the straps to avoid reaching for her phone.

Charlie's face warmed. "That sounds great. Just let me know when you're ready."

Shel smiled, thanking him.

Professor Sobol stood stocky and solid before the class, looking them over through his thin-rimmed glasses. Shel admired that his button-up shirts were always ironed and tucked into khaki pants.

"May I remind you to keep working on your documentary projects?" His voice boomed. "I know some of you might have a tendency to wait till the last minute." He was never angry, but curt and stern.

Shel had come to appreciate the class. They'd covered tools in developing the exposition, presenting arguments and counterarguments, using archival footage, staging reconstructions, conducting interviews. Shel appreciated the documentary clips he chose to show as expositions of these tools: Michael Moore's *Bowling for Columbine* as an interview approach, Ken Burns's *JAZZ* as narrative, Morgan Spurlock's *Super Size Me* as tracking a personal experiment, and countless others, including *Man with a Movie Camera* from the 1920s, *Grey Gardens* from the '70s, *The*

Times of Harvey Milk from the '80s, and *Hoop Dreams* from the '90s.

Shel saw the power of documentary to tell a story, frame history or a position, and move the emotions of the audience to potential action. Though Dr. Sobol didn't spend much time on it, Shel noticed how much emotional engagement the music engendered in the films. She thought of her experiences in Mr. Tarlaigh's class with vibration, resonance, tone, and tension, and this connection made much more sense to her now.

Later that day, Mr. Fujimoto wrote characters on the whiteboard that were more complicated than usual. Shel continued to be fascinated when he would elaborate on the context of various maxims, and she came to realize that a whole consciousness surrounded each character that integrated the sum of its people's past—its lineage, traditions, and ideals.

Today, the markings looked like this:

金繕い

And underneath, Mr. Fujimoto wrote:

Kintsukuroi / Golden Repair

"In Japan," he said, "there is a tradition that, when a piece of pottery is broken, it is not to be thrown away but mended with golden lacquer. The process is called *kintsukuroi*."

He pulled down the projector screen at the front of the room and showed an image of a blue bowl with gold striations glowing where it had been cracked. Shel's face flushed, and she stiffened in her chair. Her mind flashed back to her family's traditional Japanese bowl hidden away in the cupboard. This kind of design had been in the background her whole life, and she hadn't known what it was called. *Kintsukuroi,* she repeated in her mind.

Mr. Fujimoto went on. "It takes patient work, strong lacquer, sanding, and refinishing, but the pottery is made new, even more beautiful than it had been before."

"To the Japanese," he said, "it is not simply a mechanism of repair, however. There is a deeper philosophy behind it. The pottery does not lose its value when it has been broken but becomes more valuable because it has character. Its history becomes part of its story, and those marks are not to be hidden, but celebrated. Its spirit is more visible, glowing through where it has been broken.

"Sometimes this philosophy is connected with the Japanese concept of 'no mind,' which means beyond thought or attachment. It is being fully present in the moment, letting go of what has been or what will be, and appreciating the beauty of what is."

He had the class copy the characters, demonstrating the stroke directions and details of the figures. Then they returned to the standard curriculum, continuing the next series of numbers, common phrases, and months of the year, practicing the characters and repeating after Mr. Fujimoto to fine-tune their pronunciation.

Shel's hand went along with the motions, but her mind went to Jeremy. She didn't see how she could appreciate what happened with him. She gave a pained stare into the page. There was a part of her that wanted him back, that still yearned for the chemistry and the bliss of kissing him, being near him. She missed the way his eyes made her melt and how they'd soften with his smile when he was close to her. It was a tender reverie to get lost in, but the embrace always ended with the stab of a hidden dagger. He had pierced her open heart. Her pen slashed through a character she was writing, tarnishing the peaceful flow of the other strokes. She wanted to erase it, somehow, but Mr. Fujimoto's words came to her: *kintsukuroi, appreciate the beauty of what is.* Mr. Tarlaigh's words were not so different. *What if tension was something to be avoided? We'd be missing out on a lot of beauty.* She let the ink be and wrote on.

The next week, Mr. Tarlaigh called the talkative class to order. He seemed happy that everyone was starting to feel comfortable with one another, and he smiled, the wrinkles under his glasses becoming more pronounced.

"Alright," he said, wringing his hands, "I hope you're awake and ready, because we have more to cover, this time on 'Practice.'"

Shel and Charlie reached for their laptops in their backpacks at the same moment, and Shel slapped his hand a few times, as if he was trying to steal hers. He smiled at her and held his wrist in mock injury.

Mr. Tarlaigh reached into his bag and struggled for a moment to pull something out that kept getting caught at the corners. When he was finally successful, he held before them a vinyl record with a picture of a black man playing a white guitar on the cover. Shel looked closer and saw that it said *Chuck Berry, Johnny B. Goode.*

"Everybody know the song 'Johnny B. Goode'?" Mr. Tarlaigh slid the record from the sleeve. Some of the students nodded their heads. As he walked around the back side of his desk to the rack of audio equipment, he sang, "Go, Johnny, go, go!"

He placed the vinyl on the player, moving the arm over the thin grooves. As he dropped the needle into the track, the classic electric guitar riff fired through the speakers. Some of the students who hadn't recognized the song title whispered "oh!" to confirm their familiarity with the signature riff.

As he let it play through the first chorus, Shel listened and tried to think of when she first heard the song. It was probably at one of those middle school dances where she and Thelma were inseparable. She could see the two of them doing some kind of boogie-woogie moves and laughing. It just sounded like '50s music to Shel, a period she learned about in history class, reminding her of sock hops and Cadillac convertibles. Mr. Tarlaigh pulled the needle off the vinyl, creating a sudden squelch and white noise.

"Does anyone know what was going on in music in 1958 when this single was released?"

Greg, who always sat in the front row, raised his hand and said, "Jazz was still popular."

"True!" Mr. Tarlaigh chuckled. He pulled out his phone, connected it to the sound system, and scrolled to another track, which played old-timey, interweaving woodwind melodies that reminded Shel of a soundtrack to a silent film.

"This is music from a slightly earlier time, the 1920s, but listen to the rhythm and try to tap along with your foot," he said.

As everyone locked into the pulse, they bounced their heads back and forth, and one of the students bent an arm and started swinging it to play into the corny feel, compared to music they were used to.

"Let's count along with where we feel the groove," Mr. Tarlaigh said, and he started counting, "one, two, three, four," and then starting over again at "one," as the music continued to play.

"What are the accented beats?" He clapped along.

Shel noticed that everyone was tapping their feet on beats one and three, so she shouted that out.

"Good!" Mr. Tarlaigh pointed at her. He paused his phone and moved the needle back onto the record. "Let's do the same exercise with this song."

"Johnny B. Goode" started to play again, and the students locked into foot-tapping synchronicity with the strong groove. When Mr. Tarlaigh began counting, the groove was different than the other track. Something about it felt gritty, harder, more similar to the type of beat they were used to in current pop songs.

Shel heard him say over the track, "What beats are accented here?"

Charlie yelled, "Two and four."

"Right! One, TWO, three, FOUR!"

Shel could hear the drums accenting those beats in the rhythm.

"This is called a *backbeat*," Mr. Tarlaigh said, turning off the record. "For a long time, people were used to hearing a gentler rhythm with beats one and three emphasized. When some jazz artists and rock and roll stars like Chuck Berry and Elvis started to introduce the backbeat, there were a whole lot of people who didn't like the change. They were used to their ways, and it was uncomfortable for them to see the face of popular music shifting. Some thought it was a fad that would fade. But, obviously, rock and roll changed the course of popular music all over the world, and echoes of the rhythms and techniques in some of these early records, like this one by Chuck Berry, can still be heard in pop music today.

"It's kind of like an addiction, or a bad habit," he said. "We get used to something and it can be really hard to change it. But when we do break free, it opens up new realms of creativity and freedom of expression.

"It reminds me of a story about a guitar teacher, a great master of her instrument, who was approached by two students. The first asked her for lessons, and she had him play a bit. It was evident he'd been playing for many years with bad technique. It was all wrong, and she winced as he played. But when he finished, she put on a smile. The second student also asked for lessons, but when she asked him to play, she could tell he hadn't spent much time on the instrument at all.

"'Okay,' she said, pointing to the first student, 'I'll teach you for sixty dollars a lesson.' The student gulped at the fairly large sum of money. 'You,' she pointed at the second student, 'I will teach for thirty dollars a lesson.' The first student got all hot and bothered and said, 'Why are you charging him less? He can barely even play, whereas I at least have experience.' She folded her hands and said, 'Him I only need to teach once. You, I need to teach twice: once to unlearn your old habits, and a second time to teach you right habits.'"

Mr. Tarlaigh raised his bushy eyebrows above his glasses. "Now, I'm not saying that earlier music, or music that accented beats one and three, was a bad habit that needed to be broken in our social musical context, or that the backbeat was some kind of superior technique. What I'm commenting on is the process of letting go of the old and being open to the new. Can you see the pattern? It's easy for us to get locked into a particular 'groove.'

"Kind of like the record here." He lifted the needle and placed it in one of the grooves in the vinyl. "Johnny B. Goode" began to play again. "Once I start it," he said, "it plays the same track we've heard so many times. Nothing different. The exact same notes, phrases. It's hard to break out of the groove."

Mr. Tarlaigh lifted the needle, and the speakers squelched. "Change is uncomfortable but necessary." The mood was serious and, as he looked gravely through his glasses, Shel thought he was staring right at her. Then he laughed and said, "Because we have to move on to the next track!"

He finished class with a Bach piece featuring a violin playing a melody called a *sequence,* which was a pattern of notes that kept repeating at different pitch levels, one right after the other, like waves crashing one upon the next. He showed that the only way the composer could stop the predictable pattern from going on forever was to interject a new note in the series that didn't follow in the same pattern. Shel was reminded of what Dr. Bath covered last semester in terms of neurons and synapse pathways. "Neurons that fire together, wire together," she had said.

As Mr. Tarlaigh brought the lecture to a close, he said, "Remember, life is a musical thing..." and everyone joined in, "SING AND DANCE WHILE THE MUSIC IS BEING PLAYED!"

Shel closed her laptop with a sigh, gazing at it. Charlie picked it up and pretended to take off with it in slow-motion running steps. It snapped Shel out of her cascade of thoughts, and she laughed.

The following weeks found Shel immersed for hours in the evenings with Winters's autobiography. She picked up on chapter four, which was about Shirley's adolescence. Shel was amazed at Winters's vulnerability in sharing such intimate details of her life. The book told about how hyped-up sex had become in her mind, particularly around her movie-star crushes, and how her curiosity and craving for life experience compelled her into a relationship with a young Brooklyn stage actor.

He was an alcoholic known for getting around with women, but Shirley felt adored by him. He had given her an ultimatum that they could either go "all the way" or cut it off altogether. At first, she decided to cut it off because she didn't feel ready, but then one night at 3 a.m., drunk and emotionally wracked, she called him from a hotel room, and he came over. She ended up having sex with him to try to keep him interested in her. She was only sixteen, and he was in his twenties. Their romance continued for several months, and Shirley ended up pregnant. She figured the guy would marry her under the circumstances, but he got angry, blamed her, and took her to get an abortion. Shel fumed at the story.

She couldn't believe how many films Winters had acted in. It seemed she was always contracted to one or two roles at a time, and in her earlier years, the late '40s through the early '50s, Universal Pictures was using her for the blonde bombshell roles that Shel was most familiar with from the films her parents introduced her to—films like *Knickerbocker Holiday, A Double Life,* and *South Sea Sinner.* Shel could recite most of the actors' lines.

Shelley Winters had a background in stage acting and was often engaged with classes in the Method approach. She was famous to the public as a sex symbol but was determined to make her mark in the industry as a "serious" actress. Shel came to a story about how Winters got her role in *A Place in the Sun*, for which she won her first Oscar nomination. She hadn't seen that film, but Winters evidently played a homely factory worker named Alice Tripp—quite a contrast to her former roles.

Winters idolized the director, George Stevens, and wanted the role so badly, but Stevens kept denying her auditions because he didn't want to cast a poster girl for the unlovely role. Finally, Winters convinced him to meet with her, but he said he was so busy—she'd have to meet him in the lobby of his athletic club. So, Winters dyed her hair brown, put on a worn dress and no makeup, and went to wait in the lobby. When Stevens came out at the time they were supposed to meet, she was sitting there, shoulders hunched and her hands folded in her lap, a tired expression on her face. He didn't recognize her and kept looking at his watch, growing more annoyed that Winters hadn't bothered to be on time. At last, he was about to leave. He looked at the plain woman who'd been there the whole time and did a doubletake when he realized it was Shelley. It gave her a chance at the role, and later she officially got it when Stevens saw she could really act the part. *A Place in the Sun* won a Golden Globe award for Best Picture in 1951. Shel couldn't believe she'd never seen the film and decided to watch it as soon as possible.

Shel hadn't given much thought to what Shelley Winters's life was really like outside of her screen personas. She supposed, somewhere in the back of her mind, that it was pretty ideal living in Hollywood in the 1950s and being a big star. She knew from tabloids and news on today's stars that there was not always prettiness behind the glamour of La La Land, but the mid-1900s seemed more idyllic and innocent.

It was revealing to read another account of Winters and Rita Hayworth, both icons of the industry, being forced to go to a New Year's Eve publicity party, with Hayworth grieving her divorce from Orson Welles and Winters's husband at the time serving in the Air Force overseas. A fancy limousine arrived at Hayworth's house in Beverly Hills, and she and Winters got in the back. Hayworth said, "God, I hate holidays. I think they're the lonesomest times of the year." Winters wrote, "I reached for her hand and held it while lonely tears ran down our cheeks. We blotted carefully, so as not to mess our makeup."

Hollywood was a double life, and Winters mentioned an ongoing struggle within herself, too, between Shirley Schrift, her simplistic childhood persona who associated with noble aspirations, and Shelley Winters, who, becoming an international star and sex goddess, divorced her husband and became the mistress of married men. Winters wrote, "I spent the night...with a strange, sad actor sleeping at my side and staring into darkness, wondering what the hell had happened to the idealistic, chaste Shirley Schrift."

Yet, a part of her held on to the illusion that she would still find the perfect husband. Years had passed in her Hollywood lifestyle, but, she wrote, "I was still looking for a Paul (her first husband) who wanted to be an actor. I had not yet realized those characters are mutually exclusive. My fantasy was that I would someday meet this handsome, talented PhD actor, and we would marry and have lots of beautiful actor children, and we would act into the sunset together."

She did later think she had met such a man in the Italian actor Vittorio Gassman. It was one of those magical first introductions.

"Our staring at each other must have become obvious," Winters wrote about seeing Gassman for the first time at a play in Rome. He came over to her in the balcony booth and introduced himself, complimenting her, in Italian, on her acting in *A Place in the Sun.* They couldn't communicate much with each other through the language barrier, but, she wrote, "Under the program Vittorio held my hand, and we both kept peeking at each other. He is not a person who reveals much of himself with his eyes, but that night he was very open."

After the play, he drove her around Rome, and Winters described the romance of it like it was a dream. They went to the Campidoglio, the Roman Forum, and then up to Aventine Hill, where Gassman put his coat around her and kissed her. They got ice cream at a midnight café, and Winters wrote, "At one point I didn't know who was eating which ice cream. I guess that's what they mean by chocolate-covered kisses."

Gassman took her back to her hotel, and they went up to her room. "I tried to say, 'I don't sleep with anybody on the first date,' but my Italian wasn't up to it," she wrote. The book played off a theme when Winters would be intimate with a man. She would describe it like an old movie where the camera pans to a fireplace or ocean waves. But in this case, describing her intimacy with Gassman that night, she wrote, "I finally understood the passionate beauty of Italy, which has lasted through all the centuries, and that wherever you may wander, all roads lead to Rome. And you can't pan to anything, because it hasn't been invented in pictures or words."

Shel rested the book on her chest and stared up at the ceiling, letting her thoughts drift. That was the kind of romance she wanted to experience. She thought she'd found it that night when Jeremy first kissed her. Wondering if this perfect love worked out between Winters and Gassman, she flipped to the middle of the book and scanned through the photos to see if they would reveal their future. There were two photos of the couple on a single page and the captions read, "Vittorio and I on the lawn of our new home, newly married, when he could hardly speak English. If only we could have kept it that way." And, "The minister at the Little Church Around the Corner said, 'Even for actors, you must have your previous divorce papers.'" So they'd gotten married, and it hadn't worked out.

Did that kind of love they show in the films exist? Winters's story about meeting Gassman seemed as close to fairytale as any she'd heard, and yet they ended up divorced. Was that kind of love a lie? It's all Shel knew. She'd seen it in a hundred films, and each one had a unique twist on how crazy but magical it is to fall in love. That's how it must be for everyone, right? Otherwise, where did the script writers get it from? There must be some truth to it. Doesn't everyone deserve to find the love of their lives like in a beautiful film scene? Winters and Gassman got to, but it didn't work out. Shel remembered hearing a statistic once that the divorce rate in the US was very high.

Where do we get our ideas about love? she thought. Maybe it was different from person to person, but, in general, people were always taking in media images: on billboards, in films, magazines, TV shows, ads, songs, bombarded by these everywhere they went. It was subconscious. Music at the grocery store talking about finding the perfect love and how "I was nothing before I met you." A cologne ad showing a man and woman dressed in fancy clothes, airbrushed and sexy, embracing, his lips about to kiss her long neck, "For Eternity" written below. Was that love? The thought of this type of chemistry always excited Shel.

She thought back to last semester in Dr. Bath's class and remembered hearing that falling in love was chemically similar to eating a lot of chocolate. So, was this concept of falling in love just an addiction? She thought about Jeremy. Did she really care about his well-being and want to help him on his life journey? He made her feel sexy, and the chemical high she got when they were close bordered on blissful. She had to admit that her attraction to him was selfish.

She shut the book and closed her eyes. Her thoughts roamed again through memories of Jeremy, and her heart flitted between frames of longing for that high she felt in his arms and pain and anger at his stab of sudden separation and silence.

Then she thought of Charlie and his ease and simplicity. She smiled, picturing his impish grin. It wasn't romantic, but she accepted it for what it was. It was real. The threads of her mind wove together Jeremy, Charlie, romance, real love, Shelley Winters. A tapestry formed before her as to what she wanted to do for her documentary project.

The energy was high in Music Appreciation with spring break approaching. Shel sat in her usual spot next to Charlie. Mr. Tarlaigh's tone was softer today, though, as he introduced the topic of "Creativity" with a quote from Shakespeare: "It is not in the stars to hold our destiny, but in ourselves." He said the process of creativity, or composition, was "bringing what we resonate with into material existence," and he outlined the process on the board.

Idea – Visualization – Action – Materialization

"The 'idea,'" he said, his voice far off, "is an original thought in raw form, which leads to 'visualization'—using the mind to develop a detailed plan. Then, taking 'action' on that plan connects the mental with the physical and brings the idea to 'materialization.'"

He wasn't as interactive and playful with the class as usual. Shel wondered if it was just one of those out-of-tune days.

The topic was straightforward, but she'd never thought of the steps that had to take place to create something, and how just a hint of an idea can coalesce, with a lot of perseverance and willpower, into a material thing that others can experience and appreciate.

Mr. Tarlaigh referred to a study that Dr. Robert Sacks had conducted, in which an fMRI—a high-end brain scanner—measured brain activity while Sacks listened to a piece of music in headphones. The scanner took a second measurement while he *imagined* the piece of music was playing.

Mr. Tarlaigh said, "The brain activity was identical in both cases, but with additional activity in the frontal lobe during the imagination phase. This means that, to the brain, there is essentially no difference between visualization and materialization. So, the step of visualization is very powerful in the creative process."

Shel thought about what she was doing with the documentary and remembered the "idea" struck her when she was reading Winters's autobiography. It had been a crystalizing moment when spheres of her processing connected. Given the image of the fMRI lighting up different areas of the brain, she could see why this "idea" phase could be called a "light bulb" moment.

She closed her eyes and visualized the finished documentary. She didn't think she'd actually submit it to the contest Dr. Sobol had announced, but she wanted to experiment with seeing it screened as a finalist, the theatre full of students, her friends, and family. Feeling the heat of that packed room, she heard Charlie's score. It became real to her, and she felt her stomach waver in nervousness, like she was being emotionally x-rayed before everyone she knew. Then came the applause and a standing ovation, and her name being called as one of the winners. Maybe it was stretch, but it was her vision, and she could dream big.

At the end of class, Mr. Tarlaigh seemed to strain as he made the effort toward his usual enthusiasm in his closing words, "Remember, life is a musical thing...."

The class was right there in echoing, "Sing and dance while the music is being played."

As they packed up their bags, Shel was excited to tell Charlie about what she'd been reading in Winters's autobiography. She said, "I think I've figured out what I want to do for my documentary film."

"Oh, cool!" He turned to her.

"I'll tell you on the way out." She waved over her shoulder. "See you, Mr. Tarlaigh!"

He lifted his hand as if in benediction as they went out of the classroom.

"Okay," Shel said once they were in the hall, "I've decided to do a documentary on Shelley Winters!" She waited for his reaction.

"Shelley Winters...." His eyes searched.

"She was a famous actress from the 1950s. She was in *The Diary of Anne Frank*...that's one of your favorite film scores, right?"

"Oh...yeah!" He seemed to recall her role.

They exited Morrison Hall and stopped in the shade of a tree. She told Charlie about her obsession with Shelley Winters since she was young, and how she'd been reading Winters's autobiography.

Charlie smiled at her.

"What?" Shel said, becoming aware that she was talking with her hands again.

"Nothing." He shook his head. "Well, the offer is still there if you need music."

"Yes!" She looked into his eyes and felt her steady, calm pulse. "That would be amazing."

"When do we start?" He raised on his toes and came back to his heels.

"Well," Shel said, "how about right after we get back from break? We could get a storyboard going, and that would give you some direction for the score."

"You got it." He smiled and turned to walk to his next class.

"Oh, Charlie!" Shel wrestled her phone from her pocket. "What's your number? Just so we can coordinate on this."

"Of course!" he said.

When Shel got back to the dorm that evening, she got online and rented *A Place in the Sun*, the film Winters mentioned in her autobiography, and lay on her bed to watch.

The opening credits and music flashed in black and white on her screen. At first, the film was similar to what she was used to from her old Shelley Winters DVDs, following a handsome young actor, Montgomery Clift playing the role of George Eastman, as he hitch-hiked cross-country on his way to Los Angeles. He connected with some extended family who were well-to-do and owned a factory business and was put to work on the ground level in production.

Enter Shelley Winters in her not-so-usual role of factory worker Alice Tripp, the part she'd won with director George Stevens in the athletic club lobby. Shel hardly recognized Winters compared to the sexy image she portrayed in her earlier films. She was demure and plain in her character, wearing her hair down, unbleached, and dressed in a man's collared work shirt, untucked, over an ankle-length wool skirt.

The plot was straightforward at first. George Eastman met Alice Tripp in the production room, was attracted to her, and started pursuing her outside of work. Alice was tentative, as there was a strict company rule against coworkers dating. But George convinced her they could keep their romance a secret, and she gradually gave in to his advances, eventually allowing him into her room to begin an intimate affair.

It seemed like a lovely way to fall in love, until the plot twisted and George became enamored with a friend of his cousin, the gorgeous and affluent Angela Vickers, played by Elizabeth Taylor. George was caught between his commitment to Alice and the enticement of climbing the social ladder with Angela, not to mention how smitten he was with her. He was ready to break the news to Alice but then found out she was pregnant.

So began a long line of bad choices George made to try to have the pregnancy aborted while keeping it all a secret from Angela as he continued to develop his relationship with her. Unable to find a doctor willing to do the procedure, George finally found himself in a quandary, on the brink of asking Angela to marry him—moving into a lush life, "a place in the sun" heretofore unimagined by him—and, on the other hand, still having to deal with the mistake he'd made in getting Alice pregnant.

Shel noticed how dark it had become in the room, and the screen flashed light and shadows on the wall next to her bed. She looked at the shapeless glow, and the violin score flowed past her ears. Then, she looked back at the screen and let herself sink into the plot again.

It got creepy when George crafted a plan to drown Alice by taking her out on a canoe. He executed all the steps leading up to it, but, having her out there on the boat, realized he couldn't do it. Alice stood up, sensing George's plan, and, looking for a way to get off the boat, misstepped and tipped it. She couldn't swim and ended up drowning.

The police tracked down George days later, who was now back with Angela and speaking with her father about asking her to marry him. He admitted to being in the boat with Alice when the accident happened and was sent to trial for murder. He pleaded "not guilty," saying the whole thing was an accident, but as the facts unfolded, his motives were revealed. A final question, *Why didn't he try to rescue her?* sent the jury into deliberation.

The jury came back with a verdict of "guilty," sentencing George to the electric chair in a time when corporal punishment was more common. Angela came to see him in his cell before he was taken away and said that she loved him regardless of all that had happened. The final scene followed George as he walked the prison hall toward his end.

The closing credits played as Shel lay unmoving on her bed. Had the jury come back with the right decision? George may have had murder in his heart, but he hadn't acted on it. It was an accident in the end. But he hadn't helped Alice when the accident happened. Shel rubbed at her arms. It made her think about how many times she'd been angry or wished ill on someone else, but the convenience of hiding her thoughts and not finding herself in such unfortunate circumstances as George let her continue on with freedoms in her life. She thought about how the façade of anyone's outer life cannot hide the pain that hounds them through the years until they look truth in the face. Life is a string of choices, sometimes simple and other times extremely hard, but there is always a choice to do the right thing, no matter how dark the situation or the person may be.

Her mom and dad flashed into her mind. She hadn't told them anything about what happened with Jeremy. She thought of all her shattered relationships: Ellana, Royson, Gertrude, Thelma. They were all in the water, thrashing before her. Shaking her head, she reached to click off the light.

The March breeze was cool on Shel's skin as her parents' SUV pulled into the busy LAX airport to pick her up for spring break. Her mom and dad got out and gave her hugs. Shel thought they seemed relieved to see she was looking healthy since the last time they saw her in the hospital.

Driving back to Azusa, they asked about her flight and brought up the semester, asking how she was doing. She told them she was okay.

"I have some things I...I want to share with you guys...over break, sometime," she said.

Her mom looked at her in the rearview mirror, and then her eyes fell back on the road.

Shel turned to look out the window, taking in the afternoon sunlight, realizing a part of her missed SoCal. She noticed she was starting to feel something again inside, like blood returning to a limb that had fallen asleep. She took a deep breath.

When they got home, Shel took her bag up to her room. Everything was still set up as she'd left it with the film posters on the walls, the swim team medals, and the worn *Little Mermaid* cup in the bathroom. She hadn't been away from home even a year yet, she thought as she walked to the bookcase and picked up her sophomore-year photo. The girl behind the glass still looked off into the distance, but Shel held her to her heart and set the photo back on the shelf.

A gentle knock on the open door brought her to attention.

"Hey, Dad."

"Hey, Shelley. I just...I was wondering if you'd...well, what you thought about the Shelley Winters book."

Shel relaxed. "Oh, yeah! It's actually...really good. I'm most of the way through it. I'm going to do a documentary on it at school."

"Oh, good!" He reached one hand behind his head and scratched his hair. "So, everything else is...going well?"

"It's fine." She busied herself with unpacking her bag.

"Alright." He turned around. "Well, I'll see you downstairs for dinner."

"Sounds good." She nodded.

The dining room table was set when Shel came down, the brown and gold Japanese bowl hiding in the cabinet. Silverware clinked, and brief eye contact passed between them. Shel shifted in her chair and cleared her throat to ask her mom to pass the butter. Her dad bounced his leg beneath the table as he chewed, and they each tried to swallow softly.

The weekend passed with typical errands her mom or dad needed to run, or odd jobs around the house, just like when she was in high school. Things seemed back to normal, and Shel batted back thoughts, telling herself to let them be.

She decided to reach out to Thelma. Thinking of their last visit over winter break, she hoped Thelma hadn't been too put off.

Hey Thelma, she texted. *I'm back...are you around this week?*

She set the phone on her bedroom desk, taking out Winters's autobiography from her bag. She began to read, wanting to gather as much information as she could before her meeting with Charlie after break. She jotted down overarching ideas to use as threads for the narrative.

The title of the book was *Shelley, Also Known as Shirley,* so it made sense to bring out this dichotomy between the two aspects of her psyche that these names represented. They also paralleled the outer image of Hollywood and the reality behind the scenes. Finally, and most importantly, was the healing Winters was bringing about in her life, looking at fantasy versus reality and finding harmony within herself versus depending on someone else. This took acceptance of her mistakes, compassion for herself, her family, and the men she'd been involved with, and ended with the strength to be open and vulnerable about her struggles through her writing.

"Vulnerable. Communicating. Compassion." Shel looked over these words again and double-underlined "Vulnerable."

She set down her pen and leaned back in her chair. Her mind wandered to Ellana and what had happened in October when their parents visited. They hadn't been in touch since then. She thought over all of her relationships: with her mom and dad, Thelma, Gertrude, Royson, and Jeremy. Looking at the words she'd written around "Shelley Winters" on the page—"Bitter/Cynical," "Victim," "Broken"—Shel felt her road ahead was heavy with all she would need to bring up.

Her eyes scrolled over "Sex Goddess," and then on the Shirley Schrift side, "Innocent," "Naïve," "Idealistic." She thought of Jeremy, and her heart still flashed with anger. On the page, her eyes found "Compassion." She wanted to crumble the paper in her hands. Winters made this all sound graceful in her book.

She remembered the pang of her last conversation with Ellana and shook her head at the way she'd acted, figuring Ellana wouldn't want to continue their friendship now. But it was worth an attempt to apologize, and she called her. The phone rang a few times and went to voicemail.

"Hey Ellana," Shel said, running her finger along the lined duvet. "I'm not sure what to say except that I'm sorry. I...really messed things up for a while." Shel smoothed the comforter and took a deep breath. "Could we find a time to get together? I'd like to explain." She paused, looking out the window. "Okay, hope to talk with you soon."

She set the phone down on her bed and looked at it. It was a small step, but a start, nonetheless.

Shel needed to decide on her approach to the documentary. She could see photos of Shelley Winters being zoomed in on, Ken-Burns-style, and short clips of her acting enmeshed with audio from interviews she'd done on talk shows and news programs. Shel's fingers flew over the keyboard as these seed concepts rose and developed in her mind. There was so much potential for what she could bring to life, all fueled by a message she connected with, embodied in Winters, who had been with her all along, like a silent friend understanding what was to come and caressing her head.

Her old Shelley Winters DVDs were weeks gone in the trash, and a part of her was now saddened for the loss. She hadn't seen their place in Winters's story and had taken them at face value and for what they represented in Shel's own story—fantasy, expectations. She had yearned to separate herself from that past but now felt as if she'd cast out an old friend who was only there to help her in the long run.

Shel's phone buzzed on the bed. It was a text from Ellana.

Hey Shel, yeah, I'm happy to meet up. I'm flexible later this week or weekend. Let me know what works for you.

Shel's eyes softened. She texted Ellana back and made plans to get together after the break.

After Shel read on a bit further, Thelma also texted back.

Hey Shel, good to hear from you! I've been meaning to tell you...I met a guy a couple months ago! His name is Andy...we've been spending a lot of time together. I have this huge paper I'm working on for after break, too. I'd love to see you...just a little hectic right now!

Shel turned her head and gazed out the window. As blasé as she felt about their friendship in recent months, Thelma had always been there when Shel needed her, like a little sister. She shoved her hair out of her eyes and responded as she thought she should.

Thelma!! That is so great!! I'd love to meet him sometime. I'm around, so just let me know if there's a good time for you (and Andy?).

Okay, I will! she texted back.

Shel's thoughts rolled back to when she'd last seen Thelma

over winter break. She remembered Thelma leaning in toward her, wrenching her hands as if clawing for something that was no longer there in their friendship. They had both changed so much in the last nine months. Shel wondered what Andy was like. A part of her wanted to go back to one of those middle school sleepovers when she and Thelma were inseparable. She thought of texting her that but then snapped back. Thelma would probably think she was being too nostalgic.

Before dinner that night, Shel came downstairs and opened the glass door over the cabinet and took out the Japanese bowl. She wasn't sure why her mom kept something so beautiful out of sight but figured it was because it was old and had been broken. Setting it on the cabinet desk so it would be out in the open, she again admired the gold lacquer that joined the pieces together, glowing. Tapping the side with her fingernail, the bowl clinked, and she envisioned the sound travelling out from the center of the bowl, the striations imbuing the waves with golden light.

Her mom came in, and Shel set the bowl on the edge of the cabinet's counter, pulling her hands away and tucking them behind her back. Her mom had her face turned, carrying a tray of saucers holding soup, and she called Tom in from the den. The long-backed, formal wooden chairs scuffed the carpet as they pulled them out from the table and sat down. The only sounds were the clink of the spoon on the pesto jar and soft slurping as they bent over their soup.

After a time, her mom's voice cut in. "What was it you wanted to share with us, Shel? You mentioned in the car when we picked you up from the airport that there was something you wanted to say."

Shel probed the oil and water in her bowl. "No, it's nothing important."

"Does it have to do with what happened over parents' week-end?" Her mom's eyebrows raised with her narrowing tone.

Shel shot her eyes up at her mom's. Something shifted in her that had to come out. There was no pushing it back down this time. She tried to abate the waves of tension as they rushed forward.

"You know...fine. I've just been learning a lot, is all." Her speech quavered. "I mean, one of my professors said there's a lot of stuff that gets affected by your parents. Dad, you're always working away at your computer," she said, looking at him, "off in your own world, wherever it is you are most of the time. And, Mom, you're at work so much and never willing to really talk with me about things that are important to me, always trying to lighten it up or change the subject so it doesn't get too *real*."

Her parents stared at her, their skin loose around their jaws.

The volume of her voice rose. "And then you expect me to be able to go off on my own and be fine? As if you've done well enough to keep me fed and sit there and watch movies with me, letting me go right on thinking, 'Ah, young love,' as if there's some perfect man out there that's going to make life wonderful? You never talked to me about anything! You tell me, 'Everything's going to be alright,' and, 'Just stay strong, Shelley,' when I try to bring something up that matters to me!" Shel brought her fist down on the table and sprung up. "Well, life is turning out to look different than what you thought you were preparing me for!"

Shel's voice ricocheted around the small dining room. She panted and glared, her forehead wrought with lines, and thudded back down on her chair. Her parents were statues across from her, petrified in the thick air as the clock ticked on the wall.

"Aren't you going to say anything?!" Shel turned her palms up, and her eyes widened.

Her mom turned to her dad and started to speak in Japanese. Shel snorted, and a pounding pulsated in her ears. Her dad looked at her mom then his gaze wandered the table. "I don't know," he muttered.

Her mom's eyes flickered at Shel, and she picked up her plate and walked stoically into the kitchen. The water began to run as pans clanged in the sink. Her dad's eyes were downcast. He scooted his chair back slowly, stood, and walked into the kitchen. Shel sat at the table alone with her unfinished plate, feeling a tinge through her body. Everything was a blur—the Japanese bowl, fingerprints smudged into the table, the stair railing casting dark-fingered shadows across the living room. She writhed agaist the long-backed chair and tensed her face, trying to force up and out that festering clash in her chest. She wrestled away from her place and ran up to her room.

Closing the door and lying on her bed, Shel replayed what she had said. She thought of Jeremy and clenched her teeth, the darkness burning again in her like the night she'd gone into the ocean.

She could hear her parents downstairs talking in Japanese, their voices rising at intervals. She knew they were talking about her. Her dad's voice became loud, which struck her, as she'd never known him to get emotional or agitated. Was he arguing with Mom? He was always so passive, she figured he'd go along with whatever his wife decided to dole out. There was a climactic shout from her mom, and Shel heard a door slam. Then the house was still.

Shel's thoughts roamed to Mr. Tarlaigh's class and to Charlie. Right now, she wanted to get back to them.

As the days passed through the middle into the end of the week, Shel and her parents were mostly quiet, being cordial through necessary interactions but still unresolved from the other night. Shel felt the darkness rise up every time she thought of apologizing. Her mom hid the bowl back on the shelf, closing the glass door over it, and Shel thought of all the times she and her parents passed it by when she was growing up. In the cracks, Shel saw all that had happened this year and remembered herself as a little girl struggling in the ocean, crying on the sand. Then she saw herself inside the bowl, those cracks as places where her soul was shining through. She placed her hand on the glass and wanted to pull the bowl out again where it could be seen.

She had learned so much: Winters's autobiography, the films, the conversations she'd been having. But what was it all worth? She wanted to move beyond the tension. Thinking of all she'd learned in Mr. Tarlaigh's class, the themes threaded through the vibration she shared with others, how she interpreted the way things ended up with Jeremy or her parents or friends, how she was trying to appreciate change and variation, instead of falling into old habits of practice like a broken record. But what was the point, in the end?

Her body and mind were an instrument through which her spirit could flow, and she craved that resolution, but she had to play her part with the tension. The beauty might be easier to see after the piece was over, Shel hoped. She could see it, hear it, an intimate and overwhelming harmony aching to resonate through and out from her heart. Her near-drowning, and Mr. Tarlaigh, and her other professors had taught her so much. And yet time measured on. She couldn't stop it or speed it up, but she could listen and appreciate as best she could where she was in the flow. She pulled her hand from the glass and saw her prints there.

The last night she was home, Shel was determined to finish Winters's book. The last section described the two years she was married to Vittorio Gassman, which started out rosy as they made their transition from Italy to the U.S, but neither of them had broached the subject of whether they would live in the States or in Italy long-term. Quarrels grew more heated over time as Gassman let his disapproval of living in Hollywood be known. One time, they were throwing a house party, and Winters was making pasta for the guests. As Gassman sat and chatted with his friends at the dinner table, Winters brought out the food only to be sent back into the kitchen to re-boil noodles because they were too *al dente*. Winters swallowed her anger, but the next time, Gassman let her know they were over-cooked and accused her of not knowing how to prepare pasta. She dumped the noodles on his head!

They had a daughter, Vittoria, after about a year, but Gassman took acting work in Italy, so he was not around after the early months of her life. Winters visited him there but decided to leave Vittoria in Los Angeles because she was sick. Gassman was angry that his family in Italy would not be able to meet the baby, and so began a long string of abuses back and forth between them, including Gassman hitting Winters once, but mostly involving slights and emotional cuts to each other.

In the midst of all this, they had been hired by an Italian production company to do a film together. The energy between them was toxic on the set, and Winters, not able to be with her daughter, her nerves raw from the tension, and drowning her sorrows in alcohol, eventually had a nervous breakdown and was flown to a British hospital to recover.

She was able to finish the film by being on the set on different days than Gassman, but the tension had taken its toll on her. When production wrapped, Winters went to an opera in Venice with one of her friends, Julie, featuring the great Gigli singing *Pagliacci*. Though she felt hollow, she was touched by the music and Gigli's artistry. After the performance, Winters and her friend went backstage, and the singer welcomed them. He could see her emotional distress, complimented her on *A Place in the Sun*, and invited her and Julie to dinner with some of the cast.

As they walked the streets of Venice on the way to dinner, Winters wrote,

Something happened that I know I will treasure all my life. Singers are notoriously careful of their throats and muffle them with woolen scarves and wear woolen hats pulled down over their ears. I had been shuffling slowly along with my head bowed, thinking of how I could possibly get through the rest of my life now, when suddenly Gigli put out his hand and stopped me. He opened his muffler and coat and began to sing the great tenor aria from Tosca. The four young men with him began to harmonize, using their voices as accompanying instruments. I began to shiver, but not with cold. Gigli was holding my hands and looking straight into my eyes, and although he spoke not one word of English, my actor's antenna interpreted his meaning: "Life, even with its misery, is still life. You must relish and fight through its pain and conquer it, grow, and then the joy will come again."

Gigli and the others wrapped their throats and headed inside for dinner. Julie looked into Winter's eyes and said, "Thank God." She asked if she wanted to stay outside for a few minutes before coming in, and Winters said she did, but to please thank Gigli.

"He knows he's thanked," Julie said.

When she was alone, she saw a girl, probably about fifteen years old, standing across the street. She went to her and noticed she looked very much like herself, the young Shirley Schrift, at that age. Though the girl spoke in Italian, Winters sensed that it was her younger self catching up with her and letting her know she'll always be with her in her heart. When their conversation was over, she described, in the last paragraph of the book,

· · ·

With that I took her hand and as I did, I experienced, in some deep mysterious way, a merging of that long-buried part of myself with the rest of me. I ran then into the warmth of the Taverna Fenice. I sat down next to Maria Callas and Gigli and the rest of the fine artists at the table. At one with myself, at last I felt I belonged there.

The film star was healed in the end by music, Shel saw, by merging with a part of herself from which she'd been separated. Shel thought of her birth name, Gakki, and how she'd changed it when she was a teenager. She'd left behind more than the name at that time. In its place, she became Shelley, chasing after the fantasies she'd seen from the actress on the screen.

She placed her hand on her chest, and the tension there resolved, for the moment, as if in a warm light. Closing her eyes, the vision she'd experienced in the ocean swelled through her, golden light resounding with harmony, expanding into all space. The planets and stars melted into the joy of that light, and the gentlest voice spoke to her without words. It revealed the nature of the universe as a big picture dancing in light and shadow, tension and resolution, projected on the screen of atoms and molecules. A void cast rays of undulating waves, like those Shel had heard, felt, and followed earlier in her vision, coagulating into different rates of vibration and congealing into gaseous orbs. Gasses transformed into liquid, ice and rock, organisms, and life. People appeared on the screen as actors playing their roles. But the images and music of the spheres so allured them in those roles that they forgot that they were of the elemental light and sound that created the scenes in the first place. Shel shuddered but was again wrapped and held close in the gentle vibration.

Then, her awareness rescinded back into a circumscribed space. Even though she no longer felt herself in the far reaches of the universe, the rings of golden waves still undulated outward from her heart, and she understood the voice's meaning. *You must begin with yourself*, it spoke soundlessly to her. In her own healing, she could better love and give to others and open space for their healing. Each thought was a new wave and glow, pulsating from her core. It would be a process, but one worth going through. She might have been broken, but she knew, now, that this was the only way to harmony and wholeness, and she wanted more than anything to live in that always.

The vision faded, and she opened her eyes. Though the feeling subsided from her heart, an echo of that luminous harmony stayed with her. Closing the book, she set it next to her on the bed. She kept her eyes on it as she lay down to fall asleep, as if finding solid ground in the midst of the vast sea upon which she'd been stranded.

Spring has come and joyfully the birds greet it with happy song,
and the brooks, while the streams flow along with gentle murmur as the
zephyrs blow.
There come, shrouding the air with a black cloak,
lighting, and thunder chosen to herald;
then, when these are silent,
the little birds return to their melodious incantations.
Antonio Vivaldi, *The Four Seasons*, "Spring"

Mr. Tarlaigh wasn't in Music Appreciation that morning when Shel got back to school. The sub wrote her name on the board, *Dr. Luís*, and said that Mr. Tarlaigh was sick. She looked like she was in her mid-40s, with a short and round build, wearing a magenta business dress that pinched at her armpits. Her hair was black, straight, and cut across at shoulder length.

Shel sat next to Charlie and jittered her heel against the floor, thinking of their meeting that night to dive into the documentary. She had so much to tell him about what she'd been putting together.

"Mr. Tarlaigh was not able to send a lesson plan," Dr. Luís said, adjusting her dress. "Can someone tell me where you left off in the curriculum?"

A few moments passed, some students turning to look at each other.

"How about you?" Dr. Luís opened her hand to invite Ross to share.

Ross scooted himself to the back of his chair and sat up. "Um, well, we had just finished talking about tension, and then last week...practice...." His tone rose, almost making it a question.

Dr. Luís flipped through the textbook then turned back to the table of contents, running her finger down the chapter headings.

"I don't see either of those topics in here." She tried to smile but her eyes tightened. "Can anyone else please bring us up to date?"

Again there was silence. Finally, Shel raised her hand.

"Yes." Dr. Luís thanked her with her tone.

"Professor...Mr. Tarlaigh has been using the textbook at times, but also has...supplemented with other music and...hasn't been going through the book linearly, per se...."

Dr. Luís blinked at her a few times, her hand still on the book. "I see." She closed the text. "Well, we're going to cover late Romantic period music today, as that's where you *should* be in the curriculum at this point in the semester. Let's start with 'The Big Five.'"

She wrote on the board the names of Russian composers Mussorgsky, Rimsky-Korsakov, Borodin, Balakirev, and Cui, and next to each, their birth and death dates. The chalk hissed and bit, and the class dragged out their laptops or tablets. One of the students raised her phone and captured it in a touch.

The lecture that Dr. Luís led them through was easy to follow, and she was good at organizing information. The music was pretty, too, and other times intense. It reminded Shel of film scores from some of the classics. Mostly, her mind started to drift, though, and Dr. Luís's voice grew faint. She thought of Thelma and hoped things were going well with her new boyfriend. A part of her thought it strange that she hadn't called or followed up after those couple text messages over spring break. Their friendship went back so far, and this was a new dynamic Shel had never felt from Thelma, like she didn't need her anymore. Maybe Thelma had felt the same way when Shel was out of touch for so long after Jeremy left.

Charlie was scribbling something on his page, which caught Shel's attention, and she looked over at his desk. He was writing a series of notes on staff paper. Shel thought maybe he was dictating the melody of the last piece Dr. Luís had played. She must have leaned in, because he turned to whisper to her.

"I think I have an idea for your documentary." His pencil tapped the notes on the page.

Shel pulled back and looked at him, her eyes widening, and she nodded and smiled.

After a series of listening examples and a chalkboard full of notes, Dr. Luís said, "Okay, thanks, everyone," and set down the chalk on the metal runner at the base of the board. "I imagine Mr. Tarlaigh will be back on Wednesday, so...it was a pleasure working with you today." She took a long draw from the straw in her water bottle.

Shel and Charlie started toward the door, but Shel touched his arm and went over to Dr. Luís, thanking her for coming in. Dr. Luís pulled the bottle away and wrested her lips into a grin.

That evening, Shel walked into the study room in Moffit Library. Charlie was already there, hovering over a page and humming.

"Is that what you were working on in class earlier?" Shel set her backpack on the heavy folding table.

Charlie looked up from his staff paper, lit by fluorescents in the ceiling that poured down over the small, white, square room. His left eyebrow always lifted higher than the right when he greeted her.

"Okay, so get this…." His hands were poised over his annotations. "While we were listening to 'The Big Five' today, I was reminded of music from some of the classic films of the '40s and '50s, and suddenly this concept popped into my head. What if the score for your documentary was a medley that hinted at music from Shelley Winters films?" His hands opened, offering the idea, his eyes twinkling.

"Okay, I think that could work." Shel nodded as she sat down kitty-corner to Charlie.

"Cool. Well, I'll definitely keep crafting that, then," he said, "but in the meantime, I want to hear what you have in mind for this film so I can match the mood and get an idea for the flow."

"Absolutely." Shel got out her notebook and shared with Charlie what she'd learned about Winters through her autobiography, the films she knew so well from Winters's early career, and her recent watching of *A Place in the Sun*. "I still need to watch *The Diary of Anne Frank*, but I feel like I'm homing in on the angle I want to take through the film."

She turned a page in her notebook to the diagram she'd drawn of the two parts to Winters's personality and slid it toward Charlie, explaining that she wanted to focus on the two sides of Hollywood and how those aspects within Winters paralleled that, and how it was through her willingness to be open that she was able to find beauty in her tension and mend herself in the end.

Charlie opened and closed his mouth, and Shel tilted her head at him.

"This is good, Shel," he said, pinching his eyebrows. He swallowed and then said, "I can definitely work with this."

She gave a quick flurry of blinks and pulled her notes back.

When they left Moffit, Charlie said, "I saw the email to the student body asking for submissions for the short film contest. Do you think you'll send yours in?"

Shel squirmed. "Oh, I don't think so. I—I think I've been through enough lately." She shook her head. "It's more of a fetish project, anyway."

Charlie smiled with his usual warmth.

"Charlie…." Shel searched the ground with her eyes, then she shook her head.

He leaned toward her. "What is it?"

She found him with her gaze. "Back in the library, what was it you were going to say about the documentary?"

Charlie opened his mouth and lifted on his toes then looked down. "I'm sorry. I—sometimes I have ideas, but I tend to shove them in and take over." He looked back up at her. "I'm impressed by what you've put together, Shel. I was just struggling with whether or not to share my angle, but it's your project, and it's great."

Shel looked aside and nodded then found his eyes again and smiled.

They walked together, and Shel asked him what his other favorite film scores were, in addition to *The Diary of Anne Frank.* He said he grew up listening to John Williams and Hanz Zimmer compilations, but also loved Thomas Newman and James Horner.

"Where did you grow up?" Shel pulled a strand of hair behind her ear.

"I was born in Boston, but my mom brought me to Colorado when I was two, and we've lived there ever since, so I call that home."

"What does she do?"

"Teaches fourth grade." He turned and smiled at Shel. "I probably wasn't the easiest kid to raise." His smile fell, and he put his thumbs under his backpack straps and linked his fingers across his chest. "I've just always been really particular, you know?" He looked off, away from Shel, then turned his head back toward her. "I guess I've always felt like a bit of a loner."

They reached an intersection, and Shel reached for his hand. He gave her a soft smile and let out a breath. She squeezed his palm a few times before letting go, and they walked on.

As she got ready for bed that night, Gertrude came in, not looking at Shel or talking to her. Shel sat on the bed with Winters's autobiography open in her lap, passing her eyes over the words, though her attention followed her roommate as she set down her bag and gathered her toiletries to head to the bathroom. Shel snapped the book shut.

"Gertrude…" She cast her eyes down then lifted them.

Gertrude was turned sideways, her hand on the doorknob, but she paused and held Shel in the corner of her vision.

Shel's mouth flushed with a bitter tang, but she took a deep breath and swallowed. "I feel like I…have some things…to apologize for."

Gertrude's shoulders relaxed and she took a deep breath and stood up straighter.

"I…I haven't been the best roommate to you." Shel set the book down next to her on the bed and looked at it. "I've been in a lot of pain over the last…many months, and, I'm sorry to say, some of that has been dumped on you." She brought her eyes up again.

Gertrude's chin fell. Then she turned to face Shel.

Shel held eye contact for a few seconds then dropped her gaze again. "It's a long story, I guess," she said, shaking her head. "I guess now's not the time…" She pointed to Gertrude's toiletry kit she was still holding in front of her thighs, and they both flashed faint smiles.

"No, I guess not." Gertrude's tiny voice came out.

Shel sighed. "Maybe sometime soon."

Gertrude nodded and left.

Shel ran her hand over the cover of the book and then reached for her phone to check on emails and posts before going to sleep. There was an email from Dr. Sobol addressed directly to her, which was a first, so she tapped to open it. It said,

Dear Gakki,

The online portal evidently still listed her birth name. Shel rolled her eyes.

I wanted to check in because I noticed your grade is currently not at a passing level. There are a few assignments left, but I did some calculations and, even if you got 100% on all of them, including the final documentary, you would not be able to raise your grade enough to pass the course. As I made clear in the syllabus, it is each student's responsibility to track their grades, so hopefully this email is not a surprise to you. That being said, I'd be happy to sign an Incomplete form for you, should you decide to drop the class at this time.

Thank you,

Dr. Sobol

Shel blinked and read the email again. *Failing?!* How could that be? She'd never failed a class in her life. Not even close. Sure, she'd fallen behind in her reading and wasn't doing very well on the quizzes, and she'd missed quite a few classes, but failing? Shel thought he must have made a mistake and logged into her portal to check her grade. She had a 48 percent. She scoured over the individual assignments, looking for where he might have forgotten to give her late credit, but everything was right. She hadn't missed any assignments, but she'd done poorly on so many that they simply weren't adding up to enough, now. Shel dropped her arms by her sides and bumped her head against the wall behind her over and over. What was she going to do? How was she going to explain this to her parents?

The next day, Ellana walked into The Golden Bear with a faded, single-strapped backpack that looked straight out of the '70s. Her hair was a little longer than Shel remembered, but she still wore the same V-neck T-shirt as before. Shel watched her from the table. She'd arrived early so she could pull her thoughts together. She waved across the cafeteria, and Ellana raised her chin, acknowledging that she'd seen her. A few minutes later, Ellana squeezed through the bustle and scooted in across from Shel.

"It's been a while since the last time we sat together in here." Ellana's gaze bounced around the room.

Shel leaned forward, rubbing her stomach. "Thanks for being willing to meet."

Ellana pulled off the green plastic lid on a glass Tupperware full of hummus and carrots and began to crunch away on one. They made small talk about their classes, and then Shel cleared her throat.

"I want to tell you more about what happened last semester," Shel said, reaching her hand halfway across the table.

Ellana swallowed and set the Tupperware down.

"I should have let you in on what was going on."

Ellana's eyes locked in on Shel's.

"That weekend in October was a real dark time for me," Shel

said. "I…lost a lot last semester. I don't even remember much of those months. I don't know where I went, but I was in too deep for awhile there."

Ellana's face was long and void. "Look, Shel, I get that you were going through a lot last semester, but the way you took it out on me was not…kosher."

Shel felt a vaccuum form in her chest.

"You can't just make other people feel inferior to you, like you were born on some pedestal and the rest of the world revolves around you and your feelings." Ellana shook her head and snapped into another carrot.

Shel narrowed her eyes. "Hey, I came here to apologize, okay? But if that isn't good enough for you, then—"

"Apologize? That *you* were going through a lot? That *you* were in too deep? It isn't all about you, Shel."

"I'm not trying to make it all about me, I'm just trying to explain what was going on."

Ellana closed the lid on the Tupperware. "You just don't get it, Shel. You remind me of my sister—my *half* sister."

Shel opened her mouth, and her eyes fluttered. Ellana pushed out her chair. She tossed her head, swinging her dreads over her shoulder, and walked away.

Dr. Luís was there again the following Tuesday.

"Is Mr. Tarlaigh still sick?" Shel whispered to Charlie.

"I don't know. I hope he's okay." His brow drew to a point.

Dr. Luís cleared her throat and stood before them with her hands clasped in front of her.

"I'm afraid I have to be the bearer of some bad news," she said, looking over their heads. "Mr. Tarlaigh has been diagnosed with an illness that might keep him out for at least the rest of the semester." Her eyes pulled to the right and then fell. "So," she said with a sigh, returning her gaze to them, "I will be your sub for the rest of the semester."

Shel's mouth was dry, and she struggled through shallow breaths. As the class went on, Charlie looked over at her a few times, probably because she wasn't moving much or taking notes.

"Are you okay, Shel?" He followed her out into the hallway after class.

"I don't know." She turned and let her backpack slam against the instrument lockers. "I felt like things were finally starting to go well, but...."

Charlie nodded, frowning.

"I hope he's okay." Shel looked at him.

"Me too." Charlie lifted his hand, making a fist, and then extended it to her arm.

"I wonder what kind of illness he has."

Charlie squeezed her arm and then let his eyes wander. "Why don't we get in touch with him?"

Shel blinked at him and thought about it. Maybe he wanted privacy while he was recovering, or maybe he wouldn't be checking emails.

"At least we can reach out and let him know we're thinking of him," Charlie said.

Shel nodded. "Okay. I'll write something and send it to you. Maybe I can email him, then, from both of us."

"That sounds great." Charlie smiled.

Shel took her weight off the lockers, and they continued down the hallway.

"Do you want to connect on the documentary again this week?" She opened the door and her hair was tousled in the warming breeze.

"Let's do it," he said. "Just text me and let me know when is good."

"Thanks, Charlie." Shel smiled at him, gave him a quick hug, and turned to head to her next class.

. . .

That night after dinner, she started an email.

Dear Mr. Tarlaigh,

We heard today from Dr. Luís, our sub for Music Appreciation, that you are fighting an illness. We wanted to let you know that we miss you and are sending our best wishes. Though it sounds like you won't be back in time for the end of the semester, we hope to see you again soon, and maybe to connect next semester sometime. We have really enjoyed your class. Please let us know if there's anything you need or that we can do to help as you recover.

Your students,
   Shel and Charlie

She sent it to Charlie to make sure it sounded good to him.

The next day, Shel went to the Registrar's office and picked up an incomplete form. She filled out the course number for Documentary Film and her student ID info. She shook her head, hovering the pen over the signature line at the bottom of the page. What was she going to tell her parents? They'd have to pay extra for her to complete the course again next semester. She wiped her sweaty palm on her jeans. She needed to get Dr. Sobol's signature to make it official, so she took it with her to class.

As she folded it and slipped it into her purse, a thought shot like lightning through her brain. She remembered Dr. Sobol mentioning at the beginning of the semester that he offered extra credit if any of the students won any of the top three spots in the film contest. She did some quick math and realized that she could just barely pass the class if she completed all her asssignments between now and the end of the semester and got first, second, or third place in the contest. That way she wouldn't have to tell her parents about it, since they wouldn't have to pay extra for her to retake the class at some point, and she knew how proud her parents would be of her for winning. She could see them going to get Japanese takeout after the contest screening. They would finally have something positive to talk about again. Maybe their relationships could get back on track at that point, and they could just forget this crazy year. Shel made haste for Dwinelle Hall.

After Documentary Film class ended, Shel packed her bag in the back of the classroom and tip-toed down to where Dr. Sobol was quitting out of the PowerPoint. She could feel her chest thundering and an empty pit in her stomach.

"Dr. Sobol?" Her voice quavered.

"Yes." He looked up from his screen, adjusting his thin-rimmed glasses.

"Hi, I'm Sh- I'm Gakki." Shel extended her hand, and he shook it, then she crossed her arms, holding her elbows. "I, um, got your email about my grade."

"Right, right," he said, scratching a spot on his bald head. "Did you need me to sign the incomplete form?"

Shel uncrossed her arms and turned her palms up. "Well, I was remembering what you said about extra credit at the beginning of the semester. I think you said that if we were one of the top three winners of the short film contest that we'd get ten extra percentage points?"

Dr. Sobol knitted his brow. "Yes...."

"Well, I was thinking that, if I get the rest of my assignments in between now and the end of the semester, and then am one of the top three winners, I could—"

"Now—I'm sorry, say your name for me one more time."

"Gakki."

"Gakki. Thank you. Yes, that is true, but I don't know if that's the best course of action." He straightened his shirt. "I mean, the chances of winning are…." He cut himself short. "Look, it's up to you, but it's pretty risky. I'd recommend just taking the incomplete."

Shel put her hand on her purse but then extended it toward Dr. Sobol. "Thank you, Dr. Sobol. I'm going to give it a shot."

Dr. Sobol shrugged. "Alright. Good luck."

"Thank you." Shel turned and skittered out of the room.

On Friday night, Shel sat low against the wall on her bed, letting the week after spring break wash over her. Her thoughts reeled back to the Friday night early last semester when she'd dressed up and gone to the party at Sigma Chi. Her mind replayed the evening on an invisible screen: finding out about the party from Cindy and Lark, seeing Royson in the hallway, the loud music, meeting Jeremy and dancing with him, kissing him. The familiar softness followed by searing pain in her chest went through its paces. A part of her wondered if it was alright to be alone on a Friday night, but she sat up and crossed her arms over her chest. She wasn't alone, she was with herself, and she closed her eyes for a few moments, feeling a lightness in her limbs and heart.

She remembered that *The Diary of Anne Frank* was the last Winters film she wanted to watch to piece together her ideas for the documentary. She reached for her computer and rented the film, listening to the musical score behind the title scene, violins soaring over the backdrop of a bright sky shining through clouds.

The first scene began with an old man, Otto Frank, climbing the stairs to an attic-like apartment, where he took off his hat. The tenants of the building had seen him enter, and they came to the top of the stairs. They knew him and asked what happened, and he began to tell the story.

The scene changed to a time two years earlier when the tenants showed his family the attic as a place they could hide out, as they were Jews living in Amsterdam during the ascension of the Third Reich. Otto and his wife had two daughters, Margot and Anne. The attic seemed spacious enough for them until the tenants brought in another family of three, the Van Daans. Shelley Winters played Patronella Van Daan, the wife of Hans Van Daan, and they had a teenage son, Peter. Dynamics unraveled between the two families, the parents having very different personalities and disagreeing with each other, and Peter becoming enamored with Margot.

Winters's role, as in *A Place in the Sun,* was very unlike those Shel was used to. Her character, a middle-aged woman married to an unscrupulous man, had dimension. At times her strength shone forth in the midst of all she had to deal with in her husband and the trying circumstances as a Jew, and at others, it was evident that her own vices and weaknesses got the best of her, and she represented humanity at its most selfish.

Anne Frank, played by a very young-looking, twenty-three-year-old Millie Perkins, was vibrant. She was supposed to be only fourteen in the film, and real teenage emotions came out through her jealousy of Margot's romance and her desire for her own space and freedoms, small as they may have been under the circumstances, all of which she noted in a diary her father gave her. It's clear she understood what was happening in the changing world around her, but, probably in part because of her age though also her kindly personality, she was undeniably optimistic and thoughtful of others, in one example making presents for everyone for the holidays.

A full year passed with the families relegated to the attic, and Peter, while first annoyed with Anne, began to fall for her. Margot was passive at his shifting interest, and soon Anne and Peter were spending a lot of time together. In their innocence, they talked of love and kisses behind the closed door of his closet-room and escaped when they could to the upper level that opened to a skylight.

The families grew weary with one another and with the possibility that they were soon to be discovered because of small, accidental noises they made when potential informants were below. Anne and Peter sensed the tension and maybe had a prescient knowledge of what was to come as they told each other everything they hoped their future would be when all this ended. Looking out into the clouded sky, Anne said, "In spite of everything, I still believe that people are really good at heart." As violins carried a soaring melody, Peter kissed her, and there were noises downstairs as the Nazis came for them. She and Peter and their families were taken to the prison camps.

When the film returned to Otto and the tenants in the attic at the end of the film, he revealed that he had asked after every member of his family and the Van Daans only to learn that they were all dead. Otto found the diary Anne had been keeping and broke down, remembering the last moments he got to spend with her.

Shel let the music play over the credits and lay down on her bed, looking up at the ceiling. She imagined what it must have been like to be Anne, what fears and frustrations must have wracked her. She thought of Otto and the injustices done to him, how he returned in the end with such pain that reduced him to a hovel of a man. And she played over in her mind Anne's words, "In spite of everything, I still believe people are really good at heart."

Shel knew her situation wasn't anything like Anne's, but she couldn't believe that she would ever see any good in Jeremy. She wrenched her T-shirt below the collar. She wanted to be able to forgive him, but a torrent kept pulling her back. That distance still felt too far to cross.

Then she thought about Royson. They'd passed a few times in the dorm hallway or on the stairs over the last few months, but they'd ignored each other. It seemed reasonable enough to regress into pretending they'd never connected at all. Shel wondered if it would be the right thing to reach out to him again, to apologize. Maybe she should leave him be.

She closed her eyes, and Royson's face came to her mind. She was silent, looking at him, and then she told him how sorry she was to have shut him out. She had pushed away a good friend, one of the first she had in college. Memories flashed of them studying together and talking as they strolled across campus. Shel smiled, thinking of that ice cream social in the courtyard. A sensation came of waves of gentle light flowing out from her to Royson. They filled her, too, and she breathed easier.

That weekend, Shel researched Shelley Winters interviews and articles and began to storyboard her film, interweaving all she'd been discovering about the actress. She thought a lot about her parents in light of all this and what she'd learned from *The Diary of Anne Frank*. Folding laundry on her bed, she thought of the argument she'd had with her parents over break. Her mom and dad had always towered over her in her mind as pillars that supported her life, their moods, attention, or absence leveraging vast spaces within her, defining how she saw and interacted with the rest of the world.

Then, in contrast, she saw them as two fledgling souls in a sea of humanity, trying to keep their heads above water. She saw them in the barcarolle of clash and concord, giving their best to do good but fighting the undertow of tension inherent in the world. She stopped folding, looking at the photo of them on the bulletin board. Setting down the pair of socks in her hands, she went over to it, tracing their smiles and the curves and lines in their faces, the gray patches in their hair, and the bowed arc of their shoulders. There she was in front of them, taught and poised, ready to fly straight and far.

They had given her everything they had, so much light. And look where she was and all she was doing! How was it that there were also shadows playing out now, at the same time leaving her more severely broken than she'd ever been before? She put the clothes away in her drawers and closet, sliding the door closed and pausing to think. Crossing the room, she picked up her phone and dialed her mom's cell.

"Shelley?" her mom answered.

"Hey, mom." Shel sat down at her desk chair.

"Everything okay?"

"Yeah, everything's good." Shel sighed. "What are you guys up to?"

"Oh, you know, the usual weekend stuff," she said with a slight waver. "Out doing some errands with your father right now." It sounded like she was looking for something on a shelf.

The thought rose in Shel to keep the conversation light again, like playing the same record over and over, stuck in that groove. She opened her mouth to speak, but before the needle dropped, she closed it again and realized she had control over what she said next.

"Mom, I have some things I'd really like to talk with you about for a few minutes. Is that okay?"

Her mom was silent for a moment, and Shel bit her bottom lip.

"Sure, honey. Your dad's talking with a salesman about a new computer, so I'm sure we have a few minutes. What's on your mind?"

"Well..." Shel made a fist in her pocket. "I guess I've been thinking about our argument over break."

"Mm-hm."

"I know what I said must have been hurtful to you, but... anyway, I...." She thought her mom might cut her off, but she only heard her soft breathing on the other end. Her thoughts formed in the stillness.

"I love you, Mom. I want you to know that. I've been going through a lot this year that I haven't—well, that I haven't felt like I've wanted to share with you or Dad." She looked down to the right, pressing her phone to her ear.

"Okay, I'm listening," her mom said.

Shel forced a breath. "Well, in any case, something happened that was hard...." She felt the dark cloud moving back toward her heart, and she slid her hand along the small of her back, which was clammy with sweat. Her mind stabbed at phrases that made sense to her before.

"I mean, I wanted to tell you that I forgive you and Dad, that I see that you were doing your best when I was growing up...." The words didn't hold the same vibration as earlier. Where was she going wrong?

She heard a quick snort from her mom.

"Shel, I have to be honest. After how you came across at dinner that night, I'm not really looking for forgiveness."

"No, I didn't mean..." Shel leaned back in her chair and looked up at the ceiling. Why had this been easier with her friends? Pieces seemed to fall into place when she shared with them, and the right words had flowed. But she and her mom were on different wavelengths, their words like frequencies drifting past each other in the open air.

"Shel, it looks like your dad is ready to go. Maybe we can talk about this again sometime soon."

"Okay, Mom." Shel exhaled. "Hope you guys have a great rest of the day."

Shel threw her phone so it bounced off the wall onto the bed and she got up, shoving her chair under the desk. Pacing the room, she searched the conversation for where it had derailed. She was trying to be vulnerable, she reasoned, walking back toward the window. Maybe not every situation could resolve the same way. She'd started those conversations with her friends by opening up about herself and was trying to do the same with her mom. Her mind found a memory of Mr. Tarlaigh right after he'd played the recording of "Both Sides Now" by Joni Mitchell. She recalled how still and quiet he was, absorbing that song and its message when it was over. She missed him. "I've looked at life from both sides now…" Mitchell had sung. How do you look at life from both sides? She'd been trying to explain her side of the story, but it didn't seem to be working.

Shel pulled up the storyboard document for her film, laying her notes out on her desk along with Winters's autobiography. With the sun setting behind the buildings outside her window, she placed her fingers on her laptop keys and began to type out how the film would unfold. To her surprise, Gertrude came in.

"Hey," Gertrude said.

"Hey." Shel smiled. "You're back early on a Tuesday."

"Yeah." She set her backpack down. "Is it alright if I work here tonight?"

"Of course," Shel said. "I'm just putting together the outline for this documentary project I have due in a couple weeks. How are your classes going?"

"Fine." She gave a quick nod and sat at her desk on the opposite wall to Shel.

Shel's features softened as she looked at Gertrude, her roommate's fine hair pulled into a tight ponytail.

They both worked for a while, and after Shel had written the opening sequence of the film along with narration of the scene, she wondered if it would be good to read it out loud. She turned around in her chair and cleared her throat.

"Hey, Gertrude?"

Her roommate rotated to meet her gaze.

"Would you mind if I read this intro material to you? It'd be helpful to get some feedback on if I'm starting in the right direction."

Gertrude turned around a little more. "Alright." Her eyes were wide, and she blinked at Shel.

Shel read background information on Winters: where and when she was born and early stories of her family and upbringing. When she finished, she paused to see what Gertrude thought.

With a tiny voice, she said, "That sounds really good, Shel."

Shel shrugged, hoping she'd nailed the intro on the first try.

Then Gertrude went on, "One thing you might consider is making it clearer early on what your main point is going to be through the film. Is it purely biographical, or are you bringing out a certain side of Winters's story?"

Shel looked at her roommate, unmoving.

"What *is* your main point?" Gertrude probed.

Shel was quick to explain that Winters had two identities that paralleled two sides of Hollywood, and her vulnerability through writing her book helped integrate and heal these two sides in herself, the fantasy versus reality, and gave others space to do the same.

Gertrude nodded. "What made you choose Shelley Winters for your documentary?"

Shel grazed the roof of her mouth with her tongue, and then told about how Winters was one of her parents' favorite actresses and how they loved some of her early films, which the three of them used to watch as a family when Shel was young. It wasn't until her dad gave her Winters's autobiography that she learned more about her life and these themes for the documentary. She told her she was amazed how much of a parallel there was between Winters's life and her own.

"What do you mean, a parallel with your own life?" Gertrude squinted.

Shel tilted her head back and forth, and then leaned forward with her elbows on her knees. She began to tell Gertrude about what happened with Jeremy and what she'd been going through. As she spoke, it was as if she was watching herself from somewhere just beyond the currents of her mind. She could see herself as the girl treading through this story, but a part of her was safe on the close shore.

She remembered the poem, "The Touch of the Master's Hand," which Mr. Tarlaigh had presented to them earlier that semester about the broken violin that wasn't worth much until the Master played it and people realized how valuable it was. She looked at her body there in the chair, wrestling shadows, and the Master—that beautiful, golden luminescence, vibrant with harmony—was right next to her on the shore. It flowed into her, and she came back into her body. It had always been playing through her.

It took Shel a moment to remember that Gertrude was listening. Her roommate was staring glassy-eyed at the floor.

"Are you alright?" Shel reached out.

"Shel, when I was gone that weekend… You know, when I came back and you were still sleeping that morning?"

Shel stared down at the floor.

"I told you I was going to visit a friend from high school. Well, that was true, but…" She hesitated and looked at Shel. "I went to visit her because I thought I was in love with her." She dropped her eyes.

Shel nodded, leaning back in her chair.

Her roommate went on. "I thought she loved me, too. We'd gone to church camps together when we were younger and always got along so well. She said she liked spending time with

185

me. I wanted so many times to tell her how I felt, but the words just wouldn't come. I couldn't wait any longer. I had to tell her that weekend." A tremor went through her lips and chin. "I finally found the courage to tell her, and she said I really need to seek help."

Shel jerked her head. "Is that what *you* believe?"

"I don't know. I don't know!" She leaned forward, pressing her palms into her temples.

"Have you ever talked with your parents about this?"

"No." She sank. "They would never understand." She shook her head and whispered, "God is punishing me."

Shel took a deep breath and then exhaled, which brought the thought of the ebb and flow of waves in the ocean and what she'd experienced after blacking out. "What is God to you?" She wasn't sure if she was seeking to help Gertrude or answer her own question.

Gertrude sat back up and blinked a few times, lines of worry etched on her face. She said with rote dryness, "God is love."

Shel's eyes wandered the room, pondering that answer. "I didn't grow up with any religion." She grasped for words. "Have you ever *felt*...God?"

Gertrude shook her head. "I think so." She shrugged.

"When?"

Gertrude ran her hand along her cheek. Her eyes relaxed as she closed them. "One time was...in church when I was fifteen."

"What did it feel like?"

A gentle smile came over her face. "I can't describe. I'd never felt so completely open and yet completely loved to a depth..." She stopped, and Shel met her gaze when she opened her eyes. She looked like a different woman.

Shel nodded. "I think I know what you mean."

Shel met with Charlie again at Moffit the next evening in their usual fluorescent-white room. Charlie brought a Bluetooth speaker with him.

"Have you heard anything back from Mr. Tarlaigh?" He turned the volume knob on the speakers.

"No. I sent the email yesterday, but haven't gotten a reply."

Charlie nodded.

After Shel set up her laptop and opened the script she'd been working on, Charlie said, "I have a sampling of a musical theme for the film, if you want to hear it."

"Of course!" Shel said.

Charlie opened a software program, and a score appeared with all the instruments' parts written out note for note: violins at the top, violas, cellos, and double basses.

"All strings?"

"Yes." He pointed to the staff and traced the rise and fall of the notes. "The violins carry the melody here, as you can see. I tried to capture the soaring quality of melodies in the film scores from some of Winters's early films without copying any themes exactly." He clicked the "Play" button above the page, and Shel's skin tingled at the quality of the string samples as the composition flowed through the speakers.

The violin melody was simple, with a repeating ascending pattern of notes that was echoed by the other strings, creating a rich harmonic background. It wasn't sad, but it was nostalgic yet triumphant as the melody reached a climactic high point and the violins held out a single note. The lower strings created chords like shifting colors beneath a static image, and the theme ended on a warm, though somewhat unresolved, chord.

"A work in progress," Charlie said as he clicked the "Stop" button.

"I love it!" Shel smiled.

"Oh, good! So, I'm going in the right direction, then?"

"Yes, absolutely," Shel said.

"Alright, well, what's the latest on your storyboard?" He shifted, looking at her computer.

Shel explained the exposition which now, thanks to Gertrude's input, delivered the two sides of Winters and the parallel with Hollywood then transitioned to Winters's early life as Shirley Schrift. Then, descriptions of her first films would come next, forging Shelley Winters the blonde bombshell. Following would be the story of her unconventional audition for *A Place in the Sun.*

"Her role of Alice Tripp represented the Method side of her acting, that she was more than the sexpot the studios wanted to make of her," Shel said. "And next are stories of her relationships and how she lost touch with her younger self. I'll talk about how Winters's life and the lives of many others in Hollywood at the time were not as fantasy-like as they seemed on the big screen."

Shel would reveal the climactic point of Winters meeting, marrying, and ultimately divorcing Vittorio Gassman, and then home in on her role in *The Diary of Anne Frank*, bringing a message of compassion. The ending would show how that magical moment with Gigli singing helped her integrate Shirley Schrift and Shelley Winters and ultimately experience deep mental and emotional healing.

Charlie crossed his arms and froze with the same look he'd had when Shel showed him the less-detailed storyboard last week.

"What is it?" Shel sat up straight.

"Oh, I don't know." Charlie shrugged it off. "I told you before I don't want to impose. It's just…I have this idea, but I'm not sure where it's coming from."

"What?"

"Well, I don't want to pry, but every time I hear you talk about Shelley Winters, I almost get the impression you're talking about yourself. I wonder if this documentary needs to be less about Winters and more about…*you.*"

Shel blushed and gave a quick snort, but then let her shoulders fall. "You're right. I identify a lot with Shelley Winters." She peered across at Charlie, whose gaze held hers. "Wouldn't that be a little self-centered to make the documentary about myself, though?"

"Is Shelley Winters's autobiography self-centered?" Charlie raised his eyebrows.

"Well, no. It's vulnerable, but I wouldn't say it's self-centered." She nodded. "I see your point." She put her hands over her face. "Charlie! I feel like I've put so much work into this already. I don't want to have to go back and rewrite it!"

Charlie bobbed his head. "I think your story would make waves." He winked.

On Wednesday morning, Shel heard her phone buzzing when she got back from the shower. It was her dad. He never called her, and she wondered what was going on, so she picked up.

"Dad?"

"Hey, Shelley." Her dad's voice pinched through. "Ah, do you have a minute?"

Shel rolled her towel, fixing its hold across her chest. "Yes, I'm just getting dressed."

"Listen, I'm in San Francisco for a conference today and... well, I was hoping maybe we could...meet."

Shel shook her head. "Oh! Cool!" she said, her eyes darting around the room. "Yeah...yeah, I'm free after four p.m. Do you want me to meet you somewhere or...meet at the dorm?"

"I'll, ah...I'll meet you at the dorm at four. There's something I've been meaning to share with you."

"Okay. Well, I'll see you then, then," she said in staccato.

. . .

She had a hard time concentrating in Documentary Film and Japanese class, wondering why her dad wanted to meet. Did it have to do with the argument she'd had with him and her mom over break? Did something else bad happen?

When she got back to Foothill that afternoon, she waited outside on the corner for her dad. He was right on time and, parallel parking the rental car near the entrance, pulled a black case out of the back seat that looked too small to be a suitcase. He was wearing a suit and tie and came up to give Shel a hug.

"Hi, Shel." He patted her back.

She walked him up the stairs and, when they stepped into her room, he looked around for a moment and then asked if he could sit in her desk chair. Shel waved him on as she sat cross-legged on her bed.

He set the dark case at his feet. "Well, you're probably wondering why I wanted to get together like this." He reached his hand over his head to scratch the back of his neck. "You know, in light of what happened…when you were home last…I wanted to tell you something I've never told you before." His brow pinched. "What you said was…well, it hurt your mom and me."

Shel opened her mouth, but her dad held up his hand.

"But," he said, "it hurt because there's truth to it."

Shel's face was set.

"Your mom and I aren't perfect. We know that. We've been doing our best, sometimes flying by the seat of our pants, to give you a good life."

Shel's features smoothed, but her eyes held him.

"You never knew your grandparents, my parents, but I've told you a little bit about them. Well, I never told you about a particular time…with my father."

Shel remembered the photo of her dad's parents on the stair landing back home, her grandfather in a business suit and tie, jacket buttoned at the top rung. She thought of her dream and felt a shock in her heart.

"I was eighteen, about as old as you are now," her dad said, "and I wanted to go to college to study music. My parents had me take violin lessons starting when I was very young, but just as a way to make me well rounded so I could be a…a successful businessman like my father. Well, I loved the violin, and since about my sophomore year of high school, I had been trying to convince my father that music was my calling and that the only way I'd go to college was if I could study it. There was an audition date coming up at USC, and I was determined to get in. He got angrier every time I brought it up, until he finally said that the instrument was a bad influence on me and said I couldn't play it anymore…ever."

Shel couldn't move. Her muscles were tight. Why had she never known more about her grandparents? Her eyes widened with him mentioning the violin.

Her dad's body was wiry in the chair, his suit loose on his frame. He pulled his shoulders back.

"Well, I wasn't about to let him deter me from my passion, so later that evening, I was in my room where I usually practiced, and I picked up the violin and dug into Vivaldi's 'Winter' movement from *The Four Seasons*. I know you probably don't know it, but it's one of the loudest, fastest pieces I could play. I was on fire, the bow flying over the strings, my fingers dancing on the fretboard. The instrument and I had become one, and as I closed my eyes, I felt so alive, as I always did when I played. I was in flow in that moment, and I didn't hear my father come in. He grabbed the violin out of my hand. I was so surprised, my heart…" He clenched his chest. "He threw the violin against the wall. It hit the metal radiator, and the wood cracked. Then he turned and left."

Shaking her head, Shel leaned toward her dad. Then she rocked back, holding her head.

"I was…I was crushed, you know?" He shrugged and took off his jacket. "The audition was only days away, and I didn't see any way, at the time, that I could find another instrument. Even if I could have borrowed or rented one. I didn't see the point of going on like this if it meant being disowned by my father. I—well, I cried for hours that night, saying goodbye to that dream, that fantasy, to that instrument I'd played and loved for so many years growing up."

He took a deep breath and his chest fell as he stared far off into the memory. "It wasn't a week later that I applied to study computer science at USC…instead of music."

He turned and picked up the small dark suitcase he'd carried in, and unzipped it, revealing his broken violin. Her dad took it out of the case and showed it to her. Shel gasped in recognition of the snapped neck and splintered body. She covered her eyes and massaged her temples, forcing quick breaths in through her mouth.

Her dad looked at it with hunched shoulders then set it back into the case and zipped it shut. Then he straightened, his eyes brightening. Shel rested her chin between her hands, trying to steady the sway of her thoughts and vision.

"But," he said, a gentle smile easing over his face, "there's more to the story. When your mom and I had you, we were trying to decide what to name you. Your mom loved the name Reneé, which is French—You know your mom's adoration of all things fine art and design. But I asked if we could name you Gakki, which means 'musical instrument' in Japanese. Hence, you were Gakki Reneé Henka. I wanted to name you Gakki to remind myself that you should be able to live out your dreams."

Shel's gaze didn't leave her dad.

He sunk into the chair again, crossing and uncrossing his arms. "I—I thought it'd be good to tell you all that, but…." He shook his head.

Shel's palms became clammy, and she grabbed her pillow, balling it up in her lap. "Dad, I…." She didn't know whether to thank him, tell him about the dream, hug him, or tell him she needed time to think about all this. It sent shivers down her spine that she would dream about the same violin that her dad just showed her.

"It's okay. It's okay," he said, standing. He started to put his jacket back on but then threw it over his arm. "Maybe I... shouldn't have bothered you. I just...." He scratched the back of his neck, looking at the ground.

"No, I...appreciate it, Dad," Shel said, swinging her legs over the edge of the bed and standing up, her hand still on the comforter.

He nodded and made quick eye contact with her, giving a grafted smile. He picked up the violin case. "Well, I should probably get to the airport." He sighed.

Shel's lungs tightened. Should she tell him about the dream? About what had happened last semester? About all she'd been going through? Her eyes wandered as she looked for the words to start.

"I love you, Shelley." He stepped toward her and gave her a kiss on her forehead.

"I love you, too, Dad." She walked him to the door.

Reaching for the handle, he turned and said, "You know, your mom would never say this, but... Well, you know her parents came from such little means. They could never...provide for her what... What I mean to say is that your mom has worked really hard to make sure you don't have to... She loves you, Shel. Mabye give her a chance, too."

Shel lowered her head and nodded. Her dad opened the door, and she waved as he shuffled down the hallway. A part of her wanted to call after him, but her head buzzed, and she felt dizzy trying to sort through all these thoughts crashing down on her.

SCENE 12

*M*r. Tarlaigh's email was the first Shel saw when she got online the next morning. She hovered over it a moment and then clicked.

Dear Shel and Charlie,

Thank you very much for your kind note. I have greatly enjoyed having you both in my class. As you know, this was the first time I taught it this way. There were certainly some things this semester that gave me the courage to step outside my comfort zone a bit. I found out over the winter break that I have a glioblastoma, a type of brain cancer that acts very quickly. I was given the diagnosis that I have about six months to live. I know this will probably come as a shock...it certainly has for me. However, I've been doing my best to take it all in and think about how I want to spend my remaining time.

As sweet an offer as it is, I don't think there's anything you can do at this time, but I do wish you both very wonderful journeys ahead. Life, indeed, is a musical thing...sing and dance while the music is being played.

Regards,
  Guy Tarlaigh

Shel craned her neck forward, reading the words again. Her eyes began to swell as a montage of Mr. Tarlaigh smiling or singing out of tune or raising his eyebrows and looking out over the tops of his glasses flashed before her. She pushed her chair back and shook her head. *Why didn't he tell us sooner?!* They must have given him the wrong diagnosis. He was his normal self in class with them just weeks ago.

Her next thought was to call Charlie, and she picked up her phone and dialed. It was still early, and she hoped she wasn't waking him.

He answered right away. "Hey, Shel!"

She spoke fast. "Hey, Charlie, did you see Mr. Tarlaigh's email?"

"No, I haven't checked it yet. What did he say?"

Shel read it to him. When she finished, all she heard was the quiet hiss on the other end of the line.

After what seemed like a long time, he finally said, "We gotta go see him."

Shel stood up and paced. "What do you mean? He said there was nothing we could do."

"I think there is," he said. "I'm not sure what it is yet, but I get the sense that it would be good to go and see him."

Shel stopped and looked out her dorm window, the phone to her ear, crossing her other arm over. "Okay, well, I can email him back and ask."

"That would be great," Charlie said.

Shel didn't have any classes on Fridays, so she sat down on her bed with her laptop and composed the email back to Mr. Tarlaigh, saying that she and Charlie would love to see him. When she finished, she clicked open her script for the documentary. Her mind kept returning to Mr. Tarlaigh, but she tried to focus on her assignment. She remembered what Charlie said about making the film about herself. She thought of her dad's story, that he'd named her Gakki and how she'd never known it meant "musical instrument," and that it signified expression. She *could* tell her story.

Opening a new document, she began to rewrite the script, starting with the night she'd run into the ocean in search of something she didn't know how to find, and how she'd almost lost everything but had returned to tell her story. She wrote about Jeremy, about her childhood and Shelley Winters and Thelma and her mom and dad and the dream about her grandparents; about music and film and the friends she'd met at Berkeley, and Mr. Tarlaigh and her teachers—all of these people who, knowing it or not, helped her when everything she knew had snapped and cracked, to start to mend those pieces back together.

When she finished, it was early afternoon, and Mr. Tarlaigh had responded to her email:

Hi Shel and Charlie,

Actually, I would love that. My wife and I will be at home this weekend. Why don't you two come by for dinner tomorrow night at 6?

4343 Montglenn Rd.

Orinda, CA 94563

GT

The next night, that is where they headed. Shel's Civic hummed eastward along CA-24, exiting at Moraga Way and winding through a maze of smaller streets to reach Montglenn Road. It was a beautiful mid-April evening, the sun waning through the trees, shadows fluttering on the road and driveway as they walked to the front door.

The Tarlaighs' house looked like it had been built decades earlier but was well maintained, with a dark wood exterior outlining a single-floor design that stretched down the property from the drive. Charlie opened the screen door to knock, and Shel looked down at the welcome mat. It had a couple music notes on it and read, "That Will Bring Us Back To Do," from *The Sound of Music*.

They heard steps against the hardwood floor inside, and a woman with streaming black and silver hair and dark skin answered the door.

"You must be Shel and Charlie." She had a wide grin and buttery tone. "I'm Wilma, Guy's wife." She invited them in.

The house smelled of pine, and Shel saw a rosemary candle burning in a small room off the hallway as Wilma showed them to the living room. The space opened from the dark passage to a large, thick-carpeted space with two sofas and a row of bookcases, connected to the kitchen, which looked like it had been remodeled. A granite-countertop island separated the rooms. Large glass doors revealed an arboreal yard, lush and green in the spring bloom. Mr. Tarlaigh leaned forward from his place on the sofa, set down a book, and rose to greet them. He looked healthy, Shel thought, just as he had the last time she saw him in class a week and a half ago.

"Hello, there!" he said through a grunt as he stood.

"Hi, Mr. Tarlaigh!" Shel walked over and shook his hand.

"I take it you met my lovely wife, Wilma." His smile couldn't altogether hide the red in his eyes.

They nodded, looking to her as she waved him off on her way into the kitchen.

"She's preparing a three-bean casserole, one of my favorites. Do you both want some wine?"

They shook their heads.

He motioned them over to the wool, gold-and-red-checkered couches, and they sank into the cushions across from the other sofa where Mr. Tarlaigh was seating himself again. Shel noticed the book he'd been reading on the coffee table: *Jonathan Livingston Seagull*. She'd heard of it but hadn't read it. There were other books and magazines on the table, a small remote that Shel matched with a stereo on the bookshelf, and a chessboard whose pieces looked like they had been long at battle.

The shelves were lined with volumes, most with titles Shel couldn't see, but she caught a large-font *BACH* next to *Jurassic Park,* leading into leather-bound classics that ran the length of the lower shelves in adjacent cases. The rest of the library was eclectic, populated with hardcover and paperback copies of different widths, heights, and colors.

"Have you read all these?" Shel motioned with her chin.

"Oh, no!" He laughed. "Most of those are Wilma's. She teaches literature at Berkeley."

"Oh, cool." She nodded.

After a pause, Mr. Tarlaigh cleared his throat. "How is Music Appreciation going?"

Shel turned to Charlie, who said, "It's a bit of a shift since you left."

Mr. Tarlaigh looked at the floor and bobbed his head a few times.

Wilma rattled some pots, putting something away, and then exited through another door.

"How did you meet?" Charlie smiled, moving his head in the direction of the kitchen.

"On campus. We were both involved in a summer program for high school students." He grinned.

"Was that when you were doing your undergrad?" Shel placed her hands in her lap.

"No, that was only a few years ago, actually." He chuckled and gave them that look over the top of his glasses. "I've been married twice before."

"Oh!" Shel blinked and looked down at the shaggy carpet, kneading her hands.

"One thing I've learned," he said, reaching for a glass of wine on the table, "is that sometimes your mistakes can lead to your greatest blessings."

Shel looked up, and his smile was warm, and he drank to his words and winked at them as Wilma came back into the kitchen.

A timer beeped, and she called across. "Soup's on!"

As they sat around the dining table in the room beyond the kitchen, they heard more about the literature program from Wilma. Charlie asked about her favorite book, which she had a hard time choosing, but she loved *A Farewell to Arms.* Shel hadn't read the book but had seen the 1932 and 1957 versions of the film, and that started them in on the topic of adapting the novel to cinema, and then to discussing the tragic end of the story, which left them all wiping at their eyes. When the food was gone, they sat back in their chairs, sipping decaf in candlelight.

"Mr. Tarlaigh"—Shel's voice lilted from the silence—"what were you planning on teaching us for the rest of the semester?"

He was unblinking, focusing on Shel. Then he said, "Come with me. I'll show you."

He got up and kissed Wilma on the forehead, thanking her for preparing the meal. Shel and Charlie's praises followed, and she waved them off, telling them that meant a lot to her. They followed Mr. Tarlaigh down the dark hallway to the pine-scented room they'd passed on the way in. Inside, he turned on a light to reveal a messy music room. An upright piano sat flush with the back wall, sheet music strewn on its face and top. The guitar he'd played in class rested on a stand, and his violin hung on the wall.

He sat down at his desk, cleared off a stack of papers, and pulled the computer keyboard toward him, lighting up the desktop screen. Clicking through a few folders, he opened one entitled "Music as a Metaphor for Life." In it were documents named after the subjects he'd been covering in class. Shel recognized Vibration, Resonance, Variation, Instrumentation, Practice, Interpretation, Tension, and Creativity from class, but there were three more: Simplicity, Balance, and Performance. He opened the "Simplicity" document, and it wasn't a class plan as Shel expected to see but was laid out like a book.

"They're each chapters," he said, scrolling through the pages. "I'm almost finished editing all of them, and am hoping I'll have time to publish them as a textbook. I'm spending almost all my time on it now to get it done. I didn't get to these last three chapters in class, but I'll email them to you." He pulled up a draft, attached the files, and hit "Send." "You'll have to let me know what you think."

Shel thanked him, and he walked over and grabbed the violin off the wall.

"I think we still have dessert waiting for us in the kitchen," he said with two quick raises of his eyebrows, "and you can't have a dinner party without some live music."

Wilma had put out small bowls of chocolate ice cream with raspberries, and while she, Charlie, and Shel stood around the island eating, Mr. Tarlaigh played some old Celtic fiddle tunes that had them all tapping their feet and moving their heads. Shel watched Mr. Tarlaigh rise on his toes, the wrinkles on his face melting away as he closed his eyes and rested his head on the violin. She turned and saw Wilma clapping and crying and hoped she would always remember her husband this way. Shel certainly would.

After the music ended and the bowls were empty, the Tarlaighs walked Shel and Charlie to the door. They all said goodnight and that they hoped to see each other again. Wilma walked them down the driveway.

"I wanted to thank you," she said.

Shel and Charlie didn't know how to respond.

"Since getting the news, things have been a little heavy around here, as you can probably imagine. Guy has always loved teaching, and having you two around really lifted his spirits. I know it'll be a memory he'll hold on to through what's to come."

Charlie and Shel hugged Wilma.

When they got in the car, Shel said to Charlie, "I hope she'll be alright."

"Me too." He squeezed her hand. "I think she will. I think they both will."

They drove off into the dark.

SCENE 13

$\mathcal{I}$t was time to call Thelma. Shel had ignored her calls for too long and figured Sunday was as good a day as any for a long-overdue catch-up. The dial tone rang and rang, but Thelma didn't answer, and it went to voicemail. Shel didn't know what to say, so she hung up and watched her screen as Thelma's name disappeared into black.

Shel tried to put her mind into revising her script. She could only get so far with her thoughts spinning around between Thelma, her mom and dad, Ellana, even Royson and that awkward passing a few weeks ago. A tug, like something expanding, trying to push its way out of her chest, compelled her to get out of her room and scout locations where she could film. Though all she had for a camera was her phone, she got some "B-roll" footage of herself in the dorm room, walking the path through the tunnel of trees to campus, at Moffit, Dwinelle, Wheeler, Tolman, and Morrison—the halls where she'd spent so many hours her freshman year. She went by the Golden Bear, all the while propping up her phone at artistic angles to the university backdrop and posing for the camera by looking into or beyond it, walking by, or sitting at a distance in the frame.

When she got back to the dorm, she uploaded the videos and created a new project using the stock film editing software on her lapop. She dragged and dropped the clips into a rough sequence and played with filters, exposure, and transitions between them, entranced by what could be conveyed through a simple play of light and shadow. She lost track of time until her stomach reminded her she should have a late dinner.

That evening, when she got back, she opened the attachments that Mr. Tarlaigh had emailed. The first of the last three chapters was "Simplicity." Mr. Tarlaigh used the song "Somewhere Over the Rainbow" to talk about how something could be simple but still have depth:

Let's begin by looking at the renowned song from *The Wizard of Oz,* "Somewhere Over the Rainbow." This song is a great example of the simultaneity of simplicity and depth. If we look at the melody, we see it is just the notes from a major scale, all within one octave, following a basic pattern of an octave leap followed by a descending motion back to the root. Pretty simple.

Now, here's where the depth comes in. What is the film *The Wizard of Oz* about? Dorothy finds that she's not in Kansas anymore, but in Oz, and the whole movie is about her trying to get back home. Along the way she meets some traveling companions: the scarecrow, tin man, and lion. Ultimately, she meets the wizard and gets back home.

Now let's take a closer look at the melody. In music theory, the note this melody starts on is called the "root" or "home note" or "Do." The melody then jumps up a whole octave, as far away as you can get from "Do" without making the melody too high to sing. Then we get a gradual return to "Do" with four melodic phrases before finally arriving back "home."

If we compare the features of this melody to the plot of the movie, we could make the connections that the octave leap represents Dorothy finding herself "not in Kansas anymore," the four phrases represent the four main characters she meets along the way, and the return to "Do" represents her return home. We can certainly say these are interesting correlations with the plot of the movie. This is simplicity with depth.

He included a quote from a book called *The Artist's Way* by Julia Cameron:

> Simple does not mean simplistic; nor does it connote dullness. It is uncomplicated and readily understood, like a Rembrandt etching, or Lincoln's Gettysburg Address. No wonder that the adjectives "striking," "elegant," and "classic" are often coupled with the word "simplicity."

Shel had thought of simplicity as dumbing something down, but she could see Mr. Tarlaigh's point that it could also be about having a vision and finding the most graceful and purposeful way of bringing it to materialization. When nothing was overstated or in excess, it gave the idea more power. She would keep that in mind as she edited her script and footage. It didn't need to be complex, just genuine…with depth. Shel pulled her laptop closer as she read, letting the unveiling of melody and lyric guide her.

The time had gone by faster than she thought when she checked her phone. She scrolled ahead to see how much she might still cover in the next chapter before bed, but she yawned, so she eased the screen shut. She was about to walk to the bathroom when she froze. The scene came to her of Mr. Tarlaigh writing out the creative process on the board with the words *visualization* and *materialization.* She had visualized apologizing to Royson, and that did help her feel more resolved, but she could also act to bring it from mind to matter.

She decided to write to him. Tearing a few sheets from her notebook, she began a letter that started from the beginning of her story. She didn't get far when it seemed too long and verbose. *Simplicity,* she reminded herself. She started again, and her thoughts became elegant phrases tracing the essential message she needed to convey: that she was sorry, had been going through a lot, and was sad to lose his friendship. She didn't have any expectations going forward but at least wanted him to know that she didn't take their conversations for granted. They had meant a lot to her and had helped her, and she thanked him for that.

She walked down the hall to his room. He was in there, as usual, ensconced at his desk. Slipping her hand around the door frame, she left the note on the floor just inside the entryway then scuttled back to the bathroom and slipped out of view, her hands jittering. She rubbed them along the sides of her jeans and listened to the buzz of the fluorescent lights over the mirror for a moment before washing her face.

Shel needed a good place to shoot A-roll, and Charlie agreed to explore Morrison Hall with her for the right spot. Neither of them had spent much time in the building except to enter and walk the staircase to the second floor for Music Appreciation. Today, they descended the stairs to the lower level and continued down to the basement. A long, concrete-walled hallway extended before them, caged bulbs staged between shadowy intervals.

"This is creepy," Shel said, "like a catacomb."

"Yeah, I'm not sure we're supposed to be down here," Charlie said, looking back toward the staircase, "but let's at least see what's at the end of the hall."

They crept past unmarked doors until there was a sharp right turn they hadn't seen from the stairs, and a door ajar at the end of the arm. It was quiet, and Shel and Charlie's steps echoed in the stale tunnel.

"Hello?" Charlie pressed open the door, knocking a few times.

The room was dark, though it seemed that light came from somewhere far in the back, and Charlie's voice didn't carry. It was muffled by something. Shel heard him feeling along the wall a few paces into the room. The lights flickered overhead as he hit a switch.

The contents of the space materialized before them. Shelves upon shelves of folders and old, dusty books repeated, as if in a mirror, down the length of the room.

"What *are* all these?" Shel's mouth went slack.

Charlie pulled a folder from one of the shelves. "Scores."

"Scores?" She looked over his shoulder.

"Thousands and thousands of musical scores. Some of these might be copies of original manuscripts. They've probably all been digitally archived." He looked down the stacks as if upon a treasure trove.

"Really?" Shel ran her hand through her hair and then siezed Charlie's shoulder. "What do you think are the chances we could find Vivaldi's 'Winter' movement from *The Four Seasons*?"

Charlie turned to her. "Only one way to find out."

It only took him a moment to decode the letter and numbering system on the sides of the shelves.

"It looks like we're at the beginning of the alphabet here," he said as he walked deeper into the room. His voice became fainter, "H…I…J…."

Shel was sure they weren't supposed to be in there but decided to follow. Everything smelled musty, like a long-sealed tomb. She found Charlie at the far end, flipping through one of the frail books.

"Found it!" He smiled. "We're in luck. It's a copy of an original manuscript. Now to just get to the 'Winter' movement."

He turned the pages and then handed the score to Shel. It was brilliant and intense, a thousand dots and lines arched and beamed together with penciled notes of "tutti," "allegro," and "forte," and cycles and variations of ascending and descending patterns.

"Wow," Shel whispered.

Charlie nodded next to her. "Let's see if there's a place to sit and look at this."

They followed the maze to the back of the room, where they discovered an antique wooden bench beneath an angled window that let in light from above. Shel sat, and the thin planks creaked.

"Shel." Charlie froze.

"What?" Her heart beat faster.

"That's the spot." He motioned at her with both hands.

"What are you talking about?" She looked around.

"The spot to film your monologue!"

She gazed up and saw that the rays pouring in from the window spotlighted her, and the ancient bench was an artistic contrast to the concrete wall. She balanced the "Winter" score on the back of the seat.

"Perfect!" Charlie laughed. "Do you think you can be ready to film tomorrow?"

Shel started to nod but then realized the door might have been left unlocked by accident. It was possible they wouldn't be able to get in again, she told Charlie.

"Good point," he said. "What do you want to do?"

Shel reached into her backpack and took out her laptop. "Let me review the script for a few minutes, and then let's film."

"Absolutely." Charlie jumped and clapped and then picked up the score, thumbing through it again.

It was a slow process to memorize the sequence, but she decided to give it a shot. She handed Charlie her phone, and section by section, take by take, Shel made her way through her story. For a while, she forgot Charlie was there, he was so still and absorbed in what she was saying. Shel remembered it was the first time he was hearing all this, but she didn't feel shy with him.

That night, as she downloaded the clips onto her computer, she saw something in the quality that gave her goose bumps. She couldn't tell if it was the setting or the way Charlie had framed her in the lens, or if it was how comfortable she seemed, or all of those things together, but it had a vibe to it.

She spent the next few hours editing the A- and B-roll together, her voice from the A-roll audio narrating throughout. When she was done, she attached the file for Charlie to add the music.

I think we're onto something, she included in the message, and then typed, *I think I'll submit it to the contest, after all.*

The next day, after Sobol's class, Shel's phone buzzed in her pocket. It was her mom.

She never calls on a weekday morning, Shel said to herself. She had some time before meeting with Ellana again for lunch, so she picked up.

"Mom?"

"Hi, Shelley. I had a little time between clients today, so I wanted to call to finish the conversation from the weekend."

"Oh, okay." Shel knitted her eyebrows and blinked, looking around. She found a quiet corner outside Dwinelle.

Her mom's tone was natural. "I've been thinking about it, and I really need an apology from you."

Shel jerked her head. "An apology?"

"Yes, what I haven't heard you say since our conversation almost two weeks ago is, 'I'm sorry, Mom.' So, instead of continuing to be angry, waiting for you to come around to it, I realized I just needed to bring it up."

The words settled, but Shel's stomach stirred. "I don't think I owe you an apology for anything." She could hear her own voice quaver. "I was just trying to share where I'm at with things. I wasn't trying to hurt you."

"Well, you did."

"Well, I'm sorry *you* felt hurt by that." Shel's voice rose a notch. "I can't take responsibility for how you respond to what I say."

"Shelley." Her mom's tone took an edge. "You're not hearing me. You need to apologize."

"You can't tell me what to do anymore, *Mom*." Then she shook her head and exhaled.

She thought of all she'd been learning and sought anything that could help her. She groped at the concepts that had been so clear as she read and wrote about them. Now they blared and hissed like a bad radio, far from tuning in with the harmony she'd felt in her vision. She dropped her shoulders. The tension in her heart eased and she put her hand to her chest. Joni Mitchell's song came to her mind, and she could almost hear the singer's voice. *I've looked at life from both sides now.*

"Mom," Shel said, "I don't know how to resolve this with you, but I don't want to fight." She took a deep breath. "I hear you that you want me to apologize. I don't feel the same way right now, but I want to understand your side. Can you tell me where you're coming from?"

"Shel, your dad and I have done nothing but try to help you all your life. It just seems like ever since you went away to college, you've been changing into a different person...like over Family Weekend...and over Christmas I didn't feel you were really with us. Then, you suddenly yell at us during spring break, and... Shel, I've always done everything I can to be there for you."

Shel paused before responding. "I know. I know you have, Mom, and I know I've been distancing myself. It's just that we've never really talked about...harder stuff, and every time I try to bring up what I've been going through—"

"Shel, there you go again. You're making it my problem, that I haven't done this or that when I've given you everything. Look where you are, studying film at UC Berkeley. Do you know how hard I had to fight to get into USC when I was your age? And then do you think that scholarship was easy to keep? I didn't have it nearly as easy as you."

"Yeah, but that's *you*, Mom. I'm a different person with a different life. Okay, I have it a lot easier in some ways. I get it. But that doesn't mean that I don't have my own struggles and that I'm not trying to deal with them in the best way I can. I'm trying to do everything I can with the opportunity you and Dad have provided for me...I just—"

"Look, Shelley. I get that you've been going through some hard things, maybe with a relationship and it's gotten you down and all that, but you can't *let* it get you down. You've got to stay focused on the positive and take advantage of the opportunity that's before you. You have the chance to be everything you can be, and I know how much potential you have—all that joy and excitement you had as a little girl."

Shel lowered her head and thought about what it must have been like for her mom trying to navigate life when she was younger, and raising a daughter in the midst of it all. She thought about what she knew, now, about what her dad had sacrificed for her, too. Tears came to her eyes, and she choked out, "Yes, Mom."

"Honey." Her mom's tone softened. "You know we love you. We just want what's best for you."

"I know." Shel thought about the Japanese bowl in the cabinet.

"Okay, well you just hang in there through the end of the semester, sweetie. Your dad and I are both looking forward to having you home again this summer."

Shel sniffled. "Okay."

"Alright. Bye, sweetie."

In Japanese class that afternoon, they practiced pronunciation, placing the accents on the appropriate syllables and forming vowels and consonants that had felt foreign but were now becoming more natural to her. She thought about her name, Gakki, and its meaning, "musical instrument." She appreciated learning more about her family's language and felt more connected to her parents and grandparents. She wondered if the dream of the broken violin would return.

That night, Shel read the last of Mr. Tarlaigh's *Music as a Metaphor for Life* chapters. The one on "Balance" began with a quote, this one by John Powell:

Many people think that music is entirely built on art, but this is not true. There are rules of logic, engineering and physics underlying the whole creative side of music. The development of music and musical instruments over the past couple of millennia has depended on a continuous interplay of art and science.

Shel thought of Shelley Winters and the two parts within her, and how she'd learned to balance them—an interplay between fantasy and reality. She thought of herself in the same balance between Gakki, the child in her, and Shel the teenager and, now, young adult.

Mr. Tarlaigh used the example of Indian classical music to explicate the balance of art and science. The *tala,* he said, was the rhythmic element and could be equated more with the scientific side. Different from Western concepts of three- or four-beat rhythmic cycles, the tala could have as many as twenty or more beats to a cycle before repeating. "Raga Puriya Kalyan," performed by Ravi Shankar, contained eleven beats, which looked like this:

The melody, or *raga*, on the other hand, was more improvisational over the foundation of the tala. The raga, therefore, could be equated with the artistic side. Using a particular scale of notes, Ravi Shankar improvised a playful melody while the steady tala was held by a performer on *tablas,* a type of Indian drum.

"So," Mr. Tarlaigh wrote, "it is the combination of structure and improvisation, science and art, that has been the foundation upon which Indian classical music has stood for millennia."

Shel remembered the story of Shirley Schrift fusing with Shelley Winters, and the resolution Winters felt at that moment.

Mr. Tarlaigh also spoke of balance in terms of using all the concepts he'd covered in the classes and chapters to continue to learn about life through music. In the chapters, he'd spoken of

Vibration, Resonance, Form, Variation, Instrumentation, Practice, Interpretation, Tension, Creativity, and Simplicity. A performer might work to balance these elements and use them as a basis for deepening mastery. In life, a person might use these elements as a basis for developing the body, mind, soul, emotions, a sense of purpose, and relationships.

As a way for a performer to analyze ability in each of these areas, Mr. Tarlaigh demonstrated a chart with all the chapter headings around the outside:

The center of the wheel represented low ability, and the outside of the wheel represented high skill level. So, placing a dot at each of the areas, a performer could assess where strengths and challenges lay and could track growth over time. Similarly, a person could place body, mind, soul, emotions, relationships, and other important aspects of life around the outside of the chart and track growth over time. The important thing to remember was balance. Too much attention to any one of these areas could be detrimental, as could neglecting any of the areas. Fusion and integration were key, each part interlinked with and affecting the others.

Shel thought of all the elements that had come together, leading to her documentary, each of them a gleaming striation in her memory: her body and all it went through with Jeremy and the ocean; her mind opening through Mr. Tarlaigh's class, psychology, language, film; her soul awakening through Winters's story and roles to a greater consciousness of vulnerability, connectivity, and compassion; her emotions, like tension and resolution, ebbing and flowing to realms she'd never had to face before; and the splintered relationships that she was trying to re-mold and make new. In her mind, she placed these around the edge of the wheel and connected them with lines which glowed into the hollow.

Mr. Tarlaigh had sent only one more chapter. Shel clicked it open and read the final lesson, on "Performance." He explained that, in the career of a performer, half of the success was in mastery of the skills and personal, intimate connection with the spirit of the music, but the other half was in sharing that with the audience. He wrote:

It's great, no doubt, to be rehearsing, even totally alone, and to be really deeply feeling the connection with the music. But what's even better is to feel that connection with the music while other people are in the room. The experience then expands into them and there is a shared understanding, a simultaneous, in-the-moment, "we all just felt something together," recognition that somehow connects our hearts and minds, makes us more sympathetic toward one another, more accepting and loving.

Shel thought of Winters, her vulnerability and sharing through her book. She thought of the experience she'd had in the ocean with waves of vibration, her sense of self expanding in all directions with her heart as the center, connecting her with everything around her. In that, she had known what it was to be filled, but she would have to choose on her own, in the depths of emptiness, to share herself and the echo of that fullness with Ellana and Thelma, and Charlie and Gertrude and Royson, and her parents. It wasn't until she was open that she'd be able to move again toward that harmony.

Mr. Tarlaigh explored the cellist Yo-Yo Ma and how he accomplished this in his performances. About his masterful performance of Edward Elgar's *Cello Concerto in E minor, Opus 85* with the Baltimore Symphony Orchestra, Mr. Tarlaigh wrote:

Yo-Yo Ma's brow is furrowed with deep concentration and absorption in the moment with the music. This internalization makes way for authentic expressivity, as though the music is originating spontaneously from him in that moment. The cello becomes a tool for sharing the music he feels and is generating from within....

Yo-Yo Ma said, "I've always thought the sound that you make is just the tip of the iceberg, like the person that you see physically is just the tip of the iceberg as well." Through the sound Yo-Yo Ma creates in this performance, we are offered a glimpse of what is beneath the surface, both within the musical piece and within him as a person. It is this openness that allows him to connect with the joy of the music, and share that experience with the audience.

In the very last paragraph of the book, Mr. Tarlaigh wrote:

"Whatever our approach to music and life might be, the point is to enjoy the journey. We could say that life is, essentially, music. It is vibration; it is beauty, and tension, and resolution. We are all a part of this music. It'll be fun to see where this masterful composition goes, and be in awe as we listen for the role we get to play in it. Philosopher Alan Watts said, "[Life] was a musical thing and we were supposed to sing or to dance while the music was being played."

Sing and dance while the music is being played. Mr. Tarlaigh had said that to them so many times. And now his part was almost over. One day it would end for Shel, too. She only had so much time, as does a performer once the piece starts, to have that intimate connection with the harmony and share it with others. She wanted to sing and dance, for herself, for Mr. Tarlaigh, and with everyone around her whom she loved so much.

Another current still pulling at her feet was Jeremy. He appeared to her, now, from a new angle. She wondered where his pain came from. Picturing him in her mind, he no longer wore a smile and magazine clothes, mocking her, but instead was hunched over in a chair, a dark hand pressing down on his neck. To this boy, she reached out and held him against her chest. She cried, but it was no longer in brokenness. A flood of light flowed through her to him. Shel whispered, "I forgive you, Jeremy," and a piece of her that had snapped at the center of her heart was mended in place.

Even if through a broken instrument, like in "The Touch of the Master's Hand," she could give that harmony. In fact, like Mr. Fujimoto's kintsukuroi, golden repair, the cracks were needed for the light to shine through.

She closed the document and began an email back to Mr. Tarlaigh, thanking him for the chapters. He had helped her so much this semester, and she wanted him to know she would do her best to live and pass on what she had learned.

"I hope all of you uploaded your documentaries in MOV format online before class today." Dr. Sobol's voice boomed. "I will not be accepting any late submissions on this one, since it's your semester project."

The prior evening, Charlie had emailed the documentary back to Shel with his score included and a *Yes!* in response to her deciding to enter it into the contest. Before bed, she had sent the film to Dr. Sobol through the class portal along with the contest submission request, closing her eyes as she hit "Submit."

Dr. Sobol was preparing them, now, for the final exam in two weeks, which was also when the final screening round of the competition would be held. Shel hoped her film would be chosen, as only the top twenty submissions would be screened, but she wasn't holding her breath. The finalists would be announced in a week, next Thursday. The screening would be the Thursday evening after that, during finals week, in Dwinelle C-25, where Hadaway's Introduction to Digital Video Production class met last semester.

Shel had begun seeing posters advertising the competition around campus, and the latest email to the whole undergraduate student body included an announcement about it. She would go even if her film wasn't selected. It would be fun to see what her peers were creating, and she was sure Charlie would want to go with her.

When she saw Charlie in Music Appreciation, she was beaming.

"Well, it's submitted," she said as she sat down next to him.

Charlie nodded, pinching his lips. "Congratulations, Shel. You've put a lot of work into that. It's already a great success in my book."

"Well, you played a big part in it," she said.

She reached into her bag just as Charlie leaned for his and she slapped at his hand, making him smile.

Dr. Luís had transitioned into twentieth-century music. Today, she was explaining the avante garde period, showing them a composition by John Cage called "4'33"." The concept was that the entire performance was to consist of silence, the musicians posing to play at the beginning of each movement but then relaxing and sitting tacitly until the end of a prescribed time. Cage's point, Dr. Luís suggested, might have been to question and expand the boundaries around what we consider "music" to be. Perhaps it was any and every sound that happened in the theatre, organically, during the movement. Even Dr. Luís, Shel thought, though disapproving of Mr. Tarlaigh's approach that first day she subbed, couldn't help but talk of music as a metaphor for life—life as a musical thing.

The days crawled as Shel waited for the following Thursday, when the finalists would be announced. Early the next week, Mr. Tarlaigh had still not emailed back after she'd thanked him for the book. She hoped he and Wilma were doing well enough and that she and Charlie could go visit them again, maybe as soon as the semester was over.

Thursday morning Shel woke to Charlie calling, and she lunged at her phone.

"Shel." Charlie's voice shook. "Have you checked your email yet?"

"No," she whispered, rubbing her eyes. "What is it? What happened?"

"You made it…your documentary… It's in the top twenty!"

Shel popped up and maneuvered with as much stealth as she could to her desk, trying not to wake Gertrude. She opened her computer, and there it was, an email to the student body announcing the top twenty finalists. She'd also received an email from Dr. Marlin, the Chair of the Film Department, congratulating her on her short documentary being selected as one of the films to be screened in the final round of the competition.

"Oh my God!" she mouthed into the phone.

"I know, it's amazing." Charlie was giddy.

She covered her mouth with her hand and stepped into the hallway, sitting down against the wall. "Charlie, we have to celebrate! I need to call my parents. I *have* to invite Thelma and Ellana. I need to thank Dr. Sobol. What am I going to wear for this?"

"Slow down, slow down." Charlie laughed. "First take a deep breath, and then you can take it a step at a time."

She closed her eyes and let the air flow into her lungs. The good vibrations resonated in and through her, and she smiled.

When she got off the phone with Charlie, she texted her parents.

Hi Mom and Dad, I have some good news! I created a short film this semester that made it into the top 20 in a contest here at school, and it's going to be screened on May 12th!! Want to come up?

Then she texted Thelma and Ellana, telling them that she really needed them at this screening, that it would explain so much.

She showered as fast as she could and got dressed, leaving a note for Gertrude about the contest and inviting her. Her chest swelled, and she hummed as she flew out to door to Music Appreciation.

SCENE 14

$\mathcal{W}$hen the big night arrived, Shel flipped through her wardrobe, debating in front of her mirror which outfit was most appropriate for the screening. After multiple dresses and blouses lay scattered on the bed behind her, she decided to go casual and put on a pair of jeans and her $E=M(Scene)^2$ T-shirt, pulling her hair into a simple ponytail and wearing her glasses. She looked at herself in the mirror and winked at her reflection.

People were packing into the theatre as Shel and Charlie, sitting in the front row, turned their heads to see the last remaining seats taken and a line forming along the back wall. Shel's parents made the trip up and sat to her left. She hadn't heard back from Thelma or Ellana, so she figured they wouldn't be there.

There were so many faces to take in as Shel stole glances over her shoulder. She looked for Gertrude, who said she'd be there, and finally spotted her at the far end of the room sitting between others in conversation. She wondered if she should go invite her roommate to sit with them but glanced down the front row to find it filled. She was grateful Gertrude had come and smiled her thanks across the room, even if her roommate couldn't see her.

About to turn back around, her eye caught Ellana in the back row. She thought of waving, but was far enough away in the crowd she wasn't sure she'd see her. Shel wondered if Royson had received her note and if it had smoothed the rift between them. She looked for him for a long time but didn't see him.

She hunkered down in her seat and bunched her hands over her heart. Her chest was pounding as she closed her eyes, and something like a prayer surfaced that her film could somehow reach her parents, her friends, and that things could return to a semblance of the way they had been.

The house lights dimmed, enshrouding the audience, focusing all attention on the podium at the front of the theatre. Dr. Marlin came forward and tapped the microphone.

"Good evening, everyone." She smiled. "We're very happy to have you here for what is becoming a new tradition for us at UC Berkeley. This is our third annual undergraduate short-film contest!"

The audience applauded.

"As you probably know by this point," she said, "what you're about to see tonight are the top twenty finalists from over one hundred and fifty submissions we received last week. Our film faculty have put in a lot of extra hours to select these finalists, so let's start by thanking them."

The audience applauded again as a handful of teachers stood to receive the cheers. Students called out a few "whoos" and professors' names. Shel heard a guy in the back shout, "SO-BOL!"

Dr. Marlin began again. "We have a few special guests with us tonight who will be selecting the top three winners."

She introduced Nora Bellinsky, director of the San Francisco International Film Festival, and Shel turned to look at her mom, who raised her eyebrows. Dr. Marlin welcomed Leslie Framm, who worked in post-production at Pixar, and Ballinger Glass-man, who was a film critic for the *San Francisco Chronicle*. They each stood, in turn, to greet the audience with a wave. Shel felt her stomach drop. It was one thing to have seen their names on the email Dr. Sobol sent out months ago, and another to be sitting across the room from these industry giants…who were about to watch *her* film.

"We'll now begin our screening," Dr. Marlin said. "Congratu-lations to *all* our finalists. I hope you enjoy the show!"

The audience applauded one last time, and Shel could feel the tingle in the room as the podium spotlight faded and the screen lit with the title and opening credits of the first film. She wasn't sure who the other finalists were but assumed they sat inter-spersed through the crowd. She also didn't know what order the films would be shown in, as there was no program.

The first one was by Amil Sleiman, entitled *Backstroke*. It depicted a fictional relationship between a Czech government official and his mistress, the title being a double entendre on him hiding this relationship from his wife and how his daily routine of swimming laps was the only time he could forget about the pressures of his life and the choices he was making. There was no music except when the minister was in the pool. Simple piano chords were touched and held out a long time as he began the blind stroke. Shel was impressed with the film quality and the message that people and their choices were not always as black and white as they might seem.

The crowd clapped at length for the film. Shel saw the guest judges making notes. How could she compete against that kind of skill and talent? The thought passed through that maybe there had been some mistake in her novice documentary being selected.

Two more films showed, one an animated feature about a virtual reality character that becomes too real to the player, and the other a comedic silent film with a honky-tonk score about two college guys who go back in time and are trapped in the early 1900s, not able to convince anyone where they'd come from. Shel thought she caught obscure references to *Bill and Ted's Excellent Adventure.*

And then, there it was. Charlie's string score began with a single violin playing the ascending melody as the title flashed against the black background: *The Broken Violin.* Those words faded into, "A Memoir by Gakki Renée Henka," and then, "Music by Charlie Bassett." A cello joined the violin with a complimentary melody when Shel's image focused into view, lit by the vertical window in the Morrison basement, Vivaldi's "Winter" score in the background. Out of the corner of her eye, Shel could see her dad nodding. On the screen, she introduced herself by her Japanese name, "also known as Shelley, or Shel," she said. As she began her story about the ocean, the scene changed to her balancing on a curb, walking away from the camera. At first all that could be seen were her feet, but as she stepped farther from the lens, her whole body came into view. An effect of waves undulated through the image, and the brightness flickered like old film.

More strings joined the ensemble, beginning a gentle rhythm, Shel taking the audience back in time to her first days of the fall semester and the boy she met. She told how she never heard from him after that fateful night, accompanied by increasing tension in the score. This cut to Shel in her dorm room, holding her head between her hands on her bed, her body curled in a ball. Red light flashed as if from an alarm or prison cell as she picked herself up and went to the mirror, mascara running down her face.

Her image crossfaded with one of a young, blond Shelley Winters in a halter top, and the string melodies hinted at the soundtrack from *South Sea Sinner.* Shel described how she used to watch the "blond bombshell" with her best friend in high school, and the fantasies that formed around the time she changed her name to match the actress's. The first photo of Winters changed to the plain factory worker Alice Tripp in *A Place in the Sun,* and Shel quoted short passages from Winters's autobiography: how the actress's fantasies of Hollywood began to splinter as the two parts within herself, Shirley and Shelley, grew more distant. Then came an image from *The Diary of Anne Frank,* Winters playing an older woman. Shel quoted the line, "In spite of everything, I still believe people are good at heart," and said it was pivotal in Winters finding resolution after her divorce.

Winters's photo morphed back into Shel's at the mirror, and she told about how months went by in a blur, and her relationships splintered around her. But one class, Music as a Metaphor for Life, as she called it, helped her to bring all she'd wanted to hide out into the open. The scene cut back to Shel narrating in the ethereal light of the music stacks, and she related the story of her dad's broken violin. He had named her Gakki, musical instrument, and she had been broken, but she gathered the pieces and, though they could never come together in the same way, she'd learned how to mend them into something more beautiful than before.

A visual of her writing "Gakki" in translucent Japanese characters overlay another scene where she sat at a distance from the camera. The score returned to the single violin melody as Shel told the story of that broken-down violin in "The Touch of the Master's Hand" and the Master who restored its worth. As she said "Master," a deep golden light washed over the screen as the strings dipped into a deep harmony, and she read the last three stanzas of the poem that Mr. Tarlaigh had begun in class:

And many a man with life out of tune,
    And battered and bruised with sin,
    Is auctioned cheap to the thoughtless crowd
    Much like that old violin.

. . .

A mess of pottage, a glass of wine,
    A game and he travels on.
    He is going once, he is going twice,
    He is going and almost gone.

But the Master comes,
    And the foolish crowd never can quite understand,
    The worth of a soul and the change that is wrought
    By the touch of the Master's hand.

Shel, sitting afar in the frame, then got up and began walking toward the camera. Her voice narrated that a friend in her music class helped her start to tell her story. As she shared herself with those around her, some of her relationships had begun to mend. She found she had only seen the surface waves of who they were, and of who she was, and was beginning to understand how much depth lay beneath. In spite of everything, she could now say, she believed people were really good at heart, even herself. Shel had walked right up to the camera until she was so close that all that could be seen were her open eyes as she looked into the lens. Everything went black, and the music stopped. Only Shel's voice then pierced the void: "That's how I learned to tread the darkness...and glow again."

Full, rhythmic strings filled the void with powerful chords and a soaring violin melody as a bright image lit the screen, showing Shel's hand touch the leaves on the path to campus she'd walked so many times, then of her singing and dancing in front of Dwinelle Hall in fast-motion like an old home video, running up the few stairs and turning around and smiling, and then of her standing on one of the balconies at Moffitt, the camera at her back as her hair blew in the wind.

The music decrescendoed one last time to solo violin, and the shot returned of her beneath the basement window. As the melody ended, the only audio was the sound of her taking a deep breath in, and then releasing it. She looked at the camera and smiled, and the screen cut to black.

Silence hovered over the audience for what felt like minutes to Shel, and then applause enveloped her. She didn't know if it was louder or longer or more enthusiastic than it had been after any of the other films, but it felt amazing to be surrounded by so much support and good will, having laid herself so open. She turned and smiled at Charlie. Her dad, she noticed, had been crying. She peered over at the judges hashing out notes, wondering what they thought.

The next film started, called *Generations*, which leapt, *Memento*-like, between phases of the female character's life, revealing how much perspective can change over one person's lifetime. Shel tried to focus, but her mind replayed all that had just happened. It felt so different watching in her dorm room versus with an audience. She rubbed her temples, thinking of sitting through so many other films before she could hear from the judges or talk to anyone to know their impressions. She set her hands in her lap and looked up at the screen, but then her leg started to jitter.

The other shorts continued to be very good. It was somewhere around the twelfth or fourteenth film that the audience was introduced to Isidora Ruíz. The title of her short was *Conveniente Olvidar (Convenient to Forget)*, a documentary about her home country of Guatemala and the genocide and civil war that had occurred there so recently: the 1960s and '70s. She told some of the story of Rigoberta Menchú, who was a child during the time of the atrocities and was now an activist who had won the Nobel Peace Prize. She revealed that, growing up in Guatemala, she had never heard much of this recent history of her nation. The younger generation was choosing to forget what happened. Her documentary was dedicated to those who had suffered, that the past be remembered and interwoven with the present and future of Guatemala.

A few people around the room stood up when Isidora's film ended, prompting a cascade of others to rise. Shel glanced at the judges, but they gave nothing away. She felt heavy in her seat. This documentary covered international issues and brought light to something important that was so much bigger than Isidora. Shel let herself sink into the chair. *I've been spending so much time wrapped up in my own issues this year.* But she remembered what Charlie said, and how Winters's autobiography had helped her. Then, the image from her vision came to mind, vibrations going out in all directions with her heart as the center. Shel placed her hand on the arm rest and hoisted herself up with everyone else to honor the film.

After the last film played, Dr. Marlin came to the podium.

"Let's give one more round of applause for *all* those who submitted films, and to acknowledge the range and diversity of expression that just occurred through a simple play of light and shadow on the screen."

The theatre flooded with waves of sound as everyone stood.

Dr. Marlin announced a twenty-minute intermission while the judges corroborated, and many people filed out to use the bathroom or mingle with others in various sections of the hall. Shel hugged Charlie, and they looked at each other. He gave her two light squeezes on the back of her arm and grinned.

Her dad held her close with wet eyes. "It was really sweet to see your birth name on such a wonderful work of art," he said in her ear.

Then Shel turned to her mom, whose face was flushed. She looked like she was trying to compose herself and then turned away and excused herself to the bathroom.

Shel watched her go and nearly tripped over the seats as she turned toward the aisle. She needed to find Ellana and walked toward the doors, rising on her toes to see if she could catch her in the back row. Along the way, she saw Gertrude and shuffled through the crowd to where she was sitting, talking with a girl next to her. Her voice bubbled, and her movements were fluid. Shel's eyes widened, and she grinned.

"Hey, Gertrude!" Shel said as she wriggled past the people standing by the seats.

"Hey, Shel!" Gertrude beamed.

"Thanks so much for coming!" Shel gave her a hug.

"This is Liza. We just met," Gertrude said as Shel shook Liza's hand.

"Good to meet you!" Shel said.

Liza said, "We were just talking about your film. It's very brave."

"Oh, thank you!" Shel blushed.

"She's my *roommate*," Gertrude said, looking at Shel and opening her arms wide.

Shel winked and smiled, thanking them again for coming, and meandered past the back-row seats toward the lobby. She passed Dr. Sobol, who caught her eye and gave her a thumbs-up and smiled. Shel smiled back and went out the back doors. She looked at all the faces in the lobby and wended through the groups of people chatting, wondering if Ellana had left. But then she finally spotted her alone, leaning against the wall in the corner by the main entrance.

Shel approached her with her hands folded in front. "Hey," she said, and bit her lip.

"Hey." Ellana turned her head and looked out the glass doors. "You did a great job"—she flashed her eyes toward the theatre —"on the film."

"Thanks." Shel's gaze wandered.

Ellana pushed herself off the wall and faced Shel. "Seeing what you've been through… I was maybe a little harsh last time we talked." She adjusted her shirt at the collar. "You're not entirely at fault, Shel. Yes, I was hurt that day in October. I thought we were close friends, and it was hard to see some side of you I didn't know attacking me. But I went into my own shell, too."

Shel relaxed and wanted to say something. She extended her arm, her palm up, but then brought it back to her side.

"The thing is, I'd felt that kind of attack before…from my sister. I guess she never liked the idea of our dad remarrying, and so I've been a target for her: 'the daughter of Dad's second wife.'" Ellana mimicked her sister's voice and looked away. "If she wasn't straight up ignoring me, she would remind me in other ways that she was better than me. I followed her around everywhere, you know? I wanted to be accepted by her. We grew up, of course, and became more mature and stuff, but that programming is deep in us now, and whether it's her intention or not, I still feel like some peasant on the outskirts of her castle."

She looked at Shel. "When you lashed out at me, I turned back into that little girl. I felt myself, in that moment and for weeks afterwards, wanting to reach out to you…not to check in and see how you were doing, but to see if you still accepted me. It scared me because I thought I'd left that little girl behind. I didn't want another relationship in my life like the one I have with my sister."

Her pause made Shel wonder if she was telling her their friendship was over, but then she went on. "The truth is, you made me look at a part of myself I was hiding from. I don't know how to not hide anymore, but I thought about reaching out to you…to talk like this."

Shel took a step forward and held Ellana's hand.

They stood there a moment then Ellana rolled her shoulders back and stretched. "Well, as much as I would love to stay and see if you win, I do have a final tomorrow I really need to study for, so maybe I'll…." She nodded toward the door.

Shel smiled. "Let's chat again soon. Maybe I can call you once

I'm back in SoCal after finals are over."

Ellana placed her palms together at her heart, tipped her head to Shel, and pushed open the door.

Shel stood there and watched Ellana skip down the stairs outside. There were five minutes before the winners would be announced, so Shel walked out the doors into the night. Looking at the surrounding buildings on campus, she leaned on the entryway handrail, remembering driving up the coast from Azusa ten months ago. She had wondered, then, glancing across the deep blue-gray expanse of water to the horizon, what this year would bring. If she had known what she would have to go through, she might have turned the car around. She looked down at her feet, followed the line of her jeans over her T-shirt, and put her hand on her heart, which had pounded the first time she came across campus to Wheeler and Dwinelle, broken in her bed after Jeremy left, fallen in the ocean that night, and begun to remold in Mr. Tarlaigh's class.

Shel looked up and saw a girl coming up the steps who looked like a younger version of herself, the one in the sophomore year photo. Time fell into slow motion as the girl's eyes met hers, smiling and seeming to wink at her. Her hand still on her chest, a warmth glowed there now, and she wouldn't trade it for anything.

Charlie shuffled out from the door. "You alright?"

Shel looked at him and rocked herself forward off the railing. "Yeah, I really am." She put her arm through his to walk inside. The lights flashed in the lobby, and people filtered back to their seats.

Dr. Marlin tried to quiet them down. "Okay, everyone," she said, "our judges have reached their final decisions."

The chatter calmed to silence, and Dr. Marlin invited Nora Bellinsky to announce the winners.

Nora placed her hands on the podium. "First of all, I want to convey on behalf of the judges how impressed we are with the quality of artistry coming from this young generation."

The audience applauded.

"I think contests are a great thing to be doing in a college setting like this. A challenge pushes students to new levels of expression they might not have known existed within themselves."

She turned her attention to a piece of paper in front of her on the podium.

"It was a very difficult process, but we have selected first-, second-, and third-place winners from tonight's screenings, which I'll announce in reverse order."

Shel's heart dropped into her stomach. She thought of her grade in Documentary Film, what she'd have to tell her parents if she didn't win, how her mom would probably jump and down in excitement if her film was going to be shown at the San Francisco International Film Festival. Out of the corner of her eye, she saw Charlie turn to look at her.

"The third-place winner, who I understand will be receiving a professional-quality video camera, is…."

Shel held her breath.

"…Vikki Gordon for her film, *Generations!*"

The applause swelled. Shel had been so lost in thought after her own short screened, the name hadn't registered to her. But when Vikki came up to shake hands with Nora and Dr. Marlin and receive the video camera, she recognized her as the main character. Shel thudded her hands together.

Nora spoke again. "The second-place winner of the internship at Pixar is…Amil Sleiman for *Backstroke!*"

Amil also came forward to thunderous accolades, shaking hands and receiving a certificate representing the internship invitation.

Shel let her back slide down the chair. She felt nauseous, and her body began to shake uncontrollably.

"And the first-place prize for the opportunity to screen their film at the San Francisco International Film Festival and shadow *moi*…." Nora flipped her hands to point at herself and paused with her mouth open. A few in the crowd started laughing and applauding.

"Let me first say," she said, taking a breath, "that this young woman shows rare talent. The other judges and I agree that she has real potential to be one of the next great documentary filmmakers."

Shel's chest was bursting. Was she describing her?

"The first-place prize goes to…Isidora Ruíz for her film *Conveniente Olvidar, Convenient to Forget!*"

The audience stood and cheered for Isidora as she came to the front and shook hands with the judges, bowing to the gracious reception. Charlie turned to Shel, his eyes soft.

Shel couldn't breathe. Was this still in her imagination? A coldness drained her body, and she felt small in the large, loud room.

As everyone poured out of the theatre after the closing remarks, Shel, her parents, and Charlie remained seated in the front row. Shel slouched in the seat, and no one said anything to her.

With a deep breath, she pushed herself up out of the chair. "I should go thank the judges. I'll meet you in the lobby," she said.

Small groups of students stood around the judges. Shel waited a couple minutes to talk to Nora and then Leslie. She introduced herself to them as Gakki Renée Henka, and they said that she'd made a solid film and should keep at it. She waited to talk with Ballinger Glassman and again introduced herself.

"Yes, I know who you are." Ballinger squeezed her hand. "I was very impressed with your film."

"Really?" Shel curled her toes on her sandals.

"Yes. I was making a case to Nora and Leslie that the raw

content was some of the best of the evening. That kind of honesty is what got me into journalism. It's like a pebble dropped in the water."

Shel jerked her head, but he moved on, asking what year Shel was in school.

"Oh, I'm just finishing my freshman year."

Ballinger nodded. "I'll be excited to see how you develop over the next few years." He looked at her as if seeing some possible iteration of her future.

"Thank you so much!" Shel shook his hand and bowed her head to him, smiling. When she turned around, her mom was waiting for her in the aisle. Everyone else had gone to the lobby. Her mom's face was drawn and her chin high. Shel lowered her head and marched over to her.

"Shelley," she said as Shel turned to look at her. Her mom's movements were restrained. "When you said you were going to showcase a film you'd made, I thought it was going to be based on something from your class, not…" Her eyes brimmed over with tears, which she wiped away. She went on in a broken voice, "Not about *you*."

Shel wrinkled her brow and looked down. Maybe this was the last straw, and she'd really hurt her mom with this.

Her mom put her hand under Shel's chin and looked into her eyes. "I'm very proud of you."

Shel put her arms around her mom.

They stayed a long moment in that embrace, and then her mom pushed back, holding Shel's arms. "You know, maybe it's time to bring that bowl out in the open, on the dining room table."

"What?" Shel looked at her and tilted her head.

"The Japanese bowl. I saw that you set it out when you were home last, and I…" Her throat caught, and she looked at Shel through puffy eyes. "I think it's time we should set it out where it can be seen. It's such a beautiful piece, really. It'll be there next time you're home."

Shel beamed then lowered her gaze again. "Mom, there's something I have to tell you. I…thought I was going to be able to pass my Documentary Film class with this competition, but I didn't win, so I'm not going to pass, and I should have tried harder, and you guys are going to have to pay for extra credits, and…"

"Shelley." Her mom put up her hands. "Shelley, we'll figure that out later, honey. Right now, let's just… I'll tell you what we're going to do. We're going to go with everyone and get Japanese takeout."

Shel gave a quick laugh and wiped her eyes. She hugged her mom again, and they walked out to the lobby.

That night, after the competition, Shel fell into a deep dream. Her grandparents again came out of the mist and bowed low to her. She bowed as deeply in return and looked down to find the violin in her hands. The neck, where it had been splintered, was now smooth. Shel ran her thumb over the work that had been done. She could tell where it had been broken, because gold striations glowed where the cracks used to be. It looked like it had taken patient work, strong lacquer, sanding, and refinishing, but it had been made new, even more beautiful than it must have been before.

Understanding what she was to do, she lifted the violin toward her grandparents and bowed her head low, offering back to them what they had placed in her hands. Her grandfather took it and held it close to his chest. As he did, the spirit of the instrument shone. He pulled the bow across the strings, making a warm tone.

Then a peaceful sound surrounded that tone, and her grandfather nodded at her. She looked down at her chest and found it vibrating with golden light through cracks and fissures. At the center, her heart glowed with that warm light, and she leaned her head back to feel the depth of that harmony.

Opening her eyes and looking ahead again, her grandparents had vanished into the mist.

SCENE 15

*T*he next day, having finished all her finals, Shel stayed in her pajamas. Her parents were going to be there for a few days to help her get out of the dorm that weekend. They'd made plans to get together that afternoon, so Shel sat on her bed and emailed Mr. Tarlaigh, expressing on behalf of herself and Charlie that they hoped he was doing alright. She let the memories of last night's contest wash over her and smiled. Then she got out her shiny silver suitcase and looked around her room for what she could start packing. She grabbed her clothes from her closet and threw them on the bed. Walking back over to the closet, she saw the Shelley Winters poster she'd thrown back there months ago. She pulled it out and scrolled it open. Winters was beautiful with her long legs and lipstick smile. She rolled it up again, and her eyes landed on the actress's book on her desk. She placed the poster under her arm and flipped to the last page. She didn't remember reading a short addendum Winters had added there.

TO BE CONTINUED, I HOPE...

P.S. Shelley Winters A.K.A. Shirley Schrift are now firmly fused together. In this life journey, perhaps I'm sometimes vague about what took place in which year, but conversations of long ago have come back almost word for word. All these things I've written about are exactly as they happened. Some things are even exactly as I wished they hadn't happened. Perhaps a few things are exactly as I wished they happened. However, I will never know the difference...nor will you.

Shel closed the book and zipped it into a pocket inside her suitcase. Then she set the poster down on the far side of her desk. Maybe someone would find it when they cleaned the rooms and want to keep it, or even next semester a girl might come across it when she's unpacking for the first time at college.

When she checked her email again, Wilma had responded and said that Mr. Tarlaigh was in the hospital. It was the John Muir Medical Center in Orinda, room 1471, and she and Charlie were welcome to come visit. She called Charlie, and he said he would love to go with her, but he had a final later that morning. So she replied to Wilma that she would stop by in an hour or so.

Wilma sat by the bed and held Mr. Tarlaigh's hand as Shel poked her head around the door and knocked quietly. Wilma got up and gave her a hug, taking the flowers she'd brought and thanking her in soft tones. Mr. Tarlaigh was sleeping. He had lost a lot of weight, Shel noticed. His scraggly beard was longer than usual, and he rested peacefully, taking long breaths with the aid of the respirator.

Shel and Wilma sat down at the small round table a short distance from the foot of the bed.

"How's he been?" Shel twisted and pulled at a few strands of her hair.

Wilma frowned and looked at her husband. "Not so good."

She leaned forward, her elbows on her thighs, and her large beaded necklace swayed to and fro.

Shel pursed her lips and turned to look at him, too. He stirred, and his eyes drifed open.

"What are you two commiserating about?" His voice was thin and dry.

Wilma stood up and walked back to the bed and took his hand again. He looked at her, and his eyes warmed. Shel took a few steps forward, and he turned his head with effort to see her.

"You finish?" he said.

Shel grinned. "Yeah, I had my last final a couple days ago. I even had a short film I made get screened last night. Charlie did the music for it."

He nodded. Then he closed his eyes and seemed so still and breathless that Shel looked up at Wilma. But then he opened his eyes again and lifted his hand just enough to point at something on the table next to the bed.

Wilma jumped. "Oh, I almost forgot." She picked up an envelope with Shel's name on it and handed it across.

Shel took it and ran her thumb over the scribbled letters. She looked up at Mr. Tarlaigh. "Should I open it now?"

He shook his head. "You'll know."

She nodded and held it by her thighs with both hands.

Wilma ran her hand over his forehead, and he closed his eyes again. "He probably needs to rest."

Shel nodded and came around to give Wilma another hug. "Let me know if you need anything."

Wilma gave her a pained grin, and Shel padded across the room to the door. She turned around and looked at Mr. Tarlaigh then slipped out.

When Shel got back to campus, she noticed Thelma had texted.

Hey Shel. I'm sorry I wasn't able to be there for your screening.

It's been a busy week with finals and such. I did get your link, though, and watched. It's so good, Shel. Please give me a call when you can.

As she walked back up to her room, she dialed Thelma and waited through a couple rings.

"Shel?"

"Hey, Thelma!" Shel smiled.

"It's good to hear your voice." Thelma's tone was flat.

"Mm." Shel followed the design on the carpet to her door. "I'm so sorry, Thelma. I feel so bad for not picking up when you called all this semester. I've just been in a very weird place."

Thelma didn't respond right away. "I know. I got pretty down not being able to reach you."

Shel unlocked her door and sat in her desk chair, setting down the envelope from Mr. Tarlaigh. "I don't know what to say. I wish I could make it up to you. You're my best friend, Thelma, and I didn't mean to…shut you out."

"Yeah. I don't know, either." Thelma sighed. "I watched your film, and it all makes sense. Everything just feels…different now, though."

Shel leaned her head back and looked up at the ceiling. "I know. Sometimes I wish none of this had happened, and we could just go back to those times in the basement watching movies together."

After a pause, Thelma said, "Did I just hear you say 'movies'?"

Shel laughed. "I guess so."

"I haven't heard *that* since middle school." Thelma exhaled. "I don't know, sometimes I do wish we could go back to that time. But I'm not sure it was so simple. Things look nostalgic when they're far enough in the past."

"You know what I was thinking recently? Why did we always hang out at my house? I think we only went to your house, like, a few times through all those years. I feel bad about that. It wasn't even on my radar."

"I mean…." Thelma's voice searched. "I guess I just looked up to you and your family."

"Looked up to us?" Shel shook her head.

"Yeah, it always felt like you had it all together, and your parents are so chill and nice. I was always just happy to be a part that. I don't know. You felt like the big sister I never had."

Shel nodded. "I think I felt that, too, but it never occurred to me, consciously. You've always been like the sister I never had. But after what happened with Jeremy, and us getting together over winter break, I…I don't know…. I feel like I just shut down."

Thelma was silent for a moment. "I can see that." Her voice was softer. "After enough calls and not being able to reach you, it really made me think. I put you on a pedestal, I think, and when I saw you hurting like that, it scared me. I saw that I needed to finally find my own feet."

Shel waited for words to come. "Listen, I hope we'll always be friends, you know? That might not look the same for us as it did in high school, but that's…okay."

Thelma breathed then her tone lightened. "Is that a good 'okay,' or are you hacking a lung?"

Shel couldn't hold back a laugh. "It's a good 'okay.'" After a pause, she said, "What are you doing this summer? I can't wait to see you soon!"

"Well…." Thelma breathed in through her teeth. "I'm hanging out with Andy."

"Right!" Shel adjusted her position on the chair.

"Yeah, things are going pretty well. He's an architecture major, and we have great conversations, and he's into classic films."

"That's so cool." Shel kicked at the drawer in her desk.

"Yeah! He's from Michigan, so he's kind of outdoorsy, but also nerdy with math and stuff." She giggled.

Shel had to laugh with her. She looked at the picture of the two of them on her bulletin board and rested her feet on the ground.

"Well, I hope to meet him sometime soon. Don't worry, I'll find things to busy myself with this summer."

"No, no, I want to hang out with you, too, I just wanted you to know I won't be around…all the time."

"Mm-hmm." Shel's sound caught in her throat, but she let it come up and out.

"You okay?"

"Yeah. Change is just hard sometimes, you know?"

"Yeah, I do. Things might never be the same, but they can still be really good."

Shel leaned forward and rested her elbow on the desk, putting her chin in her palm. "You're still the best, Thelma."

A few days later, as her mom and dad helped her pack some last items into her suitcase and the box they'd reconstructed, Shel checked her phone and saw that Wilma had emailed. Tears came to Shel's eyes as she read the words. Mr. Tarlaigh had passed away in the early hours of that morning. She was planning to hold a small memorial service for him in a few days, and she wanted to make sure Shel knew she and Charlie were invited.

Shel told her parents what was going on then called Charlie. As the phone rang, she remembered that they didn't have to be out of the dorms until Thursday, so she could stay for the memorial.

Charlie picked up. "What's up, Shel?"

She told him the hard news, and he became quiet. She told him about the memorial and asked if he wanted to go.

He didn't respond right away but then said, "Yes. I can stick around until then. I definitely want to be there."

Shel made plans with her parents for them to take some of her stuff back with them on the plane, and she'd drive the rest down on Wednesday, after the memorial.

When they left for the airport that evening, Shel gave them both hugs, holding them close.

"Thank you," she said, looking in their eyes.

They looked back at her with warm faces.

Shel reached into her purse. "Almost forgot." She pulled out one of the packages of Tokyo Banana cakes they'd sent her in the care package. "Just in case you get hungry on the flight."

"Ha!" Her mom took it and put it in her satchel. "Thanks, honey."

Shel winked and waved as they drove off in their rental.

On Tuesday, Shel and Charlie drove to Mountain View Cemetery in Oakland. As the highway lines flew by, Charlie beat out the rhythm on the dash to "Free Fallin'."

After the song ended, he turned to Shel. "What do you think you'll do this summer?"

Shel looked out her window and then back at the road. "I don't know yet. I think I need some time to process everything that's happened this semester, maybe spend some time at home… maybe get a job and save up to help my parents cover the cost of the class I'm going to have to retake."

Charlie bobbed his head. "That sounds good." He straightened the crease in his slacks then turned to look at her. "I think you probably know by now, but I really like you, Shel."

Shel glanced at him and grinned. "Thank you, Charlie. You are such a good friend to me. I—I don't know if it's what you're saying, but I don't want to define this right now."

Charlie folded his hands in his lap and lowered his head. "I understand."

"I don't mean to turn you down. I'm…not. I just need time…to figure a lot of stuff out."

He took a deep breath and said, "Shel, you're my friend, and I care about you. I respect what you're saying."

She looked at him, and his smile carried its usual grounding effect. "Thanks, Charlie."

When they arrived at the memorial, they saw Wilma with a small group of people huddled near a wall, and they walked over. She greeted them, and when they gave her the flowers they'd brought, she said, "Oh, you two!" and waved her hand, but then took them and added them to those in a metal cylinder next to the place that held Mr. Tarlaigh's ashes. She told them that Mr. Tarlaigh had finished editing his book before he passed, which they were very glad to hear. She had the whole group stand in a semicircle and, after thanking everyone for coming and saying how much Guy would have loved to have them all together, she read the message she'd had inscribed on the plaque over Mr. Tarlaigh's remains: *A true Musician who played his part well, and whose Music will be missed.*

Some people told stories about Mr. Tarlaigh, and it was fun for Shel to hear about his younger days. Then everyone came forward, one or two at a time, put their hands on the plaque, then gave Wilma a hug. Shel and Charlie strolled along the cemetery grounds and found a bench on a hilltop that looked out over the city.

They sat in silence, listening to the birds and distant traffic, looking at the foggy haze that connected highrises with trees and the green grass of the cemetery park.

"It's a crazy thing, isn't it?" Charlie said.

"The cemetery?" Shel squinted.

"No, all of this...whatever all of us are doing in this...place." He looked up and made a circular motion with his hand.

"Yeah." Shel's voice became distant. "I wonder where Mr. Tarlaigh is now...what he knows."

Charlie nodded. "He probably sees the bigger picture, reasons for things we don't understand while we're here in the midst of it all."

Shel smiled, remembering the way Mr. Tarlaigh used to raise his eyebrows and look over the top of his glasses. Then her smile fell. "It's not an easy place to be, down here," she said, recalling the image from when she'd visited him in the hospital—how thin and frail his body was. Then she remembered the envelope he'd given her that day and took it out of her purse. She opened it and unfolded the note made out in his scribbly handwriting.

Dear Shel,

I thought this would be the best way to thank you for helping me make the biggest transition of my life. You see, when I found out in early January that I had this illness, I couldn't sleep that night and drove to the beach to take a walk and get perspective on the whole thing. I saw someone lying on the beach and ran over, gave CPR, called the police, but then got nervous and headed out of there as fast as I could once they arrived. When I met you in class, I didn't recognize you until a few weeks in when you answered a question. It jolted me out of my misery over my fate and made me realize it was time to teach the class the way I had always wanted to. When I got too sick to keep teaching, I had time to write it all down and finish my book. Truly, I think if it wasn't for you, I wouldn't have enjoyed these last months of my life, which has made all the difference to me, and to Wilma.

All the best to you in what's to come,

G.T

Shel wiped tears from her eyes, folding the note back into the envelope. Charlie asked what that was and if everything was alright. She shook her head but then nodded. "Do you mind if we make another stop before heading back to campus?"

Charlie tilted his head. "Where do you want to go?"

Ocean Beach stretched out before them into the water that flowed to the horizon. As they neared the waves, Shel stared off into the vast space and took a deep breath.

"You okay?" Charlie's voice carried on the breeze.

"Yeah. Maybe I could just use a minute alone," she said.

"Of course." He meandered down the coastline.

Shel let her feet sink into the wet sand, the surf coming up over them and then receding away, hugging her ankles. She had fought against its current, and it had taken her under but let her see its big picture and the part she needed to play. In her mind, she bowed to the dark tension that had broken her and the Master whose hand had brought out her worth. She looked up between color-drenched clouds, and a single light winked through the atmosphere. As far away as she knew it was, it seemed to smile at her. How this could be, she couldn't say. Maybe there would always be some mystery in it.

She breathed with the waves as they broke and rebuilt again, feeling the rhythm in her body, in her heart. The rhythm was life's clock and reminded her of the tick of frames going by on a classic reel, like a Shelley Winters film.

The sun melted into the water and disappeared as a fading projector light, and she shivered in a gust of wind. Shel thought of her parents and Charlie, Thelma and Ellana, and wanted to hold them all close, never wanting them to fade. But then a thought flashed from what Mr. Tarlaigh had said all semester.

The point was to sing and dance while the music was being played. She lifted her feet to go on and do just that.

SPECIAL THANKS TO:

Rachel Weaver, Lynnette Horner, Marco Flores, Mitch Handelsman, Amy Huff, Jessica McGaugh, Laurie Baefsky, Donovan Raitt, Sean McNamara, Caroline Stump, Maria Tsuruta, The Lighthouse Writers Workshop in Denver, Colorado, and my wife and family.

Made in the USA
Coppell, TX
27 August 2021

61320192R00144